ICE STATION

ICE STATION

A MARINER NOVEL

PETER TONKIN

Severn House

Tonkin

This first world edition published 2011
in Great Britain and in the USA by
SEVERN HOUSE PUBLISHERS LTD of
9–15 High Street, Sutton, Surrey, England, SM1 1DF.
Trade paperback edition first published
in Great Britain and the USA 2011 by
SEVERN HOUSE PUBLISHERS LTD.

British Library Cataloguing in Publication Data

Tonkin, Peter.
   Ice station. – (Mariners series)
   1. Mariner, Richard (Fictitious character) – Fiction.
   2. Offshore nuclear power plants – Fiction. 3. Nuclear
   crisis control – Fiction. 4. Sea stories.
   I. Title II. Series
   823.9'14–dc22

ISBN-13: 978-0-7278-8042-0 (cased)
ISBN-13: 978-1-84751-356-4 (trade paper)

All Severn House titles are printed on acid-free paper.

Severn House Publishers support The Forest Stewardship Council [FSC],
the leading international forest certification organisation. All our titles that
are printed on Greenpeace-approved FSC-certified paper carry the FSC logo.

MIX
Paper from
responsible sources
FSC
www.fsc.org FSC® C018575

Typeset by Palimpsest Book Production Ltd.,
Falkirk, Stirlingshire, Scotland.
Printed and bound in Great Britain by
MPG Books Ltd., Bodmin, Cornwall.

For Cham, Guy and Mark

As always

PRELUDE
Hook

Vanya Vengerov, Second Lieutenant and officer in charge of the nuclear barge called Ice Station *Zemlya*, cupped his hand round his lighter-flame and the end of a Sobranie Black Russian. The cigarette was one from a packet he had purloined on his last visit to the Executive Suite in the fabulous Kempinski Hotel to update the owner on the progress they were making here. And to voice some of his continuing concerns. Those few he had dared to voice now. No more than the tip of the iceberg. As he sucked the smoke into his lungs he coughed, shoved his fists deeper into his raincoat pockets, and thought that if he kept this up he wouldn't live for much longer.

By *this* Vanya meant both the smoking and the stealing of property from the unnerving owner, Mr Felix Makarov, who had a reputation for ruthlessness that made Stalin seem as benign as Father Frost at Christmas. The fact that he was bringing deepening concerns to the attention of the man he most vividly suspected of being at the root of them. And the fact that he was sneaking around a deserted dry dock at night, shaking like a leaf, waiting to meet a contact from the local Prosecutor's office. To try and put into words his increasing certainty that there was something murderously dangerous going on aboard his command, carrying proof stolen from his absent captain's quarters. Any one of those things, in his experience, was likely to shorten anyone's life expectancy.

But Vanya didn't know that he was already dying. That, quite apart from the toxic and radioactive particulates likely to be contained in even the most exclusive cigarette smoke, his whole burly body was already infested with a murderously insidious dusting of Uranium 235, and its quaintly named *daughters* Lead 210 and Polonium 210. A talcum-fine powder that had been applied to the man-made lining of his nylon coat. In a very short while indeed, he was destined simply to start disintegrating from the inside out. Then he would rot to death in a matter of hours and there was nothing anyone could do to save him. An apt way to murder someone on a nuclear facility, perhaps. He was a man who appreciated irony; and he might have seen the wry logic of it, had he known. But of course, he had no idea, and preoccupations that were apparently much more urgent.

The massive anchor groaned where it dangled high above him on the outward flare of the vessel's blunt forecastle. The bulk of the shipyard was actually situated behind him; this section seemingly untenanted in the darkness, with only the massive hulk of the nuclear ice station reaching thirty metres upwards into the starry sky above his left shoulder.

The long voyage from Arkangelsk to St Petersburg's Baltic shipyard had been pleasant enough, for most of the seafaring had been done by the captains of the tugs *Ilya* and *Ivan* who had pulled the powerless vessel here, though two more powerful English-owned tugs would join them for the long journey back. Vanya had used the time to try and train up a couple of junior lieutenants called Brodski and Kuznetsov with whom he would be working during the rest of the voyage; all the way back out through the Skagerrak, up north of Norway, then past Arkangelsk all the way to Leningradskiy, near Wrangel Island thousands of miles to the east. And he had also used the time to make friends with *Ivan*'s captain Boris Gagarin, who would be one of the four tug skippers pulling them there along the newly commercialized North East Passage that joined the Baltic to the Bering Strait, gateway to the Pacific.

Vanya had first turned to Gagarin when things changed so suddenly and unsettlingly so soon after they arrived in St Petersburg and dragged *Zemlya* up here into Dry Dock Four for her final fitting; something he did again and again as things became more and more disturbing, until he had decided to call in the authorities.

Unthinkingly, Vanya threw the gold-coloured cigarette-butt away and pulled his black raincoat tighter around himself, shivering, although the clear night was warm and humid. The gesture made him aware of the ID badge pinned to his uniform lapel beneath the black nylon coat. В Венгегров, it said; his name in Cyrillic script. That in turn pulled his mind back to the interview he had given Joan Rudd, the film maker who was doing a documentary on the whole enterprise. She liked the Cyrillic writing on the badges and the notices aboard. Otherwise, *Zemlya* looked just like every other big boat afloat, she said. Especially as she hadn't been allowed into the reactor rooms yet. It was in that interview, thought Vanya, that some of the concerns that had been bubbling beneath the surface of his conscious mind had come to the fore and begun to form unsettling patterns. He hoped he hadn't said too much, then or later.

In St Petersburg all sorts of new crew members and ancillaries had come aboard and begun to settle in, most of them recorded by Joan Rudd's cameraman; some of them interviewed. A captain had shown up, with Felix Makarov, the owner, grimly in tow. Captain Sholokhov, who looked unsettlingly like Adolf Hitler, and a fat lieutenant he favoured called Oblomov – not unlike Hermann Goering. It was not *their* fault, they explained to the restless and unhappy Makarov, that things were beginning to fall behind schedule. They had all gone off to his suite at the Kempinski Hotel to discuss matters.

They were succeeded by caterers and galley staff, stewards and attendants, many of the latter simply breathtaking girls with come-hither eyes. Rather less attractive maintenance and supply men, whose duties were likely to overlap with the deck officers' once *Zemlya* set sail again after the reactors were installed and the English tugs arrived. The first of the operations teams, checking on the computer hardware and software even before the reactors came aboard. The tall, scholarly widower Professor Kirienkho and his team who were in charge of the reactors themselves and who would effectively run the floating power station once it had been tugged the length of the old Soviet Union and anchored off Leningradskiy. The team he brought along with him. And the security.

It had been the arrival of the security team that had really started to raise Vanya's hackles, he supposed. They were Spetsnaz to a man. Coldly ruthless special forces, trained to kill. Ready, willing and able to kill. Happy to kill. More threatening than the old KGB. Highly skilled, well equipped, far too well armed for Vanya's taste. Responsible to no one else, certainly not to the captain or his lieutenants. Answering to no one but their commander. And he acknowledged no superior except for Mr Makarov.

When they had started placing CCTV cameras everywhere aboard, both Vanya and Professor Kirienkho took their concerns to the Spetsnaz captain. With no result. So they took them to Mr Makarov at the Kempinski. In the taxi from the docks to the hotel, the two men had exchanged a disturbing range of disquiet. The professor shared the lieutenant's worries about the general situation aboard, and, apparently, had concerns of his own about the state of the reactors that were coming into the reactor rooms, about the computer systems designed to control them, and even about some of the people on his own team.

In a kind of *folie à deux*, like children egging each other on to greater and greater excesses, they wound themselves up. No sooner did they arrive at the hotel than they retired to the bar and added vodka to their increasingly lively grievances and within half an hour they had managed to gatecrash a meeting in Mr Makarov's suite.

There were four men in the main room of the suite with Makarov when the professor and the lieutenant lurched in. Two were ships' officers – the Hitler-like Captain Sholokhov and his sidekick Oblomov. Two were not. One was a familiar-looking open-faced, almost boyish Indonesian who had been aboard on a visit already and who proposed to come along for the ride until *Zemlya* was anchored safely off the north Siberian coast. He represented potential buyers for the technology – perhaps for the barges themselves. The other was a gaunt, intense-looking man of more advanced years. His sallow, ivory-skinned skull of a face was bracketed by two unsettlingly large black hearing aids which completely concealed his ears. His glance was enough to stop the two tipsy men in their tracks; far more disturbing even than Makarov's icy rage.

The owner took the two interlopers through into one of the inner rooms which, Vanya remembered, looked across the square towards the Hermitage. While the professor unburdened his soul, the lieutenant lingered by the door, his interest piqued by the stranger with the scary eyes and the unsettling hearing aids. The men were speaking in a mixture of Russian and a language the lieutenant could not understand, but he heard the stranger say *Yamin* – which he recognized as the name of the open-faced young man; and captain Sholokhov called him Mohammed. And he thought he heard Mohammed Yamin call the stranger *Sittart*. But he couldn't be certain and the man's reaction to the speaking of his name sounded negative. There was a scraping of chairs. The slam of a door.

The professor's brief talk with Makarov resulted in the old man being given a week to think things over and a first-class ticket for a flight home to Moscow while he did so. Vanya received short shrift. Get back aboard and do his duty no matter what he thought or feared, or look for another berth. People able to run a nuclear power station were quite a rare commodity. Sailors were ten a *kopek*.

So Vanya had gone back aboard, but started looking more closely still at what was going on around him as the Spetsnaz team wired everywhere for CCTV and the professor's assistant Dr Leonskaya oversaw the final preparation of the newly fitted reactors.

Each evening when his duty was finished, Vanya would sneak off the vessel to meet Boris Gagarin at ФπагMAH, The Flagman Bar, on Stacheck Prospekt where they would drink vodka, eat dried fish *vobla* snacks and put the world – and *Zemlya* – to rights. They would probably never have gone any further than talking had not Lieutenant Brodski found them there three nights later and told them that Professor Kirienkho had been killed in a car crash on the slip road in from the MKAD ring road in south west Moscow. 'He was on his way to see his wife. She's buried in the big cemetery at Kuntsevo, apparently,' the young man said brutally. 'Pretty convenient. He'll be with her for good, now, what's left of him.'

It was after Brodski left that the suddenly sobered Vanya said to Boris, 'That's too convenient to be an accident.' Suddenly he did find he was in immediate fear for his life. But he couldn't see why. Or from whom the threat was likely to come. 'Who do you think I ought to take this to?' he asked at last. 'And don't say Milisia or FSB because I've had trouble with the authorities in the past. And my brother at the Nuclear Inspectorate would only get pulled in again.' So, after a while the clear-headed, shaken men decided that Vanya would best refer his worries and suspicions to the office of Sergei Zaitsev, the City Prosecutor. But indirectly, through secret contact via Boris, so that he could get further proof if any more were needed.

Vanya had sought proof earlier this particular night; first pleasurably by bedding the delectable and very willing Ivana, steward in charge of the upper sleeping-quarters, and stealing the pass key that opened the captain's cabin while she snored quietly in satiated slumber. A key he planned to return when he slipped back into her bed later. Then, more nerve-rackingly, he had continued his quest in the captain's cabin itself, before he had contrived to steal past the security cameras and come down to the meeting place that Boris said he had arranged for him, pausing only to slip back into his empty cabin and pull on the cheap black nylon raincoat that he fondly believed would allow him to melt invisibly into the shadows – as it had done every night when he slipped over the side to go drinking with Boris.

So, here, now, at the end of it all, Vanya was standing wrapped in his poisonous black raincoat in the shadows beneath the flare of *Zemlya*'s bows with the wind gusting through the hawsehole and the anchor chain above, waiting to meet a contact from the City Prosecutor's office, wondering if another Sobranie would shorten his already limited life-expectancy, still unaware that the radioactive toxins in his system were by now fast-destroying the cell-structures in his eyes and ears, behind his nose, in his throat, lungs and stomach, loosening his hair and making his gums start to bleed

He was beginning to feel nauseous, and was wondering where the nearest toilet was, when there was an abrupt, sharp *clang* from somewhere high above him. A gathering rumble. Then everything was overwhelmed by an ear-splitting rattling. Someone screamed, '*Look out! Look out!*' And *Zemlya*'s starboard fore anchor hit Vanya directly on top of his decaying head. As it weighed the better part of one hundred thousand pounds it stamped him out of existence like a giant's foot squashing an ant. Just as he never knew that he was dying of radioactive poisoning, he never knew what hit him – or what a lucky escape it actually represented. One moment he was alive and dying horribly – the next he was cleanly and absolutely dead.

Then the chain the massive anchor was attached to continued to rattle down on to the mess on the dry dock long after the man from the Prosecutor's office had taken to his heels and fled. When the startled crewmen who got to the scene of the accident first arrived, there was little to see beyond a pile of anchor chain.

When the chain – and the anchor – had been winched back into place, there was so little left on the dockside that Captain Sholokhov and Mr Makarov both agreed that the best way forward was simply to hose the slipway clean and hold a service at the water's edge.

As the Prosecutor's office made no formal report of the contact, the paperwork was completed as swiftly as the memorial and Ice Station *Zemlya* slid down the slipway greased with her late First Officer's blood, only a couple of days further behind schedule after all. Fully crewed and well equipped, she was tugged out into the Norwegian Sea where the Heritage Mariner tugs *Erebus* and *Terror* supplemented the efforts of *Ivan* and *Ilya*, pulling the floating nuclear Ice Station *Zemlya* north, into the Arctic Ocean and east along Siberia's Arctic coast, towards Leningradskiy and Wrangel Island just north of it.

Pevek

'*Look out! Look out!*' screamed Robin, her face twisting with terror. 'Richard! Look out!' Her wide grey eyes burned. Her cheeks were pale with shock. The golden waves of her hair seemed to fly as the power of the howling wind took hold of them. 'Richard!' she screamed again. 'Richard! Look out . . .'

Richard Mariner sprang awake from a brief, uncomfortable nap, his mind still haunted by the vivid vision of his beloved wife's face. Uncharacteristically, he did not come into full wakefulness but stared around, blinking until he remembered where he was. Then, still subconsciously acting under Robin's nightmare direction, he looked out of the window. And almost shouted with shock.

The sleek Sukhoi Superjet 100 S7 Airlines aircraft swooped out of the low overcast that had shrouded it for the last hour or so as Richard had dozed and all he could see terrifyingly close beneath the plane was water. Then the fuselage tilted further and his exhausted gaze was dazzled by the sunlight glancing off the restless surface apparently inches beneath the port wing tip. His massive hands spontaneously closed on the armrests of his seat, and it was a testament to the men and women at the Sukhoi factory that he did not tear them free. But he shook himself at once – physically as well as mentally; 'Get a grip, for God's sake,' he growled.

At the sound of his words, the hostess, hurrying to her seat for landing, turned and looked down, shading her grey-blue eyes with long honey lashes. She had been covertly watching the massive passenger throughout the flight, fascinated by his size and by the aura of restless energy and power he exuded. The way his ice-blue eyes met hers on occasion, sending goosebumps down her forearms and inner thighs, for all that his gaze was distant and distracted.

'You wish for something, Captain Mariner?' she asked, her English throaty and coloured exotically by an odd mixture of accents delivered in a husky tone that a number of men had found irresistible.

Not Captain Mariner, sadly. He shook his head. '*Nyet*,' he answered baldly.

In his big navy-blue British Warm overcoat, his massive frame looked like the body of a great black bear wedged into a cage that was far too small to contain him, she thought, even though he had two seats to himself. A sudden, dazzling flash of arctic light defined the angles of his face like a spotlight on a film star. The beak of his nose, the almost brutal mouth, the square, dark chin; the fine white scar like the duelling trophy of a Hapsburg prince along his cheekbone. She saw his eyes narrow as he read the Cyrillic letters of her name-tag: AHHa.

'*Spasibo*, Anna,' he concluded.

She continued towards her seat with a little moue of regret, a sensual shiver and a resurgence of goosebumps all along her inner thighs, at the way he had growled her name from deep in his cavernous chest. It was men such as this who might offer her the next leg of her long escape from the Muscovite suburb of Kuntsevo towards the bright lights of some dream of a life like the ones she saw in all the magazines.

Richard watched the air hostess walk away, but his mind did not really register what he was looking at. As the nightmare vision of Robin's screaming face receded, he was too busy telling himself to stop behaving like a child. He knew very well the S7 Siberian Airlines jet was not really about to hit the freezing southern outskirts of the Arctic Ocean, it was simply throttling back in its final approach to Pevek Airport.

Richard was simply exhausted by more than seventy hours of travelling. Hours that had pulled his increasingly weary imagination back in time from his current position as CEO of Heritage Mariner, one of the largest shipping companies in the world, to his earlier work with Crewfinders, when he had dashed all over the world at the drop of a hat, taking the place of navigating officers who had been hurt or killed mid-voyage and needed replacing with the utmost urgency. Usually within twenty-four hours.

He had made it from London to Kerguelen Island in the Antarctic Ocean in forty-eight hours once, he remembered. London City Airport to Chicago O'Hare and on to Thunder Bay in thirty-six. Gatwick to Gander in twenty-four. Heathrow to Hormuz in eighteen. And now, Heritage House to Pevek in seventy-two of the eighty-odd hours since he had seen Robin in the flesh. But short of hiring – or buying – an executive jet and coming out here direct, this was the fastest he could get from London to the back end of the world.

As the Sukhoi's wheels bashed on to the concrete flags, bounced and bashed again, Richard was jarred back into the weary present. He looked away northwest across the Siberian Sea, up towards Wrangel Island and the pack, which lit the horizon with that familiar ghostly brightness.

Richard buttoned up, dismissing his wife from his mind at last, then he stooped, lifted his briefcase off the spare seat and hefted it, feeling the odd, familiar combination of books, paperwork and extra-thin laptop it contained. An apparently contradictory catalogue of contents that reflected the nature of their owner, he thought. A little bit of cutting-edge, twenty-first century Apple hardware closeted with determinedly nineteenth century papers and fountain pens. And the book in the middle of the mix was Fergus Fleming's *Ninety Degrees North*, the story of the race to reach the North Pole from the 1700s to the 1900s. By and large a tale of incredible heroism leading to inevitable tragedy, all contained within the Arctic Circle, his own resting place for the next few days at least. Up beside that strange, unsettlingly bright northern horizon. Dealing with the formless, nameless dangers he suspected were waiting for him there, aboard Ice Station *Zemlya*.

Stooping automatically to keep his all-too preoccupied head clear of the cabin ceiling, Richard walked stiffly down to the front of the plane, last in a line of passengers who all seemed much keener to get here than he was himself. 'Goodbye, Captain Mariner,' said the striking hostess with the seductive accent and come-to-bed eyes.

'*Dasvidanya*, Anna,' rumbled Richard, still hardly sparing her a second glance, and he stepped out on to the steps, straightening luxuriously.

Baggage claim and customs were fast, efficient and courteous. His paperwork was scrutinized briefly, stamped punctiliously and returned with a smile. By the time he got through immigration his big suitcase was circulating lazily on the luggage carousel. The little airport's waiting area was small but functional. It boasted a bar serving food and drink. Half a dozen tables surrounded by a couple of dozen chairs. A panoramic window looking west across the bay.

It was seemingly filled by a giant of a man wedged uneasily into a spindly chair. And the fact that he was wearing a full Arctic uniform of sealskin trousers tucked into sealskin boots, sealskin parka with wolf-furred hood, simply added breadth to his massive stature. Especially as the parka was open to reveal a garish shirt of warm brushed double cotton weave in lumberjack tartan, open in turn at the throat to reveal a high-buttoned woollen vest. His skin was a little pallid, telling of too much time on the ice, and his beard was ragged and unkempt. Kate Ross, his wife, was clearly also well out of the way, thought Richard with a smile. The first smile since Heathrow had fallen away beneath him three long days ago.

'Hi, Colin,' called Richard as he strode out of the official area with his briefcase in one hand and his travelling case in the other. 'Glad to see you made it OK. Been here long?'

'Half an hour,' answered Colin Ross, heaving himself to his feet. 'Long journey. Short wait. So far.'

'Tell me about it!' Richard put his case down and reached out to shake hands with his friend and sometime associate. 'How's the ice business?' he asked. Colin spent most of his life at one end of the world or the other.

'Busier than ever,' answered Colin, the words drawn out by his Highland brogue. 'I've been up on the ice cap for the better part of a year this time, going from one station to another. Bit of a holiday from the Antarctic. Busman's holiday. How're Robin and the twins?'

Richard closed his tired eyes for a moment and Robin his wife was there again, but not the nightmare vision this time; Robin as she really was, reed thin, golden haired, her grey eyes calm. 'The twins are just back from their grandparents' place in the south of France. As far as I know they're all camping at Cold Fell just outside Carlisle before going up to Edinburgh for the Fringe. The twins have work experience before their studies start again in the autumn. Robin's off back to Heritage House in just over a week to hold the fort while I'm away. What about Kate?'

'Kate gave up and went home for the summer. But there's so much going on up here – *independently* of your floating nuclear power stations . . .' The tones were frosted with almost Calvinist disapproval.

'They're not *mine*,' said Richard as the pair of them eased themselves into the slightly rickety chairs. 'Well, Heritage Mariner might be getting involved with Ice Station *Zemlya*. If the whole concept of nuclear facilities floating off coasts all over the world starts to look safer and more profitable, at any rate. We've certainly been happy enough to supply the tugs now that our work in the North Sea is beginning to scale back. That's why we're here after all. To see what's going on with the Ice Station and the tugs, and to check out the place they're planning to anchor her. Where did they pick you up from?'

'From a *proper* ice station. *North Pole Forty* on the Petermann ice island. Well, the Russians call it *North Pole Forty*. The Yanks call it *Omega* – or they're supposed to. Most of us just call it *Trudy*, after the Canadian Ice Service

officer who first saw the Petermann island had broken free
of the Greenland glacier back in the summer of 2010.'

'Trudy. I like that. Where's *Trudy* now?'

'Half in Canadian waters and half in Alaskan waters,
drifting west towards Siberian seas, just south of the pack.
My old stamping grounds. They choppered me off *Trudy* and
into Barrow then flew me down to Fairbanks – then on across
here. Thirty-six hours door to door and everything smooth
as silk. I don't know who did the paperwork on it, but it
must have been a miracle-worker.'

'Audrey at Crewfinders,' said Richard as though that
explained everything.

In Colin's experience, it did. 'Say no more. She set you
up too?'

Richard leaned back, undid his coat buttons but left his
jacket closed. 'BMI business class from Heathrow to
Moscow Domodedovo in one of those big new Airbus wide-
bodies. Domodedovo to Anadyr on a Transaero MS 21, also
business class, thank God. Then Anadyr to Pevek on the
S7 Siberian Airlines one-class Sukhoi they're turning round
now. Just on seventy-two hours with a couple of stopovers
I don't ever want to talk about.'

'And still one leg to go before we reach our final destination. Is this a good time for a briefing?'

'I'm not sure. I guess so. I'll tell you what I know, but
we'll have to wait for Felix Makarov to get the full picture.'

Colin grunted. 'I've always tried to steer clear of the
Sevmash boys,' he growled. 'We don't fit into each other's
world view, Felix Makarov and me.'

Richard nodded understandingly. He knew quite well that
in all Colin's long association with Richard and Heritage
Mariner, the world-renowned explorer and ice expert had
managed to stay clear of what he, not very secretly, thought
of as the shadier side of Richard's business. And that meant
steering clear of Felix Makarov and his partner Max Asov
who together made up the Russian business empire known
as the Sevmash Consortium.

With Richard's occasional involvement and more than
occasional investment, Sevmash were world leaders in
retrieving gas and oil from the vast fields beneath the Kara
Sea using the TITAN 10 series of submarine tankers. They

were moving into Siberian oil and mineral extraction, and had more or less bought the frontier city of Leningradskiy to the southeast of here.

They owned and ran the huge facilities in Archangel which broke up, disposed of, and reused derelict oil-tankers at huge profits. They owned most of the ship building facilities in St Petersburg. More recently, they had built the barges for the huge floating nuclear power stations like *Zemlya* which the Russians were pioneering and getting ready to sell all round the world.

And now they were the men responsible for the first privately financed, commercially built floating nuclear power station: Ice Station *Zemlya*. The next generation on from the *Akademik Lomosov* Government-funded series, the first of which was currently in Vilyuchinsk on the Kamchatka peninsula. The next few of which were designed to be positioned all along the north coast of Siberia. There was even supposed to be one coming into the bay off Pevek here, to supply power to the region to the south. Unless the Sevmash alternative could come in more cheaply and efficiently – and, as a test-bed, supply power down as far as the oil and mineral fields of Leningradskiy and Mys Shmidta nearby. But Richard and Colin had been called to this godforsaken place because things were not going as well as expected. Because things, indeed, were going dangerously wrong.

'Now you've arrived, it won't be long before Felix Makarov shows up,' Colin observed.

'True. So we'd better get on with anything we don't want Felix to be privy to. Do they have coffee here?'

'Coffee, tea and vodka. I've tried the coffee. The tea's simply got to be better. There's a samovar over by the bar.'

Felix

Richard and Colin stood shoulder by shoulder looking out through Pevek airport lounge's elderly panoramic window. The view was impressive and improving but the draught was dreadful, especially as the north wind began to pick up.

Richard sipped his steaming tea. 'That's where the local government people are going to anchor the next nuclear power station they get from Rosatom in St Petersburg, the *Akademika*,' he said, balancing the volume of his words between the immediate rattling of the windows and the more distant possibility of eavesdroppers. 'Unless they go the commercial route with Felix Makarov and his Sevmash boys. Which is, of course, Felix's plan. And part of the pressure here. The Rosatom product's a bit of a brute. It's little better than a steel-hulled hulk five hundred feet long, a hundred feet wide, thirty feet freeboard with a draft of twenty feet. Two reactors capable of producing seventy megawatts of power or three hundred megawatts of heat. Enough to keep a fair-sized city going. They just have to finish the shore-based connection facilities . . .'

'*And* build the city,' added Colin dryly.

'That's the next point,' said Richard. 'Makarov and Co. have got the city. Leningradskiy. It sits on a gold mine – literally – and is only a few miles north of the new Gazprom oilfields that promise to be even bigger than the Sevastyanovo field down near Irkutsk that the Russians opened in 2010. And it's only a couple of miles south of the airforce base at Mys Shmidta, currently being upgraded for civilian use. Add in the power – especially if they are supplying it themselves – and it's a licence to print money. To print *more* money.

'And that's independent of the fact that they may well have a highly commercial proposition in their new floating reactor in any case, especially if it can power a port as well as an oilfield. Yet another stepping-off point for the Russian move into the Arctic Ocean. And of course a planned stopover for bigger and bigger ships on the North East Passage run from Murmansk and the Kara Sea Oilfields to the Bering Strait, the Pacific and all points south. North as well, come to that, now that BP and Rosneft are planning to start drilling in the more challenging polar environments.

'All in all, a perfectly positioned floating power station, which, if the pictures, drawings and specifications I've seen are anything to go by, is *not* a brute. *Zemlya* can deliver everything the *Akademika* can – same output from the nuclear plant and so-forth – but she's more elegant, more artistically designed . . .'

He ignored Colin's *harrumph,* which said exactly what the ice master thought of aesthetics in the commercial world, and proceeded.

'But most importantly, *Zemlya*'s cheaper to buy, maintain and run. She's designed to be completely self-sufficient for her thirty-year operating life. The reactors are self-contained. That means no by-products. There's no waste of any kind that goes into the environment, just waste-storage units the size of commercial containers that are replaced in each servicing cycle. Clean energy, no environmental impact. When she's in place, no carbon footprint.'

'And she's as pretty as a picture into the bargain,' rumbled Colin sarcastically. 'Positively decorative. So what's the problem? Why do they need us?'

Richard sipped his tea thoughtfully and answered in measured tones. 'This is only gossip, you understand. But my commercial intelligence people at London Centre keep their ears to the ground. And my people are aboard two of the four tugs pulling *Zemlya* into place, they're not aboard the station itself.

'All in all, there are elements of the problem that are so obvious that they can hardly be secret. Time, for a start. The whole project is two months behind schedule and the weather is closing in early this season. Lately, the project has been bugged by delays that might, it seems, have been caused on purpose. The opposition is government funded after all. And we are talking the Russian government here! Not to mention the fact that there are a range of outside interests who do not want this technology to proceed too fast in any case. Environmental warriors. Greenpeace . . . We crossed swords with La Guerre Verte a couple of years back – they are the al-Qaeda of environmentalists. More legitimate players. Big oil – and that doesn't just mean the States, Shell and BP. It means the Middle East, Indonesia. Russia itself.

'But, all that aside, what is needed now more than anything is harmony and close-working if they are going to get the increasingly dangerous job done in time. With national agencies, local government, Uncle Tom Cobleigh and all. And aboard as well as ashore. But then there's the typical Sevmash approach – high profile, high risk. They're pumping this for as much publicity as they can manage – and, as we all know, publicity can go two ways in the twinkling of an eye. Look at . . .' Richard named the last couple of worldwide celebrities who had most spectacularly fallen from grace.

'Sevmash have the world and his wife watching – with heaven knows how many supernumeraries aboard *Zemlya* itself. Independently of the sixty or so permanent staff needed to man her, maintain her and keep the reactors safely on-line. Visiting experts, potential purchasers – or their representatives. They've stretched even their financing to the limit – and then some. Not even my intelligence people know who the final few backers are, but it'll be people who take big risks and play for keeps.

'So, there's a Newscorp news reporter aboard, with an extra crew making a documentary about the whole project. Destined for prime-time TV – Fox, in the States of course, with trade-off to CNN or some such. Fox Australia – covering the whole of Indonesia into the bargain. The BBC are asking to see a copy of the finished product. So everything has to be perfect. And apparently it's *not* all perfect. And there's something else. Something more worrying still . . .'

'Like what?' demanded Colin suspiciously, raising his voice against the thunderous battering of a sudden squall. 'This final bit of financing? Some really shady *éminence grise*, some particularly nasty ghost in the machine?'

'I don't know,' answered Richard. 'But I know a man who does. And this looks like him landing now.'

The squall of wind intensified; became a downdraught. The wheeling birds were scattered by the sudden arrival of a big Mil helicopter. One of the new Mi 38 models in the sea-rescue rig with keel and floats for water-work, though the bright yellow fuselage with the Sevmash logo looked too heavy ever to float. It was a medium-sized workhorse machine, crewed by two pilots and an engineer, with seats for thirty passengers and enough power to lift six thousand kilos of freight. On this trip, however, it carried one man and a briefcase.

Felix Makarov strode across the apron to the airport building with the tails of his black leather coat whipping around his ankles, revealing a red silk lining that matched his tie to perfection. His black Astrakhan hat was pulled down so low that it almost met his straight, thick eyebrows at the front, and disappeared into the black mink fur of his collar at the back. He walked tall even under the rotors of his chopper, stared down his long nose with intense brown eyes and gave off the same sort of sparking energy and charisma as Richard. The wind pulled the black leather back into wings behind him as he strode forward, and even at this distance Richard could see that the charcoal grey of his perfect two-piece had almost certainly been hand crafted and been maintained in the meantime by someone who would have given the inimitable Jeeves a run for his money.

'Welcome to both of you,' he said as he shook hands with Colin. 'We have much to discuss. But first . . .' He swung away and crossed to the samovar. Disdaining the venerable vessel, he leaned forward, calling to the barman. In a moment he was back, clutching a tumbler of clear, slightly oily liquid. 'Stolichnaya,' he said. 'And not Elite, either. I had hoped for good old-fashioned Imperial but I think I cleaned them out of it the last time I passed through. So this will have to do. It will still keep the cold at bay. *Nasdravye!*'

Neither Richard nor Colin drank alcohol, but that had never bothered Felix who had all the social sensitivity of a charging rhinoceros. He knocked back the vodka and slammed the glass down on a nearby table as though it had been a shot glass rather than a tumbler. 'We have some time here while the chopper crew complete the turnaround, then we'll be off. I'd rather discuss the most important matters while we're in the air and I can be sure of security, but I can fill you in on general background now, answer any immediate queries. But before we start, does either of you need anything to eat or drink – other than the tea? I can hardly recommend the food here I'm afraid. But I have something more appetizing laid on for you aboard *Zemlya*. Still, if you're desperate . . .'

Both men shook their heads, so Felix, still acting as host, pulled the table with his vodka glass on it over to the window and the three of them sat around it. 'Now,' he began expansively. 'Where shall we begin?'

'Nice chopper,' said Richard, starting the conversation, as was his habit, a little way away from where he wanted to end up.

'Well fitted, too,' boasted Felix contentedly. 'It has everything except a really pretty air hostess.'

The three of them looked at the brightly coloured, strikingly new-looking machine. Then Felix's crack about the air
hostess clicked in Richard's tired mind. 'You should poach
the one we had on the S7 jet up from Anadyr,' chuckled
Richard without thinking. 'Her name was Anna . . .'

As chance would have it, the Sukhoi's flight crew came
through into the bar at that very moment, and Felix would
have had no trouble in working out which of the girls Richard
was talking about, even had his brooding gaze not seen the
name-tag AHHa on her lapel. The two pilots and six assorted
cabin attendants and hostesses all carried overnight bags and
coats. Heaven alone knew where they were heading – there
were no hotels in Pevek – and they did not look to Richard
like happy campers at all.

Felix's eyes fastened on Anna, and his expression went
from preoccupation to amazement and back. He glanced at
Richard and was gone in a leathery flap of coat-tail and a
cloud of his favourite aftershave, which Richard recognized
as Eau Sauvage, like a very upmarket vampire. 'I was
joking . . .' he said to Colin, half amused at Felix's antics.

'I didn't think Russians did *joking*,' Colin answered, his
voice chilly with disapproval. 'Felix certainly doesn't!'

The pair of them watched the massive Russian sweeping
up to the suddenly nervous-looking flight crew. 'He isn't
behaving as though there's a major crisis happening or
impending,' mused Richard.

'That means nothing,' shrugged Colin. 'The whole of Ice
Station *Zemlya*'s power facility could be going as critical as
Chernobyl and he'd still be swilling vodka and propositioning
pretty girls.'

'I thought you said you didn't know him all that well . . .'
said Richard, struck by the accuracy of Colin's cynical insight.

'I said I avoid him, not that I don't know him! Perhaps I
avoid him because I know him all too well!'

Mil

When Felix returned he was in an ebullient mood. He waved at his friends and made a sharp left turn towards the bar. A glance across the room revealed to Richard's quick eye that the bemused S7 flight crew was one member short. And that there was no sign of Anna. 'It's like Jean Anouhil's play *Becket*, isn't it?' said Colin, following Richard's gaze. 'That scene where the king comes across a woodsman's pretty daughter in the forest.' He tried his best to sound like Peter O'Toole – but still sounded more like Sean Connery: '*Have her washed and sent up to my bedroom . . .*'

Felix arrived with a fresh glass and a full bottle of Stolichnaya. He put the bottle and the glass on the table, looked at them for a moment, frowning. 'Now, to more serious matters,' he said, leaning forward to fill the tumbler. 'Ice Station *Zemlya* has a crew of sixty-nine. The three shifts of engineers overseeing the nuclear power output are the most important in many ways. Certainly, their training, disposition and comfort are the most crucial. We don't want them worrying about anything except their reactors. Especially as a good number of them are doubling up as maintenance and so forth when they are not on duty in the reactor rooms. And that number is designed to rise over time.' He broke off apparently noticing with some surprise that his glass was empty. He filled it up and tossed it back before he leaned forward conspiratorially and continued.

'Then there are *Zemlya*'s crew. She needs no naval engineers because, like the older *Akademik Lomosov* models, she has no motors. She's effectively a huge barge. We did have a couple of what we might call civil engineers in place – electricians, plumbers and so-forth – but now the off duty reactor teams or turbine men will cover all that too. She needs a team of navigators to keep watch while she is under way, like any similar vessel, even though she is being pulled

from one place to another by the four big ocean-going, ice-
breaker-tugs we have attached to her now. Two of yours,
Richard, and two of our own. But once she is anchored and
permanently in place they will move on. Both the tugs and
the navigating officers. But we envisage a permanent doctor
and small medical team, appropriately trained of course. And
then there are the stewards, cooks and so-forth.'

He freshened his drink again and continued, 'Zemlya isn't
a cruise liner – by no means – but we have a top-flight
hospitality unit looking after our comfort at the moment and
we'll leave a pretty-strong team aboard when we have her
set up, self-sufficient and running smoothly . . .'

'Because the reactor people need to be stress-free and
contented, long-term,' growled Colin. 'Or something unfortunate might happen – like Chernobyl or like Three Mile
Island.'

'But in the meantime there are people aboard who are even
more important than the reactor teams . . .' added Richard
smoothly before Felix could react. 'Prospective purchasers.
Newscorp news reporters. Documentary makers . . .'

'Too right!' answered Felix in an unsettlingly accurate
Australian cadence. 'They've been coming and going at an
incredible rate. It's been like Red Square on May Day, I can
tell you. But it's beginning to calm down now.'

'Probably because Pevek is a pretty hard place to get to,'
said Richard feelingly.

'Whether you come from west or east,' added Colin.

Felix nodded and reached for the remaining half bottle of
vodka. 'Things'll be easier when Zemlya's in place, though,'
he said. 'She'll not be too far from Leningradskiy and when
we finish updating the airport at Mys Shmidta, we'll be able
to fly people in there and chopper them out to Zemlya without
too much trouble. Like the medical team, the chopper crew
are going to be on the permanent staff. If anything goes
wrong, the Mil can evacuate the whole station in three trips.
Then of course longer-term there'll be the new port facility
– if we can get the backing.' He lowered his voice and glanced
around. 'We're even getting sniffs of interest from Beijing
in that aspect – now that they've finished work on the new
port city of Hambantota. But that's really hush-hush. Who
was it that said "such knowledge is dangerous . . ."?'

Frowning at the thought, Felix leaned forward to pour himself another vodka, as Richard drew in breath to tell his associate that Samuel Johnson had actually said that knowledge *without integrity* was dangerous. But as he did so, a shadow fell across the table. The three men looked up. A short, square man in a pilot's uniform was standing at attention with his head and shoulders framed by the panoramic window. 'We are ready to go, Mr Makarov,' he said formally. 'The tanks are full, the flight-plan is logged, and the new crew-member is aboard.'

'But she has nothing to serve to our Very Important Passengers!' said Felix, surging to his feet, his mood changing in a mercurial instant. 'Get a case of Stolichnaya from behind the bar and we'll follow you out at once.'

Fortunately – at least in Richard's eyes – the chopper pilot was a good deal more down-to-earth than his employer. So that, when the three men had sorted themselves out, handed coats to the new Sevmash helicopter air hostess – still wearing her S7 uniform – and taken their ease in the big, comfortable seats, four of which faced each other round a fold-down table, Anna was able to offer coffee and tea as well as vodka.

As the Mil lifted off and swung away northeast, across the Pevek peninsula and over the Arctic Ocean proper, Richard and Colin sipped Lipton's Yellow Label tea while Felix pushed his vodka glass aside and became more focused. He lifted his briefcase on to the table, snapped it open and the three men gathered round it. Felix pulled out a bundle of documents – papers, diagrams, photographs – and got down to business. The considerable amount of vodka he had consumed so far had no discernible effect on him. Even his breath seemed innocent, smelling of nothing more than Parma Violets. 'The problems started suddenly and unexpectedly,' he announced, 'soon after the first approach from China – via some mutual friends in Manila. Ice Station *Zemlya* was ahead of schedule at that stage, as you know. Hull built and reactors ready. Our Archangel and St Petersburg shipyards did a really top rate job on her, and at first it seemed there would be no trouble. The reactors went aboard and were certified. Her tests went smoothly. It was only when your two Heritage Mariner tugs *Erebus* and *Terror* arrived in early June to help *Ivan* and *Ilya* move her from Archangel to Wrangel, and the

first whisper came in from Manila as I said, that things began
to hit barriers. But even by that point there had been a couple
of accidents.'

Richard and Colin glanced at each other. Richard had
already listed all the usual suspects, but even he hadn't thought
to add the Chinese or the Indonesians to the mix. Now, they
really did play hardball, he thought. No wonder Felix was
looking unusually nervous. During the next few moments,
however, Felix focused on *Zemlya* herself, and so added little
to what Heritage Mariner's commercial intelligence staff had
already discovered or surmised. The usual tale of government
and corporate foot-dragging: central government worried
about competition for their own massively expensive project,
local government caught between a better price and the pressure of contracts with Moscow and St Petersburg already on
the table; Big Oil everywhere from Texas to Timbuctu to
East Timor, not to mention Gazprom and their hangers-on;
environmentalists of every shade and legitimacy.

But then, abruptly, there was a change in the seriousness
of the information as Felix continued from his last
revelation.

'. . . and just before Professor Kirienkho could come
aboard permanently, he was killed in an automobile accident
on the MKAD – the Moscow ring road. That held us up too,
of course, but his second in command Dr Marina Leonskaya
pulled things together. She is an impressive woman. You will
meet her. But the point I am making is that Kirienkho's death
was only the first of a series of fatal and near-fatal accidents
and incidents that have slowed us down and put our people
at risk. At first these things happened ashore. The Second
Lieutenant was crushed on the slipway, for instance. Tragic.
But once we were under way, they began to happen aboard.
And not just aboard *Zemlya*. *Ilya*'s captain Boris Gagarin
vanished three days ago – that's when I decided to call you
in, Richard. Our best estimation is that he got drunk and fell
overboard. But he's long gone – and he's not coming back
either. *Ilya*'s First Officer is in command. But in the meantime, the Newscorp people are beginning to ask some very
pointed questions and we want everything to look normal.
Even if it's starting to smell a bit suspicious to me.'

'So the long and short of it,' said Richard, 'is that you

want me to put on my Sherlock Holmes hat and start looking for clues?'

'Yes and no. You have every reason to be aboard. You're the only person we could think of who could show up at this point without raising too many eyebrows. You'll fit right in. And because of who you are and what we've done together in the past, you can go everywhere and see everything. No problem. But yes. Keeping your eyes open.' Felix gave a bark of laughter. 'At the very least, you'll be a perfect distraction.'

'But let me get this clear,' repeated Richard. 'Are you seriously worried that there might actually be some kind of sabotage going on? That someone aboard is actually trying to ruin this whole project – no matter what the cost?'

'No,' said Felix, frowning, backtracking suddenly, his eyes going shifty, as though he suddenly found the vodka bottle utterly fascinating. 'It's more subtle than that. Nothing has happened that can't be explained – perhaps simply by bad luck. But the extra pressure is the Newscorp reporter and the documentary team. If they come across anything that looks like a good news story then they'll go for it. You know that. We have a good news story to tell. But a bad news story will make bigger headlines. Sell more papers. Whatever.'

'Hmm,' said Richard. 'This all sounds pretty shaky, Felix. Even with the Chinese element – Moscow would go ballistic if that information trickled into the Kremlin. Or, worse, into FSB headquarters in Lubyanka Square.'

'Or, worst of all, into the Prosecutor General's office,' whispered Felix, and his hand shook a little as he reached for his vodka.

'Granted,' said Richard, bracingly. 'But if it had, you wouldn't be here, would you? You'd be rotting in Butyrka Prison. Look. I've come a long way and at some cost because you said you needed me urgently. There has to be more on your mind than bad luck, bad news, and worries about things that might go wrong – but haven't gone wrong yet.'

'You'll see.' Felix looked around, as though even here there were enemy ears eavesdropping. 'When you get aboard, you'll see.'

'And me?' asked Colin, leaning forward with a frown. 'What about me?'

'You're part of the longer game,' said Felix. 'Ice Station *Zemlya* is currently destined to be anchored off the coast. In the Arctic Ocean. There's a bay there, but it's blocked by ice. But we have to promise that she'll sit there pumping out power for thirty years – or our plans of getting a port facility built beside her will all come to nothing.'

'You should be fine,' said Colin. 'Especially with global warming pulling the pack edge up closer to the pole each year. That's what opened up the North East Passage in the summer of 2010, anyway.'

'But you haven't thought it through, Colin. We envisage a problem that you – and, perhaps, you alone – can help us with.'

'And what is that?'

'*Trudy*. North Pole Forty. On the Petermann ice island, a hundred miles of berg ice. It is grinding along the north coast of Alaska now, predicted to stay just clear of Barrow and Prudhoe. But after it crosses the Bering Strait, it could well swing south of Wrangel Island and come grinding along the north coast of Siberia crushing everything in its path.'

Felix looked out of the window suddenly, gesturing down so forcefully that the other two looked down automatically; where they saw the upper weather deck of the elegant vessel *Zemlya* as she seemingly swooped upwards out of the sea towards them. 'Everything in its path,' repeated Felix. 'Including Ice Station *Zemlya* and her two nuclear reactors.'

Reception

Ice Station *Zemlya* was a beguilingly pretty vessel, thought Richard. As the Mil flew over and around her, settling on the best approach for landing, they were given a clear view of all her lines and angles. Her hull must be the better part of two hundred metres long. She was thirty metres and more in the beam. Although she was basically a barge, she was shaped like a ship – a square-hulled vessel to be sure, but still with a proper ice-strengthened cutwater at the front of a suitable forecastle crowning an almost elegant bow. Her stern was high and fully rounded too.

And yet her existence as a powerless barge was emphasized as well. Great hawsers stretched forward from capstans on her elegant foredeck and were secured to the sterns of two battered and filthy-looking ocean-going tugs, which seemed almost to have been chosen to clash with *Zemlya*'s clean lines and sparkling paintwork. At her sides, spick and span Heritage Mariner ocean-going tugs snugged up against her, with great protective inflatable fenders keeping the working hulls apart. They were lashed by short hawsers at bow and stern, able not only to thrust her forward but also to turn her right and left as well.

Felix leaped down the steps ahead of Richard and Colin, who paused to exchange a word with Anna the air hostess. It was Felix, Richard noticed, who exchanged some words with the cameraman and sound engineer who were preparing to add this episode to the raw footage of their documentary, focusing all his charm and energy on a striking, intense-looking woman with long black hair. Her face was vaguely familiar – Richard assumed she was a TV reporter. It was Felix who decided on the pecking order as soon as he was satisfied that the cameras were rolling, assigning places with brutal efficiency as Richard and then Colin came past Anna and on to the chopper's steps.

Felix performed the introductions as Richard finally stepped on to the icy, gusty deck to find himself confronted by a considerable committee of welcome. Once again, his years with Crewfinders made Richard quick at assessing – and remembering – people. And he was blessed with a visual memory, which meant that names and faces stuck. Otherwise, like Colin, he would be utterly confused by the information overload presented by Felix's introductions.

There was a slight, dapper man in perfect captain's blues and braid, who saluted smartly, raised his hat and tucked it punctiliously under his arm to reveal oiled black hair with a perfect parting to match his straight-cut toothbrush moustache as he offered his hand to shake. His eyes were hooded and calculating. They did not quite meet Richard's as he gave a military half bow when Richard's fist closed on his. 'Captain Sholokhov,' said Felix. 'Currently in command of Ice Station *Zemlya*.'

The captain stepped back, turning towards Colin, hand held out. He was replaced by a tall, slim young woman in a severely tailored grey suit. She had lively blue eyes that crinkled at the corners above a ridiculously *retroussé* nose. Her mouth was full and sensual, dimpling at the corner as her eyes gave a flash of a smile – before the wind whipped the short bob of her dark blonde hair into her face and made her blink and cry. Her handshake was firm. Felix said, 'Dr Leonskaya. Marina. In charge of the Reactor teams.'

The list went on. Richard linked names to faces automatically, shaking hands carefully and repeatedly, like visiting royalty, saving his questions for later. The day was darkening again, the weather closing in. He could see a squall sweeping towards them from the east. It was a dark line in both sky and sea, closing like a pair of blades as it rushed westward. As he had hesitated at the top of the helicopter's steps, he had seen it beyond the two Russian tugs that laboured in the steely water out ahead of the nuclear barge, just as his own tugs worked to port and starboard of the hull – offering guidance as well as propulsion. Now, its misty outskirts were threatening to veil the pitching old Soviet ice-breaker bows. Beginning to overwhelm the much more up-to-date communications rig on their wheelhouses. A wind, seemingly as cold and damp as a wave, slapped his face.

'Vasily Vengerov,' called Felix, sensing Richard's distraction. 'From the Nuclear Safety Directorate.' An intense young man loomed at him, more perfectly turned out than the captain in clothes that were better cut even than Felix's, who contrived to look down his nose at the rumpled Richard and the ill-shaven Colin – in spite of the fact that he had to look up at them.

'Dr Nana Potemkin . . .' Could her name really be *Potemkin*? A square, masculine battleship of a woman with thick grey hair cut short. Square face, square shoulders. Jacket and trousers. 'Dr Leonskaya's right hand.' She shook hands as though gripping a pneumatic drill. She did not nod or smile. Her whole demeanour seemed to say *I have something*

better to do than to waste my time glad-handing visitors.
Richard liked and trusted her at once.

The Russian tugs had vanished, their towlines straining
into a misty grey deluge that was making Felix shout to
overcome its stormy roar. 'We had better get below,' Richard
said, raising his own voice towards a quarterdeck bellow,
releasing Dr Potemkin's hand and glancing down the three
or four faces waiting hopefully in line behind her. 'There's
a nasty squall coming.'

They ran for the nearest door, the camera crew taking
precedence, keen to protect their equipment, and their star
reporter, by the look of things. Then Felix. Then, courtesy
of Richard and Colin's medieval notions of propriety, the
other two women. Captain Sholokhov and Vasily Vengerov
pushed forward almost as ruthlessly as Felix, careful of their
hair and clothing. All of them rushed inwards and away
without looking back to see whether their honoured guests
were following or not. Richard would have, but a big, red-
freckled hand, furred with what looked like copper wire came
down on his shoulder and stopped him.

Thus Richard met the last couple of the welcome committee
in a less ordered fashion than Felix had planned. 'So, you're
Comrade Makarov's miracle worker,' said a flat Australian
voice as a red-haired man pushed up to him.

'Am I?' asked Richard, looking back towards the helicopter
as the first shower of rain spattered across the deck like
grapeshot. The pilot was overseeing the unloading of the
bags. The co-pilot and engineer were running them towards
the hangar – there was probably an internal companionway
and equipment lift there too, thought Richard. Anna was
helping, in spite of the squall. And in spite of the fact that
she clearly had no idea of the vessel's layout yet.

'You are if you're Richard Mariner.' The redheaded man's
eyes were faded blue, narrow and shrewd. His whole stance
was challenging, as though he were a rugby forward getting
ready to scrum down.

'Guilty as charged,' said Richard, shoving out a hand.
'Though I can't promise miracles. And this is Dr Colin Ross
of the British Antarctic Survey. Mr . . .'

'O'Neill. But it's Tom. *Mr* O'Neill's me old dad back in
Paddington, New South Wales.'

'Nice to meet you, Tom,' said Richard. 'You'll be the Newscorp man I guess.'

'Got it in one. I'm a hack from way back. Started out on the Morning Herald – onward and upward from there.' O'Neill turned to a slighter figure hovering self-effacingly in his shadow. 'This shifty-looking bloke here is Mohammed Yamin of Indonesian Incorporated Oil,' he concluded. 'Don't let his baby-face fool you. He's a corporate shark from the top of the pecking order over there.'

In fact Mohammed Yamin looked anything but shifty. He had an open, smiling face, made almost boyish by a combination of plump cheeks and smooth skin. He had wide, guileless brown eyes and a snub nose that looked as though it would only gain character and maturity when its owner hit puberty. But Mohammed must be mid-thirties, thought Richard. And there was likely more to him than met the eye. His tailoring, for a start, rivalled Vengerov's. 'Indonesian Incorporated,' he said, offering his hand. 'I haven't heard of that. New outfit?'

'Very,' answered Mohammed cheerfully, pumping it enthusiastically. 'Headquarters in Manila and Hambantota. So new the paint's hardly dry. So is Hambantota, of course . . .'

Richard nodded. Hambantota again he thought. Like London buses, you waited ages for a mention of the place and then several seemed to come along at once. He knew that Hambantota was new – it was the port at the southern point of Sri Lanka that had only recently been opened, financed by loans from China, constructed with the help of Chinese expertise and labour. One of the 'String of Pearls' with which China hoped – and planned – to keep control of the nearest seas and shipping lanes. And, if Felix was being honest, hoping to get a piece of North East Passage action too.

He knew all about Indonesian Incorporated Oil, though he chose not to admit it at this stage, feeling as devious as Felix. It was an amalgamation of several suspect organizations trying to improve their image through re-branding themselves. Luzon Logging, Bogor Biofuels and Pontianac Oil Enterprises. He knew about Indonesian Incorporated because the man who ran it was Professor Satang S. Sittart, his greatest personal and business enemy. If there was anyone in Manila likely to be happy to act as go-between for Beijing and

Sevmash, then it would be Sittart. On their last meeting, Sittart had been caught up in a tsunami and nearly drowned. His eardrums had suffered irreparable damage so that now he was forced to wear unsightly external amplifiers on his head. A painful humiliation for which he blamed Richard.

The full power of the squall hit, echoing his darkening thoughts and catching the helicopter's crew halfway to safety. Richard left Mohammed shaking Colin's massive fist, put his briefcase down and ran out without a second thought to grab Anna's bag, bundling her into the dry, along with Colin, Tom and Mohammed. She looked and smelt a little like a drenched puppy. But her body seemed to burn through the stuff of her uniform like a naked flame. He put her down as soon as he decently could, shaken by the sensual impact of her. The fashionably deep-cut lapels of her tight-buttoned jacket presented a starched white blouse front that had been ruined by the downpour. White cotton now resembled sodden tissue. And it was transparent enough to show all too clearly that her bra was gossamer. Sufficiently so to reveal a dusting of freckles across the upper slopes of her breasts.

Anna opened her mouth to say something, drawing in her breath and making matters in many ways worse, but the chopper pilot came in immediately behind her and the little corridor became very crowded indeed. 'Well, no use waiting wedged here mob-handed,' announced Tom O'Neill. 'I'm off. Catch you alone for a chat about miracles sometime soon, Captain Mariner. You coming, Mohammed?' And he led the cheerful Indonesian away down the corridor to clatter down some distant companionway.

Their fading footsteps echoed strangely and were replaced by others, approaching briskly. Felix reappeared. He had used the brief interim to remove his coat and Astrakhan hat. He looked every inch the multimillionaire Russian *biznisman*. His gaze swept over the group, passing the bedraggled Anna without a flicker of recognition.

'Richard,' he said. 'I hope you and Colin don't mind bunking in together. It's a bit basic but we're still crowded I'm afraid. When you've had a chance to freshen up, both the captain and Dr Leonskaya are keen to show you round. There's a lot to see aboard *Zemlya*, I can tell you! Then there's a more formal dinner than usual planned for later.'

The cold brown gaze returned to Anna. That strange kind of recognition reawakened briefly. Then the gaze fell to the pale pink orbs beneath her soaking blouse front. The eyebrows rose in apparent surprise that he should have bothered himself with a girl who looked as though she had just showered in her uniform, even one as well endowed as this.

'The pilot will see you bedded comfortably,' he said, his eyes still on Anna's cleavage, apparently unaware that he was proving at least one of Sigmund Freud's theories to be correct. 'Right! Time's money, as Max Asov likes to point out – and we're wasting it!'

It was only when the aircrew were gone and he was turning to follow Felix and Colin that Richard realized his briefcase was no longer where he had put it.

Suite

'If this is *bunking in together*, then I'm all for it!' said Colin Ross, for whom Felix's words had conjured up visions of five men sleeping head-to-foot in a four-man tent on the Polar icecap. A situation, to be fair, he had just escaped from.

Richard shook his head, uncertain whether to be amused or outraged, distracted for a moment from his concern about his missing briefcase. The Russian's idea of *basic* comprised a sizeable sitting room with deep-pile carpet, a three-piece suite in burgundy leather, side-tables laden with books and magazines, fruit and flowers, ports for laptops, a huge flat-screen TV, and a panoramic window – securely double-glazed this time – looking away north towards the pack and the Pole. A view obscured at the moment by veils of driving rain interspersed with walls of sleet. Three doors leading inward opened respectively to a pair of decent-sized bedrooms with a luxurious-looking shower room dividing them. A glance into the bedrooms revealed that their bags had already been unpacked and everything put in wardrobes, cupboards and drawers. A feat worthy of a medal at the recent London games – had unpacking been an Olympic Sport.

Richard pulled off his damp overcoat and hung it on the back of the door, planning to hand it over to whatever valeting services they had aboard at the earliest opportunity. And his suit into the bargain, he thought. No sooner had the thought struck, however, than there was a scratch at the door. He opened it to reveal a short, deep-bosomed redhead dressed in a steward's uniform.

'I look after this room and all gentlemens,' she informed Richard in a purr that was scented as much as accented. 'You give me clothes for pressing and washing. I give you briefcase found in corridor. Is yours, yes?' She lifted her hand. It was holding Richard's briefcase. He blinked with surprise. It took a moment for suspicion to overcome relief.

'Yes,' he said. 'It's mine. Thank you. Thank you, Miss . . .'

'Ivana. I have unpacked your cases. I look after gentlemens. Anything you want, you ask for Ivana. When you want I take clothes for pressing . . .' Her eyes swept speakingly over Richard's crumpled suit. 'You dial zero on internal and I come. Every time, I come.' And she went. For four steps precisely and then she turned and came back. 'Mr Makarov says I must also give you these,' she said, reaching into her pocket and producing two credit card sized electronic keys. 'Keep secure. If you lose, I have spare. I can come any time. Come *in* any time,' she corrected herself, frowning. And off she went once more.

'Looks like we're in good hands there,' said Colin wryly.

'Yup,' said Richard, lost in thought. He slipped his briefcase on to a table and opened it, pulling out his laptop. 'Why don't you freshen up first,' he said to Colin, who was pulling off his parka – which all too clearly would not be going for valeting. 'I'll check my emails and whatnot, then do some business online.'

Colin wandered amenably into the bathroom only to find himself surrounded by mirrors – for the first time in a good long while. 'My God,' he said. He stuck his head out of the door. 'Yes,' he said. 'I'm just going inside . . .' Then, he added, grimly, '*I may be some time.*' And he quietly closed the door.

Richard gave a grunt of laughter, then he opened his laptop.

While he waited for it to boot up and get in contact with first the Internet and then his email account, he carefully went through the contents of the case. Nothing seemed to be missing. As far as he could tell it was all as and where he had left it. But, although he sometimes amused himself by playing at James Bond, he was really nothing like the spy. He had absolutely no idea whether the case had been searched or not. But the possibility made the short hairs on the back of his neck stand up once again.

As the laptop was being uncharacteristically slow to boot, he found his mind drifting off. But it didn't drift far. The suite, almost as luxurious as those he habitually shared with Robin on their travels, seemed to focus at least some of his concerns. Surely it was too luxurious for what was just a working power station when all was said and done. When *Zemlya* was anchored safely off the coast five degrees or so east of here, attached to the Siberian electrical system and pumping power – or heat or water or whatever – down to Leningradskiy and Mys Shmidta or wherever, then who in heaven's name was going to sleep here? Who would be dialling up Ivana? Dr Leonskaya? There wasn't likely to be anyone more senior or important aboard. But he couldn't see the necessity for even someone of her standing to be cosseted in such luxury. And, if he knew Felix, then the Russian would be in another suite at least the equal of this one. Probably being looked after by service that made Ivana look plain and self-effacing in comparison. What was the accommodation aboard designed for – if it could house all the extra guests and navigators who had been here during the summer so far – but all of whom would be gone as soon as the winter loomed and *Zemlya* was at anchor – wherever her anchorage proved to be. Something else to keep an eye out for while he was looking around the vessel later, perhaps. He had a strange feeling that no matter how he looked at her, something aboard *Zemlya* just didn't add up.

His email login page appeared while he was in his brown study, then vanished behind the Starfield screensaver he favoured because it amused him to be reminded of what the view ahead of Starfleet Captain James T. Kirk must have been when he and the *Enterprise* boldly went where no man had gone before. But he didn't see it any more clearly than he had seen the email page. He was still staring sightlessly at the onrushing white dots when Colin emerged from the bathroom clad in a huge white terry-towelling bathrobe, vigorously drying his hair with a six-foot deep-pile bath sheet. 'This is more like a Cunard cruise liner than a working power station,' he said. 'What do you think they'll do with these suites?' he asked more loudly. And Richard looked up, seeming to spring awake. 'I mean they're like something out of the Ritz Hotel! Are they planning to close them off? Mothball them? Let the senior staff aboard have them? What do you reckon?'

The question echoed Richard's own thoughts so exactly that he bestirred himself to try and answer it logically and fully. 'Do you know what this place Leningradskiy is actually like, Colin?' he asked, speaking slowly at first, then gathering pace as his brain began to fire on all cylinders.

'Can't say I do. Too far south to be of interest to an old ice hand like me.'

'Well I do,' said Richard firmly. 'It's like the Wild West. The whole town was supposed to have been closed down fifteen years or so ago when the government decided it was too costly to keep mining the gold. But the population refused to be dispersed. So they stayed. Then there was a revolution – an honest to God revolution – by some guys at the local air force base at Mys Shmidta. They got bored by all accounts; tooled up with their standard issue firearms and came into town looking for vodka and amusement. Mayhem. Militsia, FSB called in, the lot. Everyone except the Federal Prosecutor by all accounts.

'But still the town stayed alive. It's what, less than ten miles from the coast. Good fishing. Sizeable air force base at Mys Shmidta – where the revolting soldiers came from. Enough to keep the place ticking over. A couple of thousand diehards stayed.

'Then of course the whole game changed. Gold prices went through the roof – what are they now? The better part of a thousand pounds – fifteen hundred dollars – an ounce? And suddenly the mines began to look more viable. Speculators moved back. Then businesses like Sevmash came sniffing in case it was another Klondyke. And there was more.

Even after the Cold War, the Kremlin still kept pushing their big Bear and Backfire long-range bombers out to test the air defences over Alaska, Canada, the North Atlantic – especially after President Putin made his big announcement about resuming regular intelligence flights from 2007. The base is even being beefed up. Runway extended. The lot. Things looked up and then some. Town more than doubled in size. And that's even before Gazprom and Sevmash struck oil ten miles south and the whole thing went up like a Roman candle . . .' He hesitated, dropping his voice as Felix had done. 'Before they opened the North East Passage in 2010. Before the north coast of Siberia became the logical jump-off point for the conquest of the Arctic basin and all the oil reserves beneath it. Before the market for coastal port facilities began to mushroom. Before Beijing asked Manila to see if they could strike a deal or two.'

'But what's actually *there now*?' asked Colin, his interest piqued. 'What's it like on the ground in Leningradskiy so to speak? *As* we speak?'

'Wooden shacks . . .' Richard's voice drifted off as something Felix had said fell into place. 'So that's it,' he whispered.

'What's what?' asked Colin, unused to Richard's Olympic leaps of logic.

'This place isn't like the Ritz by accident. It *is* the Ritz. The Leningradskiy Ritz. He wants to be able to fly his clients and cronies into Mys Shmidta and show them around the Leningradskiy highlights, the gold mines, the oil fields, the port facilities as they start to come on line. Give them a sniff of the wild frontier, then chopper them out to *Zemlya* to do business in the kind of environment most conducive to parting with money.' He looked around the plush suite with new eyes. 'What is it they say?' he asked rhetorically. 'Nothing succeeds like *excess*?'

Forty minutes later Richard emerged from his bedroom, showered, shaved and steaming fragrantly. He was dressed in his smartest hand-cut blazer, pale cotton Oxford weave shirt, silk tie and grey flannels. He carried his bedraggled suit over one arm and he laid it over the back of one burgundy chair before looking up to find Colin lounging on the sofa, still looking a little like a lumberjack, with a massive Aran fisherman's pullover in natural unbleached oily wool like a yellowing snowdrift beside him, reading *Ninety Degrees North.*

'I'd have thought you'd have read that,' he said as he crossed to the phone and dialled zero. 'God knows, you've *lived* it.'

A scratch at the door announced Ivana come in answer to the simple dialling of zero. Richard crossed the room, sweeping up his suit and taking down his coat. But when he turned the handle he found himself facing not a slight, deep-chested redhead but a rigid, wide-shouldered, tough-looking young officer.

'Yes?' he said, his tone very English indeed.

'I am Brodski. Captain Sholokhov has sent me to conduct your inspection of his vessel.' The man spoke as solidly as he looked. 'If this is convenient to you. And to Mister Ross.'

Ivana stepped out from behind him. 'And I am come also. What do you wish?'

'Valeting, please.' Richard handed over his clothing. 'Colin?' he called.

'I'm fine,' said the ice master equably, putting the book down and picking up the pullover. 'It's taken years of untouched wearing and not a little bear grease to get my kit as weatherproof as it is. One touch from Ivana would undo the better part of a decade's careful work.'

'OK. That will be all, thank you, Ivana. Now, Lieutenant Brodski, lead on if you'd be so kind.'

Bridge

Richard and Colin's suite was on the upper level of the big square bridge house. In a conventional vessel, this would have been C Deck, the command bridge deck. But at first sight everything about it emphasized just how unusual *Zemlya* was. Lieutenant Brodski led the two men forward along a wide corridor floored with soft composite tiles between three more doorways – clearly leading to three other big suites.

He followed the lieutenant and the ice master through into what appeared to be a rudimentary command bridge after all. On the kind of ships Richard was used to commanding, there would be bank after bank of instruments, controls, computer screens under the wall-to-wall clear-view, all of them familiar in function if not in form. Here there were comparatively few he could readily recognize. A helm – with an apparently idle helmsman. But no power and propulsion levers beside him – no engine room telegraph at all. Because, of course, there was no engine room. By the same token, there were no movement monitors – no collision alarm radars.

Richard's eyes narrowed as his cold blue gaze raked over the instruments. There was an impressive-looking weather monitoring system and a very complex radio communications system, upon which the spruce and sprightly Captain Sholokhov was talking to several tugboat skippers all at once. The video screens of the communications system were augmented by a bank of CCTV monitors, many of them split into four-screen mode.

It looked as though whoever was on the bridge could not only communicate with a wide range of contacts – near and far – but also keep a close eye on every important space and work area aboard. And indeed, a rigid young man in military uniform wearing what looked like a forces-issue side arm was standing at ease as though carved in granite, his eyes fixed on the CCTV monitors like those of a guard-dog on a suspicious shadow.

As the captain continued speaking, Richard exchanged glances with Colin behind the soldier's back and the pair of them quietly began to look over the square, solid shoulder, scanning what seemed to be the most important areas aboard. As Richard did this, he was making a mental list of the ways in which he would direct Lieutenant Brodski during the rest of the visit. Almost at once, however, Captain Sholokhov waved his visitors forward. It was an invitation Richard was happy to accept, for he had never been aboard a barge – certainly not one even remotely like this one.

Apart from the complex radio/video link and the weather prediction system, the only advanced and familiar kit were

the depth gauges, the GPS equipment, the state of sea monitors and the various temperature read-outs for in-ship (area
by area), weather decks (top deck, foredeck and aft), air and
sea – all with clearly graduated warnings down past freezing.

Beside these there was equipment Richard was not familiar
with and which seemed to be off-line, like a sizeable section
of monitors whose function he could not begin to fathom.
He was examining this bank of blank monitors so closely
that he didn't even register the fact that the bridge had
suddenly gone silent.

'Now,' said Captain Sholokhov, appearing suddenly at his
shoulder, 'I understand you are a ship's captain, Mr Mariner,
so much of this equipment will be familiar to you. The depth
gauges, the Global Positioning System – compasses are
useless up here of course – but you will not be so familiar
with these instruments. These first ones are the central control
computers that govern even the power on the tugs. And, of
course, everything aboard *Zemlya* herself. They run from our
main generator. These others, however, are off-line for the
moment.' His open hand gestured towards the blank screens
closest to the computer control monitors. 'They are off-line
for two reasons. Firstly, because we do not yet need them as
we have enough power in our primary generators for our
current needs. And secondly, because the systems they
monitor are powered by the reactors rather than the primary
generators. Which, as the next bank of redundant screens
demonstrates, are not yet powered up themselves. Though
these, just beside them, which *are* alive, show that the backup
generator is running at optimum. Otherwise the outside
temperature of ten degrees would be the inside temperature
too, while we all sat around shivering. And in the dark of
course. As it is – and as you may see – we have light, power
and twenty-five degrees of heat in all the work areas.'

Richard was much fuzzier on the process of starting up a
power station than he was on the process of sailing it into
place. But he could see the logic of leaving the system off-
line for the moment – as long as the vessel had enough power
to function. Which it seemed to. Meaning that there was a
conventional generator somewhere aboard as well, as
Sholokhov explained and as his instruments made clear. That,
in turn, seemed a logical insurance in any case.

But the captain was sailing onwards through his no-doubt well-rehearsed speech, explaining the conservation of heat on board to keep the hull and upper works free of ice. 'Indeed, as she uses seawater as the principal heat exchange medium, she pumps out sufficient hot water to keep everything short of a major berg or ice island at bay. It is a very efficient system. All of which is monitored by these banks of screens.'

'And this hot water you're going to be pumping into the Arctic Ocean . . .' rumbled Colin, his green hackles rising at the thought of it.

'Just that, I assure you. Hot water – nothing more. These smaller monitors here observe the temperature of the exhaust water and these larger ones constantly monitor chemical composition and most especially search for any radioactive contamination. But there will be none. These reactors are the latest generation of power plants that have been working perfectly safely aboard nuclear submarines, warships and ice-breakers for almost half a century.'

'Yeah,' said Colin coldly. 'Submarines like K-19.'

'Precisely! Submarines! This technology is based on the surface ship technology. And you will find no such list of accidents and alarms for nuclear powered warships, transport vessels and ice-breakers I am certain!'

It was on this point that their visit to the bridge was ended. The captain swung away on a heel and a histrionic high leaving the lieutenant to take the pair of visitors in tow and lead them down to the main accommodation deck, where the odd-seeming layout of the lift shafts became easier to understand. Here the lateral corridor led not to one central corridor reaching back towards the poop deck but two. On the corner of each of these corridors, the lift doors stood much more logically placed. Instead of a panelled partition decorated with prints, a wall of doors faced them. 'How many personnel sleep here?' Richard asked Brodski.

The lieutenant shrugged. 'Thirty-five. More if there are wives aboard in the married men's accommodation . . .' He gestured to the area in front of them, immediately beneath the command bridge.

'Any wives aboard now?' asked Colin idly.

'No.' Brodski gave Colin a strange look. 'There are no women of that sort aboard at all. All our spare capacity is full of media people, journalists, visitors of one type or another. And us navigators of course. There is sufficient accommodation for one hundred and one personnel, but *Zemlya* can accommodate one hundred and twenty-eight if we double up.'

'One hundred and one,' said Richard. 'That's quite a few more than I thought. I thought it only took sixty-nine to run the power station.'

'It does,' said Brodski, leading them back to the lift. 'Dr Leonskaya will be able to give you precise details of who does what in that regard.'

'Then where do the extra thirty or so come from?' asked Richard as they stepped into the lift.

'You're just about to meet twenty of them,' said Brodski. 'They call themselves Alpha Team. Their leader is Karchenko. He calls himself *captain* and he has three stars on his uniform shoulder. But it's not a navy uniform, even a merchant marine uniform like mine. They're all ex-Spetsnaz. Armed to the teeth and trigger-happy. We walk pretty softly around them I can tell you.' He looked up as the door hissed open. The white light of the lift's illumination made his face look pale and gaunt. 'Security,' he said.

Security

Three stars on an epaulette were the first things Richard saw as the lift door hissed open. Three stars and a distinctive Sevmash Security badge. Then he noticed the way the captain's balled right fist rested threateningly on the butt of the pistol holstered at his side. This holster was lower-cut than the bridge guard's had been and Richard could see enough of this gun to recognize it as a state of the art OTs Pernach automatic; the latest generation, made of composite rather than metal, by the look of things. Designed to hold a clip containing up to thirty 9mm rounds and capable of firing them at a rate of 900 a minute. A hand-held machine gun designed to kill even enemies wearing body armour. No wonder the lieutenant trod softly around men armed like this.

But somebody was treading anything but softly.

'No!' shouted Dr Leonskaya. 'You will not send an escort with us, Captain Karchenko. Even if Dr Vengerov wishes to join us. I will show our visitors the below-deck facilities without your spies in tow! It is bad enough that I will have an inspector from the Safety Directorate looking over my shoulder and I simply will not have you or your men interfering. And it is my decision to make, not yours. You need to remember, Captain, that I am in command of this nuclear facility. When Captain Sholokhov and his men go and *Zemlya* is in position, safely anchored and producing power, you will answer to me – and to me alone! So you'd better start getting used to it now!'

Captain Karchenko's face was as pale as hers was flushed. Both were twisted with anger and only inches apart. Richard had an instantaneous picture of Karchenko, all line and bone even in profile. Thick white hair in a crew cut so short it was little more than stubble; one neat, tight ear; a high forehead, wrinkled with a frown; an eyebrow thick and black but as well trimmed as Captain Sholokhov's moustache. An eye so narrow as to be almost invisible. A broken beak of a nose backed by almost Mongol cheekbones. Cheeks with vertical valleys down to a lean jaw and a square chin so closely shaved they gleamed as though burned. A slash of a mouth apparently getting ready to spit – insults if not phlegm.

He towered over the slighter figure of the doctor and should have dominated her easily for she was all pink cheek, red lip, blue eye, blonde hair, and that almost comically upturned nose. Even his uniform seemed to overpower her blue cotton blouse and working jeans. But she was giving as good as she got, and was clearly not about to back down here. Richard's hand slid over the edge of the lift door, holding it wide as he watched, fascinated. In his mind, the one word that seemed to describe Captain Karchenko: Spetsnaz.

Lieutenant Brodski coughed discreetly.

The crackling atmosphere changed at once. 'Thank you very much, Captain Karchenko,' purred Dr Leonskaya, as though butter wouldn't melt in her mouth. 'That will be all. I'll take it from here.'

'Of course, Doctor.' He stepped back smartly as the three men came out of the lift. 'As you wish.' He turned towards the forward section of the bridge house where a big metal door stood in the same position as the command-bridge door two decks above. At eye level, there was a large sign which said:

Безопасность

Under that, more helpfully it said:

Security

There was no line of decorative prints cheering up this corridor. Just a solid, featureless partition that looked as though it was made of steel, as did the unusually heavy bulkhead doors that opened out on to the main weather deck beyond.

Apparently on second thoughts, captain Karchenko turned. 'But perhaps, Doctor, you would be kind enough to introduce me to our new guests before you drag them down below.'

'Of course, Captain,' agreed the doctor. 'Captain Mariner, Dr Ross, this is Captain First Class Ivan Karchenko, recently retired from our elite Naval Special Forces. He is the head of our security team. He is a man you will need to know while you are aboard. Though I'm sure he knows everything there is to know about both of you already.'

'I would hardly be worthy of my posting if I did not,' agreed the captain affably. His eyes seemed almost as black as his eyebrows and they raked over Richard and Colin like the claws of a polar bear. His left hand stayed straight down, thumb to trouser-seam, as though he was at attention. His right hand remained on the butt of his pistol. Neither offered to shake. He gave a rigid little half bow – hardly more than a nod – and turned away.

Dr Leonskaya also turned, leading the way to the far lift. As she did so, Lieutenant Brodski stepped back into his lift and at last allowed the doors to close. Richard glanced over his shoulder to see Karchenko punching a complex security code into a panel beside the door. Then Karchenko said something too quietly for Richard to hear him and, leaning forward, eye wide, looked into a little lens. Now that's what I call security, thought Richard. But somehow he didn't feel particularly secure.

'In fact,' said Dr Leonskaya as they waited for the lift, 'my domain overlaps with Captain Karchenko's on this level. Not for nothing is the security centre placed where it is. To get in off the deck outside, one must come past it. To get down off the upper decks one must come past it. At the rear of the bridge house here there is nothing but impenetrably thick steel both outside and inside. Thick steel walls that house the upper reaches of the reactor rooms – and the security men at the front are no less yielding.

'My reactor rooms fill the aft one quarter of this deck. These are the control areas rather than the reactors themselves, which are on the next level down. But there is no door in the upper level, and only one main entrance on the next level. And not even a battle tank could break through either from the poop deck or from this corridor. That's why, apart from the security centre itself there are only twenty cabins here. Each one occupied by one of Karchenko's men. And they sleep with their guns under their pillows. Seriously.'

And I believe you, thought Richard.

The lift came and the three of them climbed aboard. When it stopped one deck down, Richard found himself stepping out into a setting that reminded him of the Ritz Hotel once more. He hadn't thought through the facilities which might be needed in an environment such as this one, so what he saw came as a surprise. Especially as this section of the Ritz was bustling with activity, unlike the rest of the vessel that they had visited so far. The wall in front of Richard, one deck below the security area, three decks below the command bridge, was heavy-duty glass. Through this Richard could see on the left a sizeable swimming pool, with changing facilities and showers beyond. And to the right, a well-fitted gym with an area for weights, exercise machines, and a couple of multi-gyms beside it. There were bodies in the water, swimming with a concentration and focus that told him this was more about fitness than fun. There was a tense game of basketball in the gym. All the weights and exercise machines were occupied. Karchenko's command by the look of things, staying honed while their duties were light. But then he thought he saw that one of the basketball teams was led by Tom O'Neill, and the game was being refereed, by the look of things, by the baby-faced Mohammed Yamin. The Indonesian oil executive was puffing up and down the court dressed in Nike's finest and holding a whistle.

'There are entertainment facilities: cinema, library, Internet café and so forth beyond that, under the main foredeck,' explained their guide. 'Then, beyond them, more work areas. The forward engineering and maintenance areas – mostly stores and so forth. The aft maintenance work areas are under the poop deck behind us. It is possible to move between these areas via the lower level where the turbine halls and power connection facilities are located.

'Immediately behind us, under the sleeping accommodation for the security team, there are the galleys and dining area, and *Zemlya*'s medical facility. Then, as you will see, sandwiched between the aft maintenance work area and the sickbay are my main reactor rooms. That's where my beautiful twins are waiting to wake up. Like Snow White and Sleeping Beauty, yes?'

Marina Leonskaya led Richard and Colin aft along the corridor past the dining room, the galley and the medical facility. Aft of this there was a changing room where a little camera team was waiting, all dressed in white overalls. Nana Potemkin was with them, also in white, her powerful bulk making Richard think of polar bears once more.

Richard hung up his blazer so he and Colin could step into a matching set while Marina stepped into another, her lithe movements explaining to Richard the practicality of jeans. The tall, dark, intense and vaguely familiar TV presenter came across to them. 'Hi,' she said. 'My name's Joan Rudd.' She smiled. 'And these are Mick my cameraman and Al the sound engineer. I'm fronting this documentary about Ice Station *Zemlya*. We've filmed almost all of the visitors going into the reactor room for the first time. Is it cool if we film you as well? People's reactions have been pretty telling. Make good copy.'

'The reactors are still down,' Marina emphasized, zipping up her overalls and gesturing to a big metal door in the back wall of the changing room. 'Strictly speaking we don't even need the overalls. Let alone those things . . .' Nana had started handing out individual dosimeters. They were the size of credit cards and slipped into plastic-fronted panels on the shoulders of the overalls.

'These are new,' explained Nana. 'But they're easy to use. They check automatically for the full spectrum. Alpha, beta, gamma, X-rays even. The little panel gives a dosage reading. The little lights give a quick visual warning. Green is good. Amber not so good. Red bad. We go red, we get out.'

'It's a bore,' shrugged Marina. 'But it's a health and safety requirement – and it's good practice anyway. I think we can dispense with the headgear, though. Just this once.' She gestured at a line of green helmets hanging on the wall.

'Just this once,' huffed Nana Potemkin, with wry amusement. 'We dispense with them every time Joan and her camera show up!'

'Green does not suit my complexion,' said Marina cheerfully. 'It is bad enough that the camera adds a couple of kilos to my weight without making me look like a green-faced witch as well!' She gave a wide grin in Richard's general direction and continued her fairy-tale analogy. 'I don't want to look as though I am bringing pins and poisoned apples to my two sleeping princesses!' She punched in a code as complex as the one Karchenko had punched into the security door, waited for a moment as her iris was scanned, then pushed the big door back. The camera lights came on. Their brightness revealed a solid little antechamber and another steel door that looked, if anything, larger than the first. She looked back over her shoulder, knowing from experience that the first-time visitors would be frowning with wonder – at the least – in the face of such complex security measures. And Colin certainly was. Richard, on the other hand, was all too well aware of where this incredibly dangerous – pricelessly saleable – item was bound. Leningradskiy; Siberia's equivalent of the Wild West. He had in fact been wondering whether there would have been an insurrection in the first place if the Air Base at Mys Shmidta had been equipped with a swimming pool and gymnasium. A library. A cinema. A bevy of girls like Ivana and Anna.

But then Marina opened the second door in the same way

as she had opened the first and all thoughts were wiped from his mind by the immediacy of what he was seeing in the limited distance. Joan Rudd was there at once, between him and the inner door, pushing a microphone towards him as the beam of Mick's camera light settled on him and Al muttered, 'Sound OK.'

'Captain Richard Mariner, Chief Executive Officer of Heritage Mariner, may well be thinking of getting more involved in this project than he is already,' she was saying. 'Captain Mariner, have you ever been round a nuclear facility?'

'Call me Richard, please. And no. I have not.'

Richard opened his mouth to say more, preparing to push forward into the reactor room itself, but the door from the changing room behind him opened and Captain Karchenko stepped in. He was in overalls and bareheaded like the rest of them. Vasily Vengerov of the Nuclear Safety Directorate was punctiliously at his side, also in overalls. But he was wearing a green helmet, settled squarely on his head, strapped securely under his chin, and carrying a clipboard thick with documentation.

Reactors

With the visitors present and the cameras rolling there was no question of even the redoubtable Marina returning to the full-frontal assault Richard and Colin had witnessed as the lift doors opened; something Karchenko had obviously calculated. But, to be fair, he was the sole security representative – and for once he was apparently unarmed. Marina could hardly complain that this was the security patrol she had so vehemently vetoed. Not to mention that the presence of Vengerov, his documentation and his squarely settled green helmet caused a noticeable change in the atmosphere.

Joan Rudd carried on with her interview without missing

a beat. Behind her, Mick the cameraman stepped back through the inner doorway so that he could get a good shot of Richard's face when he finally stepped into the reactor room. 'And yet you are already involved in this project, are you not?' asked Joan.

'There are two Heritage Mariner tugs helping to move *Zemlya*, yes,' he allowed, keeping his eye on Joan as she began to move backwards, following her through the last section of the little antechamber towards the second door. 'They are called *Erebus* and *Terror*, named for—'

'Named for the ships that disappeared with Sir John Franklin and his ill-fated expedition in 1845. Yes, I know,' Joan interrupted.

'Having been to Antarctica with Sir James Ross and his famous expedition five years earlier, and brought him and his men safe home again, yes,' countered Richard cheerfully.

'The current thinking on Franklin seems to be that the ice nipped his ships and a combination of disease and lead poisoning from improperly sealed cans of food got his men. Nothing to do with *Erebus* and *Terror* themselves,' added Colin.

'And you have had long-time business associations with both Mr Makarov and his business partner, Mr Max Asov, have you not?' persisted Joan smoothly, still focused on Richard, coming back into the spotlight, and happier to be there. Her brown eyes had green and golden highlights, he noticed. And she had a little emerald pendant sitting deep in the shadowed valley of her cleavage.

But Richard had been mentally preparing his answer to this question for some time, so he was able almost to go on to autopilot as he listed the areas in which Heritage Mariner and the Sevmash Consortium had cooperated over the years. Which was lucky. Because what he saw as he raised his eyes and stepped through the second door overwhelmed him almost entirely.

The space itself seemed quite vast, though to be fair he had been in larger spaces on ships. On his huge container ships and supertankers, for instance, or the Titan series of submarine tankers he helped Max and Felix crew and run. But there was something almost awe-inspiring about this one.

It was fifty metres long and thirty metres wide; more than three decks deep – ten metres, maybe fifteen.

In the middle of the upper space hung a column of what looked like glass. Down this reached a strange array of control rods like the strings of puppets, all reaching towards the level Richard was standing on. The cameraman backed away, still filming. Joan moved likewise as though the pair of them were psychically linked. Richard followed on, entranced, still talking. He could sense Colin at his shoulder. Marina Leonskaya and Nana Potemkin moved in the corner of his vision. Captain Karchenko was no doubt somewhere behind him too.

The balcony ahead of Richard ran on out until it widened into a circle seemingly a little less than ten metres across. But then, as he moved, Richard realized that there was not one solid circle on the deck at his feet but two – arranged to look like a figure of eight. And, when he looked up he realized that the confusion of rods was arranged in the same 8-shape. Through the metal mesh of the decking, Richard looked down at the solid columns that reached, gleaming, to the very keel. Two columns, circular in section, side-by side in that figure of eight, perhaps five metres in depth. The reactors.

Richard realized he had stopped speaking, just as Marina seemed to go into overdrive as she, like captain Sholokhov on the bridge earlier, went into her prepared spiel. Although she was ostensibly talking to Richard and Colin, she was clearly keeping one eye on Joan and – especially – the cameraman. The other eye was most certainly on Vengerov and his Nuclear Safety paperwork – upon which he had begun to tick, cross and make an unsettling range of notes. Vengerov hardly looked at her. He glanced around the chamber narrow-eyed, ticking, crossing, annotating, pausing only to run one finger under the chinstrap of his hard hat.

'Floating units such as *Zemlya* have many advantages. The reactors are factory-produced and supplied as ready-made units for installation. They have integral turbines in many cases, though we have extended the turbines in this instance. The siting of the power stations is considerably simplified, therefore, as the whole vessel can be tugged anywhere in the world and only needs a basic connection system to the local power grid. Fundamentally, we just pull it to where we want it, plug it in and switch it on. The reactors are continuously operated over eight to twelve years without refuelling and maintenance. Though, of course, *Zemlya* is serviced much more regularly than that, and servicing of the reactors is built in to the general servicing schedule.' She looked at the impassive face of Vasily Vengerov who continued, seemingly, to pay no attention to her words while noting and listing every flaw and failure all around. Seemingly enraptured by his task, he was drifting away from the group, with Karchenko in tow.

'I must emphasize that Ice Station *Zemlya* is environmentally friendly,' continued Marina, raising her voice to make sure that Vengerov could hear her, no matter how far away he chose to wander. 'Refuelling, radioactive waste management, and maintenance are provided as part of the overall maintenance cycle – and all the waste produced is removed in specially designed container-sized vessels for disposal at the Sevmash facility at Arkangelsk. While *Zemlya* is on station there is no impact whatsoever on the local environment. Not even any litter. After decommissioning the "green field" concept is easily realized at its site area because *Zemlya* is tugged away and all that remains is the non-nuclear shore facility.'

She was standing with one foot on top of the nearest reactor now, simply glowing with confidence and enthusiasm. Vengerov had wandered to the far side of the strange figure-of-eight construction and was looking down into the open turbine hall below, leaning right over the safety rail at a sufficient angle to put even his securely anchored hard hat at risk – and to have Karchenko like a cat on hot bricks, ready to grab him if he went right over.

As far as Richard was concerned, Marina might as well have been speaking Greek. Now she switched to fluent gibberish, clearly trying to catch Vengerov's attention one last desperate time. Vengerov straightened, turned slowly and stepped back towards the top of the reactor. His clipboard fell to his side. Richard was struck by the truth of Marina's assessment. Under the peak of his composite hard hat, his lean face did indeed look a little green.

Richard became aware of the faintest buzzing sound, as though an angry hornet had somehow entered the reactor room. He looked around, wondering where the strange sound could be coming from. The buzzing was quite persistent now. Loud enough to stop Marina at last. Everyone else, it seemed, was equally bemused.

Except for Vasily Vengerov. The man from the Nuclear Safety Directorate reached into the left trouser-pocket of his white overalls and pulled out a little machine the size of an old-fashioned portable phone. He looked at it, frowning with almost drunken concentration.

Richard recognized it. He looked down at the credit-card dosimeter on his own overall shoulder. The figures read in the safe range, the warning light was green. He looked at Colin's. It read the same. So did Joan's, Marina's and Nana's. He couldn't see Karchenko's from here – to judge whether the two men had somehow strayed into an unsuspected danger area.

But Vengerov was holding a much more sensitive and sophisticated piece of kit. A full-blown Geiger counter by the look of things. And the urgent buzzing was its warning. A buzzing augmented by the bright red danger-light that was flashing between Vasily Vengerov's fingers.

Contaminated

Marina Leonskaya gaped at Vengerov and his Geiger counter, seemingly frozen with shock and surprise. Her expression was similar to Vengerov's own as he looked down at the noisy little machine flashing red in his hand. Joan and her cameraman stood uncertainly. The dosimeter on his shoulder was bright red too, and could have been for a while, Richard supposed. He for one had been paying scant attention to it. But now was the time for action yet no one seemed sure what to do. Even Karchenko seemed uncharacteristically hesitant.

Richard took the initiative. 'Perhaps we should continue this outside,' he suggested calmly but in a forcefully carrying voice. 'Marina, is there a way of moving your people out of

the B Deck control room above here without undue fuss and
alarm?'

'I'll go up and get them,' said Nana decisively. And she
was off towards a staircase leading upwards along one steel
wall.

'Good. Colin, if you'll lead the way out of here . . .'

As Colin turned, Richard looked at the dosimeter on his
friend's shoulder more closely. It still read safe and green. Joan
and her cameraman followed Colin. Richard was just about to
exit behind them when a clattering sound made him turn.
Vengerov had dropped his Geiger counter and seemed to be on
the point of fainting. Karchenko caught the reeling man, just as
the clipboard joined the Geiger counter on the top of the reactor.
Richard stepped back to help. Without a second thought, he
slung Vengerov's arm across his shoulders, then he and
Karchenko carried the inspector across towards the door, the
helmet-weighted head rolling from one shoulder to the other,
as though Vengerov's neck had somehow been broken.

Richard's mind was racing even as his massive frame went
into action. Every detail of the scene went into his memory
for later examination. Immediate experiences, like the weight
of the fainting man, the foulness of his breath, the Cyrillic of
the ID tag on his breast: В Венгеров. The way the urgent
buzzing of the Geiger counter faded surprisingly rapidly
behind them all took their place.

Richard and Karchenko carried Vengerov straight through
the main door, then through the second door and then on
further still into the sickbay. The inspector was unconscious
now – so they had little choice in the matter. They pulled
his dragging toecaps over the threshold and deposited him
on the nearest bed. It was only when the pair of them were
straightening that Richard noticed the security man's little
dosimeter. It was bright red. He looked down at his own.
Also red. 'My God,' he said.

'What?' snarled Karchenko, his mood obviously soured
by the incident. He had been reaching to loosen Vengerov's
headgear, but Richard's words stopped him. He followed
Richard's gaze and looked down at his flame-red shoulder.

'It's him! *Vengerov* is radioactive!' breathed Richard.

'But how can that be?' snarled Karchenko, marginally less
threateningly.

'I have no idea! But look at your shoulder! Bright red!' Richard turned and strode back into the corridor. Karchenko was suddenly close behind him, though the security man stopped in the doorway and stood guard there, duty clearly coming before safety in his mind.

Marina was still lingering in the corridor, frowning. She was holding Vengerov's clipboard and his Geiger counter. The machine was silent now. 'Can I borrow this?' asked Richard, taking it out of her listless fingers. He swept it over the clipboard and a needle on the upper meter swept round towards the red section. 'I'd put that down for a start,' he advised. Then he strode back past Karchenko into the sick room and put the Geiger counter on Vengerov's chest. The needle on the top dial flicked up into the red zone at once. After a moment it began to buzz on a rising tone, and the warning lights went to amber. Then red.

'Better keep this room clear,' said Richard. 'Captain Karchenko, you and I had better wait to see the doctor, just in case.'

They stepped back out into the corridor and Karchenko leaned his broad shoulders back against the closed door just as Nana led the technicians from the control room out, closing both doors behind her as she did so,

'Marina,' continued Richard, thinking coldly and calmly in the face of the gathering crisis. 'You will want to send a team back in to check the reactors. In the best protective gear you've got. Just in case. I've never heard of anything quite like this, but you'll want to be sure that whatever happened to Vengerov had nothing to do with your facilities.'

'*I've* heard of something like it,' said Marina, frowning as she watched the last of the workers hurry away. After a moment, when there was only the three of them left in the corridor, she continued. 'Years ago. In London. A man called Litvinenko . . .'

'Yes. Alexander Litvinenko. Died in November 2006. He was apparently poisoned with Polonium 210,' said Richard. 'It was one of the random things I checked on before coming out. Found it under "Radiation Poisoning" on Google. But the doctors in London tested him with a Geiger counter and got no reaction. Polonium apparently emits alpha particles

that can be stopped by something as flimsy as a layer of
paper – but inside the body it triggers off a chain reaction
of some sort. This is something different. Has to be if
Vengerov is emitting enough radiation to register on his
Geiger counter and our dosimeters.'

'It has to be in any case,' added Karchenko coolly. 'Unless
you think there is someone aboard who is trying to murder
people.'

The doctor arrived then, a brusque efficient young man
called Mussorgsky. He turned to Marina first for an explanation and checked her fingers as he did so, but listened to the
additions that Karchenko and Richard inserted into her report.
'Right,' he said, 'you are clear, Dr Leonskaya. But lucky to
be so from the look of things. You have done well to isolate
Vengerov and you can go now. I will deal with him at once.'

He waited as the scientist obeyed him, then he turned. 'But
I can't have you two gentlemen waiting around in the corridor.
Go into the next room and strip. It is a shower and sanitiz-
ation room. I will send a trained team to decontaminate you.
Bin your overalls and all your other clothing for decontamination. My team will check you over, scrub you down and
clean you up as necessary.' He paused, looking at the pair
of them. 'Maybe I'd better send two of my best,' he added.

Silently, shoulder to shoulder, Richard and Karchenko went
through into the shower room. Here they discovered benches,
lockers and changing cubicles as well as open, communal
showers not unlike a public swimming pool. One bench was
occupied by Joan Rudd and her cameraman, who were poring
over the playback of the footage in the reactor room. Marina's
voice explained the technicalities of *Zemlya*'s reactor system
quietly in the background, a tinny sound caught by the
camera's sound system rather than Al's. Over the top of it,
Joan was saying, 'There! You got him in the corner of that
shot, Mick. What's he doing?'

'Looking at shit,' Mick the cameraman replied. 'That's all
he does. Looks at shit and writes shit. That and fiddle with
that bloody hard hat of his.'

Richard was just about to ask whether they had any pictures
that included Vengerov's shoulder with the telltale dosimeter,
but the impatient security man forestalled him.

'Sorry to disturb you,' said Karchenko in a tone that showed he was nothing of the sort, 'but you have to leave. Now!'

Joan and Mick both looked up. Not very cooperatively. Their faces setting stubbornly in reaction to his tone.

'We may be contaminated,' added Richard placatingly. 'Doesn't radiation muck up vision recording equipment?'

'*Strewth*, he's right!' muttered Mick. 'Let's go, Joanie girl.'

Mick was halfway out the door before Joan even moved. Her moss-brown eyes rested calculatingly on Richard who was tearing open the front zip of his overall and pulling off his tie. 'If you've worked that out, Captain, then you know there can't have been anything very badly contaminated in the reactor chamber or we'd never have got the clarity of sound and digital recording we did get.'

'It crossed my mind,' said Richard, snapping the tie loose of his collar like a whip. 'And I'll be asking to see it later, unless whoever's convening the enquiry into this incident has already done so. But I'm serious. The captain and I are contaminated with whatever got Vengerov. We're stripping down and showering off now. So unless you want to join the medical team and help us, then I suggest a dignified exit.'

She shrugged and went, with hardly a backward glance.

'All this tact and cajoling,' snarled Karchenko. 'Such a waste of time.' He ripped his red dosimeter out of its holder then tore the zip of his overall down.

'I tend to agree,' said Richard, continuing to undress with a little less vehemence. 'But I do want her cooperation to look through that footage if no one else has done so in the meantime. Just to establish how soon his dosimeter started to register that he was in trouble. Where he was when it did so . . . That sort of thing. And I'm here on a Dale Carnegie mission after all . . .'

Karchenko looked up enquiringly as he trod himself out of the overalls, too careless to take off his boots at this stage, tearing the legs in the process.

'To *Win Friends and Influence People*,' Richard explained.

'Ha!' barked Karchenko, amused. He kicked the overalls into a big black bin and threw his shirt after them, reaching for the buckle of his belt as he talked. Then he thought better of it, turned, put one foot on a bench and unlaced his gleaming boots. He dropped his trousers and his shorts. His body was lean, feral, lightly furred with grey hair and marked with an arresting range of tattoos and scars. But the gaunt frame was toned; the muscle groups defined by careful diet and strenuous exercise.

Richard's own body was lean, but retained its strength through hard work not through exercise routines. His chest was deep, powerful; but Karchenko's was toned, the Russian's pectorals as defined as Schwarzenegger's, Stallone's or Statham's. Richard's belly was flat; Karchenko's was corrugated. 'I am not here to *win friends*,' the Spetsnaz officer concluded, looking Richard straight in the eye as the last of his clothing arced into the bin with an accuracy that would have made him an asset in O'Neill's basketball game. 'But I will *influence people*.'

The door opened at that point and a pair of pretty, square-bodied, freckle-faced young women in nurse's uniforms entered. '*Yzumitelno*, Captain,' said the first to Karchenko. 'I am Nurse Agna and you have certainly influenced me.' Then her cheerfully roguish eye roved over both of the considerable bodies before her as Richard placed his clothing in the bin on top of Karchenko's. 'And you may continue to do so at any time you'd like. Either of you. Now stand still, please, while Sasha and I run *our* equipment over *your* equipment. *Spasiba*.'

'Very well,' decided Agna more seriously a little later still. 'It looks like your heads and shoulders were the only areas with any contamination. Into the showers now, please.' As the two men marched obediently into the stalls, Sasha preceded them and turned the powerful jets of water full on. Then she and Agna pulled open their nurse's uniforms to reveal thoroughly modest 1950s' style one-piece white bathing costumes and slipped on big yellow rubber gloves. They followed the men in and scrubbed them expertly – and blessedly impersonally – from head to toe. In the meantime, two more nurses wearing protective gloves closed the top of the bin and wheeled it away. Now the top was closed, it was possible to see two words stencilled on it:

Загрязненный

In Cyrillic. And in English:

CONTAMINATED.

'There. Finished,' announced Agna at last. 'And almost as clean as the day you were born. You will find towels and robes in the first two lockers. Slippers too, though they will not fit. Your feet are also unnaturally large. Dry off, then return to your cabins and get dressed. Your personal clothing will be returned to you later.'

The two men silently towelled themselves dry and shrugged on white towelling robes that were really far too small for them. As Agna had suggested, the footwear was out of the question, so they padded out side by side on bare feet. They walked to the lift together, but Karchenko got out on A deck, going straight towards the door of the security section while Richard rode up to C, speculating as to whether Mick the cameraman's record of the incident might not be the only one available. Had there been a CCTV screen on the bridge recording what went on in the reactor rooms? Damned if he could remember.

Five minutes later, Richard was in the shower again and his mind had moved away from thoughts of CCTV. The ministrations of the nurses and the unusual nature of the situation in which they had tended him had made him literally ache for Robin. But she was too far away to be of any immediate help. So, trained through his years at boarding school and on single postings all over the world, he was fighting fire with fire. Or in this case, fighting fire with ice – the shower was as cold as it could go.

There was a knock at the outer door forceful enough to register over the roaring of the water and to dispel the mental pictures of Robin which were not really helping at all. Glad of the distraction, Richard stepped out of the freezing cubicle and shrugged on the towelling robe. He was halfway across the communal sitting room when the door from the corridor opened. He expected it to be Colin or – more likely, given the knocking – Ivana. But no. It was Anna.

Anna came in and stopped opposite him, her eyes wide, her lips panting, breathless with surprise – or with something else. Richard paused, frowning. Utterly unexpected feelings stirring at the sight of the young woman. She had changed out of her soaked and revealing air hostess uniform into the sort of uniform Ivana had been wearing. But it was a size at least too small for her. The curves of her body strained the material, making it hug her with nothing short of intimacy. The rain had turned her strictly brushed air hostess hairdo into a riot of golden curls. Something about the leaden overcast sky outside deepened the decided tint of grey in the depths of her wide blue eyes.

It hit Richard then, and he gaped breathlessly for a moment more as several pieces of a puzzle he hadn't even realized existed fell smoothly into place. Anna looked just like Robin. He hadn't seen the resemblance – but Felix had.

'Which is your bedroom? No one will disturb us. We can be slow . . .'

She stepped forward, her fingers going to the buttons of her straining blouse. Richard stepped back, just on the edge of tumbling headlong into the smoky depths of those steady, grey-blue eyes. 'Or we can be quick. I have no . . .' She paused, then purred throatily. 'No underwear.'

'No. Anna!' he insisted. 'I'm flattered. But I'm happily married!'

'Yes! He said this. But to my twin. To my *identical* twin. Who is half a world away . . .' Buttons parted. Lapels fell back. The matter of underwear was settled – above the waist at least. And Anna did indeed have the same sprinkling of freckles across the upper slope of the breasts so voluptuously presented by the tightness of her clothing and the shortness of her breath.

'No!' Richard stepped forward at last, all too well aware that they were just about to cross the Rubicon here, for the robe was by no means loose enough to protect his rapidly diminishing dignity.

She made that little moue of disappointment with her mouth that he remembered seeing on the plane. It was an expression blessedly unlike anything that Robin ever did. The hands became busy again. But doing buttons up this time.

'Well, *dasvidanye*, Captain,' she said, quietly.

'*Spasiba*, Anna,' he said. And this time he really meant it.

He followed her to the door, saw her out, and watched her for a moment walking away down the corridor. The way her skirt sat over the pear-shaped curves of her bottom like a coat of paint with not the ghost of a pantie line rather settled the matter of underwear below the waist as well.

Five steps down the corridor she turned. Fortunately he had raised his gaze an instant before she did. 'You want me after all,' she persisted, 'I am in with Ivana. Really, really easy to get hold of. You just dial zero. You have me. Anytime.'

Richard nodded and she turned away again. He stepped back into his room before she could smother him with any more temptation. He closed the door and leaned back against it, gasping, his head against the wood, as he wondered how long he would have to stand in the shower to get over this part of the adventure. But then his mind was distracted by the scurry of footsteps out in the corridor behind him. They went past the door, and, more for distraction's sake than for any other reason, he opened the door a fraction and peeked out.

Just in time to see Marina Leonskaya letting herself into the suite he rather thought she shared with Nana Potemkin. But there, pale and stark amongst the shadows immediately inside the door, was a naked shoulder and flank. Tattooed arm, ribbed chest, corrugated belly, defined hip, muscular thigh and calf. Lean, toned, scarred. Furred with grey, like the pelt of a wolf.

Marina Leonskaya gave a tiny gasp that carried to Richard even as he eased his door closed. '*Yuri!*' Then her door closed with a decided click.

And in the thrilling silence, Richard considered how the spark of antagonism that burned so brightly between the doctor and the security captain had another, more physical twin. And how he wasn't the only man aboard driven deep into realms of temptation by recent events.

Well, well, he thought. Well, well, *well*.

Barrier

Anna's visit left Richard on fire in ways he knew not even cold showers would help. Therefore he channelled the complex of almost overwhelming emotions into a blaze of action. The only clothes left to him were rarely worn jeans and the sort of shirt and pullover Colin Ross more usually wore. And his one pair of Timberland hiking boots; the only cold-weather gear he had consciously packed. He climbed into the outfit, grabbed a couple of apples from the courtesy fruit bowl and flung himself down in front of his laptop. He glanced at the clock on the wall and mentally subtracted twelve hours. He'd be lucky to get to talk to anyone at home.

Connection seemed better now and he hit the Skype button with a little prayer. A moment later the real Robin's head and shoulders filled the screen, behind the riot of her golden hair the spines of leatherbound volumes familiar from the library at Cold Fell. 'You look dreadful,' she said unceremoniously.

'I feel it,' he answered. 'Must be because I'm missing you so much.' Robin looked lovely. She was ready for bed in a pink silk dressing gown with a collar so luxuriously high that it was almost a hood. His fingers, rather disconcertingly, seemed to remember the almost silken softness of the robe; the languid heat of the slim body beneath it. 'What are you doing still up? It's after midnight there,' he growled a little hoarsely, the vision in the computer not really helping matters any more than the vividly tactile memory.

'Waiting to hear from you, of course.' She leaned forward. The lapels of the robe parted distractingly. He could almost smell her perfume. Her breath would be all toothpasty. 'Rough trip?' she purred.

'You don't know the half of it!' Suddenly he found he didn't want to tell her about any of it. The planes, the stop-overs, the gathering suspicions and looming dangers. The all-too available air hostess who seemed so nearly identical to her.

Her grey eyes narrowed and that tiny, achingly familiar frown creased her forehead. 'All aboard the good ship *Zemlya* OK?'

Richard opened his mouth to answer truthfully, if partially. Then he remembered what he had been thinking about Karchenko and his surveillance of everything aboard in the lift on the way up here. That surveillance included all common areas for certain. Probably reactor rooms. And possibly etherial media, including radio messages, and, likely as not,

Internet signals. Even Skype. 'Fine,' he answered, guardedly enough to make her frown deepen. 'Colin and I have to share a suite but it's like the Ritz so that's not much of a hardship. The twins?'

'The twins are out,' she said, and he smiled. She hadn't really been waiting up to hear from him at all, he thought. The only thing that ever kept her from her bed after eleven at night was maternal concern about her darling offspring. But no sooner had the suspicion occurred than the truth of it was proved. Robin's face went into profile as she looked away towards the library door. A distant disturbance resolved itself into a pair of young voices. Robin's hand closed the top of her dressing gown reflexively. Then Mary's face was thrust into frame beside her mother's. Her wide blue eyes focused on the screen as Robin leaned back to allow her access. 'Hi, Dad! What you doing keeping poor Mother up this late?'

'It's way past her bedtime you know,' added the cheerful voice of her invisible brother William.

And the slightly out-of-focus image of his beloved wife gave a simply enormous yawn. Relief at knowing all of her little family was apparently safe and well pushing Robin straight into the arms of Morpheus more swiftly than a sleeping-draught. Richard's smile deepened. He exchanged a few more husbandly and paternal words, then bade them all goodnight. He closed Skype with a wry grin and leaned back, his eyes distant. After a moment more of thought, he called up Google and searched for weather conditions in Pevek and Leningradskiy. Weathercity and Foreca informed him that squalls would be easing briefly before the next series of squalls was expected – with a really big blow due to arrive within the next twenty-four to thirty-six hours after that. He had a window of opportunity, if he chose to take it, he thought. He switched off the Internet, killed the computer and snapped the laptop closed.

When Colin came in five minutes later, he found Richard staring out at the moderating afternoon. Chewing thoughtfully on his third apple and bouncing restlessly up and down on the balls of his booted feet.

'How's the captain's enquiry going?' asked Richard without turning.

'Waste of time as far as I can see,' answered Colin roundly. He grabbed the one remaining apple and joined his friend at the window. The last of the squall was sweeping westwards over the East Siberian Sea towards distant Pevek like a ghostly giant tiptoeing away. Its skirts were grey and misty where they brushed across the still-dark sea. Its upper reaches a cloak of finely beaten gold against the brightening sky. 'Certainly is at the moment,' he continued round a wedge of apple. 'Blind leading the blind down a blind alley at midnight. With all the speed of a glacier. A pre-global warming glacier at that. Captain Sholokhov can't find Karchenko and daren't do much without him. Can't find Marina Leonskaya, come to that, and he wants to clear up something with her before he proceeds. He wants to see you too, in due course, but he's locked in closed session with Felix first.' He gave a cynical laugh. 'Nothing suspicious there then.'

'Want to do something more active?' asked Richard. 'More exciting?'

'Like what?' demanded Colin, brightening.

'Like what you're here to do. Get the chopper up before they secure it in that hangar for good and go look at our destination before any of the various glacial forces aboard can stop us.'

'You know how to do that fast enough to sneak out unobserved?'

'No. But I know a woman who does. And she says she really, really wants to hear from me.'

Anna had the grace to sound disappointed when she found out why Richard had called her so soon after her overwhelming invitation. But she knew how to contact the pilot – and did so on Richard's behalf.

So, fifteen minutes later, Richard and Colin were on the helideck beside the still-dripping Mil as the pilots and engineer raced across the bright, steaming metal towards them. 'Looks like the squall did us a favour,' said Richard.

'That and the crew's reluctance to get any more soaked trying to put her away,' Colin agreed.

'They were boot-faced enough about taking her up again as it is, according to Anna,' Richard mused. 'If they'd have had to have pulled her out of the hangar I reckon nothing less than a directive from Felix would have made them move.'

'They'll have checked with Felix anyway,' said Colin. 'Stands to reason.'

'With Felix and with Sholokhov too, I'd guess. He's in command. Nominally, at least. And *they'll* probably be up here checking on us before take-off. But the ball's rolling and they'll need to come up with a good solid reason to stop it now. We're doing the wise thing. The weather's OK for the next hour or so – as long as the sortie will take. Then it'll be time to batten down the hatches and the chance for a look-see will be gone. They'd be silly to stop us.'

'Especially as they want to keep us sweet and cooperative,' added Colin thoughtfully.

'At almost any price,' agreed Richard as Anna came hurrying out of the nearest doorway. She'd borrowed a coat but it flapped open to reveal that she was still in Ivana's too-tight uniform. Richard found himself praying she'd found time to put some underwear on. But then all such speculation stilled. For behind the hurried hostess came Joan Rudd, Mick with his camera and Al with the sound equipment, the ubiquitous Tom O'Neill. And Felix.

'Looks like we're going mob-handed after all,' growled Colin under his breath.

'Maybe,' said Richard exultantly. For he realized that the thunderous frown on Felix's face was one of reluctant defeat. 'But it sure as hell looks as though we are actually *going*.'

The three of them sat at the same table they had occupied during the flight up from Pevek. Anna came and went. Felix's humour did the same, as Richard's reasoned explanations and Colin's added weight of reassurance warred with his continued consumption of vodka. And with the fact that he did not like to be outmanoeuvred or overruled. At least he had the grace to appear more enthusiastic when Joan and Mick asked to join them. They had some questions for Colin, they explained – given where they were going. Then Richard and Felix took something of a back seat as the ice master described what he expected to find along the coast they were heading for at the better part of two hundred knots. After a few moments, they moved to another table altogether, only to have Tom O'Neill join them, keen to do a bit of probing now that he had both Felix and Richard unable to escape. 'What do you think went on in the reactor room?' he asked.

'Inspector Vengerov somehow became mildly irradiated. He's not too bad,' said Felix almost dismissively. 'The doctor expects him to make a full and rapid recovery. He won't need hospitalization – or we would hardly have released the helicopter to go scouting along the coast like this.'

'The doc give you any idea how bad Vengerov is? How this could affect his life expectancy and so-forth?'

'The incident has done the inspector a great deal less damage than the cigarettes he smokes. And he will still be able to father a fine family should he ever wish to do so, if that is what you're driving at.'

'Any idea how it happened?'

'The captain is holding an enquiry. I have no wish to prejudge anything he might find.'

O'Neill glanced over at Mick. 'Talking of the enquiry, I thought Sholokhov had impounded Mick's camera.'

'He tried,' said Felix, his tone darkening again. 'But he decided to handle things himself – only to discover that Joan Rudd can be pretty irresistible when she really goes for it. And she thought there would be some first-rate footage in this little adventure. Besides, he'll have the footage from Security when Karchenko finally resurfaces.' Felix's tone said that the conversation about the accident was at an end.

'Still and all,' mused O'Neill, 'it's yet another link in a long, long chain.' Then he changed tack completely. 'Hey, Mr Makarov, what's this Mohammed Yamin was telling me about Ludova Timber making a deal with his Luzon Logging guys?'

Felix fielded the enquiry as smoothly as a politician on the stump. 'Ludova Timber is one of Max Asov's concerns. It hardly falls under our larger corporate umbrella at all. But as I am sure you are aware, Siberian timber has been a booming export for some time; almost rivalling gold, oil and Russian diamonds. Since the floods in 1998 – and the worse ones in 2010, leading eventually to the breaching of the Three Gorges Dam – China in particular has been keen to import timber rather than to clear their own forests. But they need enormous amounts of it, and there is very little doubt that it was deforestation that led to the flooding being so destructive, particularly along the Yangtze basin. Luzon Logging also exports into the People's Republic and it seemed to Mr Asov that it would be of mutual benefit to cooperate rather than to compete. Particularly as the combined offer from Ludova Timber and Luzon Logging comprehends almost every type of wood on the commercial market – from Siberian Pine to Malayan Mahogany and Timorese Teak.'

Felix was waxing lyrical now and would have been happy to continue, but Colin interrupted him, calling urgently, 'Richard! Have a look at this! It's worse than we thought. There's a wall of ice piled up along the shore. And it stretches right across the mouth of the bay.'

Richard crossed to his friend's side and looked down through the Mil's window. The chopper had begun to lose height as the shore neared, so Richard and Colin got a clear, close-up view of the final destination to which they were supposed to be bringing *Zemlya*.

The pilot shouted something. 'Leningradskiy dead ahead,' translated Anna.

The chopper swooped upwards. The citadel of ice they were flying over became wider. Its outer edges heaved restlessly as more sea-ice was swept ashore. The coast behind it fell away southward. The resigned upward shrug of land became a low, swampy plain, threaded with silver-gilt streamlets that gathered, in the distance, into some kind of a river further inland. A little further south, on the river, a grey stain of air-pollution gave the position of the city away.

But immediately below the Mil, between the wall of ice and the low plain there was a shallow bay, its waters still, calm and as blue as a butterfly's wing.

'Here,' bellowed Felix, 'is where we will put my Ice Station!'

'We might,' whispered Colin, 'if we could make the damn thing fly!' Then he suddenly became the expert ice master Felix had summoned here. 'No, wait a minute,' he rumbled. 'Let's take a closer look at that . . .'

Enquiry

'The question remains,' said Richard thoughtfully, an hour later. 'Was Inspector Vengerov's unfortunate experience an accident or attempted murder?' He looked at the faces around the table in the Captain's temporary dayroom – which would become the facility manager's office when *Zemlya* was anchored safely and running properly as planned. If that day ever came. There was an understandable air of tension in the room, for Captain Sholokhov had completed his initial enquiry by summoning the senior people aboard to discuss his findings – such as they were.

It was not a large group. Richard was there, and he had brought a reluctant Colin, who would rather have been examining the footage Mick had filmed at the barrier across Leningradskiy Bay. But the camera was here as well, and they were taking a close look at other, earlier footage, for the pictures from Karchenko's CCTV had been of no real help at all. Marina and Karchenko were sitting well apart, and only Richard's accidental knowledge allowed him to see the glances they occasionally exchanged. Felix sat at Sholokhov's right and appeared a little reluctant to let the captain chair the meeting.

Dr Mussorgsky was still tending Vengerov. Nana was leading a team wearing protective suits and carrying Geiger counters through the reactor rooms. Two teams in fact – a team of scientists doing the work and a team of Karchenko's security men overseeing them. Marina planned to join them all for their exploration of the turbine halls. So did Karchenko. Everyone else had been locked out of the proceedings for the time being. Richard was by no means alone in realizing from the moment they got back that a range of rumours was already being disseminated through the closed society aboard *Zemlya*. What would be crucial in the immediate future, therefore, would be to keep some kind of control over what the wider rumours said. Especially before they got to the sensitive ears of the already suspicious Tom O'Neill – and via Tom and the Internet to the front pages of the newspapers worldwide.

In the meantime, Captain Sholokhov remained stolidly in charge. He was not, thought Richard wryly, a man to rush to judgement. Or to shoulder responsibility when it could be shared – and any unpleasant side effects arising from it dissipated. Especially as they were trying to come up not only with the truth, but a story that would satisfy the newspeople aboard without jeopardizing the whole business still further. Vengerov was at least the third person closely involved in the project, thought Richard coldly, who was either dead, at death's door – or missing presumed drowned, like the tug *Ilya*'s unfortunate captain Gagarin.

On the table in front of Karchenko, Mick the cameraman's video was now retrieved, reset and connected to a laptop. The sound was on mute, the quality hardly worth amplifying. Its screen showed silent images of Richard and Colin and Marina, their mouths moving like fish in an aquarium. Behind them, moving randomly and unknowingly in and out of shot, Vasily Vengerov came and went with his green hard hat firmly strapped beneath his chin and Karchenko himself as a lean shadow. The conversation round the table died as they watched the image of the Nuclear Safety Inspector as he was slowly, apparently unconsciously, irradiated.

Richard's narrow eyes flashed searching glances at the security captain and the scientific station manager to see whether any hint of the passionate spark from earlier remained. And he fought to keep his mind focused on what he was seeing now rather than what he had seen at the barrier from the Mil before the second squall forced them to cut and run for home, sucked westwards as it was like a leaf into a whirlpool by the even bigger storm that was apparently approaching from behind them. But the scientist and her Spetsnaz lover sat cold and distant, keeping their secret with icy calm. Until, when she thought no one was watching her, Marina looked across at him and her gaze lingered for an instant.

Richard looked back at the screen image of Marina, and, behind her, the smaller image of Vengerov. The inspector ticked his clipboard. He wrote some notes. The dosimeter on his shoulder showed green. He leaned almost crazily over the edge of the railings. When he straightened, his shoulder showed a flash of amber. He turned away, looking upwards. Richard read Marina's digitized lips in the foreground. '. . . safely bedded . . .' she seemed to be saying.

Bedded . . . A vision of Yuri Karchenko's wolverine flank, an echo of Marina's throaty gasp rose in his memory. Robin flooded his imagination distractingly. Robin undressed and abandoned, her face a lot like Anna's. Her breasts dusted with golden freckles, pink-tipped and perky. *Focus, man,* he thought angrily. He blinked. Karchenko was looking across the table, his gaze locked for an instant with Marina's. Colin shifted discontentedly, unaware of all this byplay, impatient to get back to a close examination of what he had seen and Mick had obligingly filmed at the barrier. It was Colin as much as his own strong will that pulled Richard into the immediate present.

They were all looking at the laptop screen once more. Vengerov's clipboard fell to his side as though all at once too heavy. His shoulder was bright red now, but oddly, it was the sudden sick greenness of his face that claimed attention. He moved, holding his head at an odd angle – *Listening*, thought Richard. Listening to the faintest buzzing. Hearing it before any of the rest of them did.

'. . . Sevmash Consortium . . .' said Marina's silent lips. The picture opened out further. Vengerov was out of focus, but visible down his left side from shoulder to knee. His pocket, weighted by his personal Geiger counter, was throbbing red.

'That's it,' said Richard. 'There can't be any doubt. Even if Dr Mussorgsky hadn't found high readings on Vengerov's head and shoulders – and higher still within that hat – that footage would give us proof. You can almost see the stuff moving down his body.'

'But how?' demanded the captain, glaring round the table. 'How can a potentially lethal dose of radioactive dust get into a hard hat in the first place?'

'And how on earth can it stay there?' asked Marina. 'If there was dust in the helmet, why did it not just blow over all of us like sand at the seaside?'

'I think I have an answer to that,' said Richard, picking up an uncontaminated hard hat brought up by Nana Potemkin at Sholokhov's request after his enquiry had made it likely that Vengerov had been poisoned by his headgear. 'Look,' he explained, beginning to articulate some of the thoughts that had occupied his mind on the flight back as Colin had gone into a brown study, thinking through the implications of what his ice master's eyes had seen. 'The main section of the helmet is made of composite. It is not subject to static electricity. We have to be particularly careful about static on tankers – even a nylon shirt can spark off an explosion, let alone a plastic helmet capable of generating static. You have similar risks here and make your hard hats of similar material.

'But look inside. The one-size hats adjust to individual heads with these plastic straps here. See? They make a kind of skullcap inside. Now these straps are polypropylene, and they do hold static electricity. So, if I rub this strap here for long enough, it picks up enough static to pull that sheet of paper like a magnet attracting iron. It's the old schoolboy magic trick where you use the static in a plastic comb to make your hair stand up or make paper seem to come alive.'

'So,' said Marina frowning, glancing across at Karchenko as she spoke, 'you're saying the inside straps on Vengerov's helmet were full of static and acted like magnets to radio-active dust.'

'Holding it in place until Vengerov put the hard hat on,' agreed Richard.

'But even if you are right and that is possible, the question remains,' growled Karchenko. 'Where did the dust come from? How did it arrive aboard? Did it come there by chance? Or was it put there on purpose?'

Is there more of it? wondered Richard. And if there is, who has it? And what are their plans for it? 'Which leads us on to the next question,' he added smoothly. 'If it was put in the hat on purpose, then who was it put there to poison?'

He looked around the table, visions of Robin and Anna blessedly far from his mind as it raced in speculation. 'And, of course, to return to an idea captain Karchenko first voiced, *who put it there?*'

Karchenko's eyes blazed. His mouth opened. Then he

frowned. Hesitated. Remembered that he had in fact specul-
ated as to the existence of a murderous saboteur. Though not,
of course, seriously.

'Let us assume that this was an unfortunate accident,'
interjected Felix smoothly. 'I have seen people in these situations – and you amongst them, Richard – leap to unfortunate
conclusions all too quickly.' His tone lost a little of its smooth-
ness on the repetition. 'After all, the logical outcome of
leaping to *attempted murder* before we have investigated the
possibility of *accident* fully is simply to invite interference
of outside authorities.'

He leaned forward almost threateningly. 'I should say that
the last time we were forced to report such suspicions after
finding a body aboard a derelict tanker we were breaking up
in Arkangelsk, it brought the full weight of the Prosecutor
General's office down on our heads. Federal Prosecutor
Yagula himself.'

His brown eyes raked round the table. Only Colin was not
frowning. Both Marina and Karchenko had blenched.

'*Yagula?*' said Captain Sholokhov after a moment. In much
the same tone as he might have said *Beria? Pol Pot* or
Himmler?

'Yagula,' affirmed Felix. 'He flew up from Moscow personally. And, of course, once he was in Arkangelsk, he occupied
himself with all sorts of matters beyond the one that had
brought him there. Many heads rolled. Some, I may say, are
rolling still.' He looked across at Richard directly, his burning
eyes at their most desperately forceful. 'We ourselves, at
Sevmash and Heritage Mariner were lucky to survive. It made
the Red Terror look like a picnic.'

'Perhaps,' said Sholokhov with sudden access to a great
deal of decisiveness, 'all this talk of murder is far too
premature. And in any case, it would be like offering red
meat to starving wolves to mention such ideas to our esteemed
guests . . .' He gestured to Mick's camera. 'Or to Mr O'Neill.
And I need hardly say that any speculation along these lines
will do nothing but damage to the crew and ancillary staff
aboard.'

'So,' concluded Felix, his voice sounding just a little smug
to Richard's ears, 'our conclusion is that Inspector Vengerov's
terrible experience is the result of a most unfortunate accident.

One that remains almost inexplicable at the moment, but one which we are looking into in order to ensure that it cannot ever happen again.'

No sooner had Felix stopped speaking than a chime sounded. Sholokhov looked at his wrist and frowned. 'That is the signal to change the watch,' he said.

Richard checked his battered old Rolex. Local time was 16.00 it informed him. The afternoon watch was over. He wondered vaguely whether they dogged the watch on Zemlya and would change again at 18.00. But Sholokhov was still speaking. 'This matter has made us late for dinner, which was held back in any case. Let's wash up now. I will call the guests to the dining salon in fifteen minutes' time. It will give me an excellent opportunity to explain what has happened to everyone before they eat.'

While I start asking one or two subtle little questions, thought Richard grimly. Because I for one do not believe that what happened to Vengerov was accidental at all. And that really only leaves us with the Karchenko alternative.

'Yagula,' said Colin as he and Richard walked along the corridor towards their suite. 'Who's he?'

'Lavrenty Michaelovich Yagula,' said Richard thoughtfully. 'He's the leading hitman of the Prosecutor General's office in Moscow. He specializes in incidents that involve foreign nationals, foreign companies, anything that the Russians might have trouble keeping a lid on internally.'

'The captain and everyone reacted like he's a kind of bogeyman.'

'He is,' said Richard shortly. 'Felix wasn't exaggerating. Sometimes I think the only thing that stopped the pogrom he started when he came up to Arkangelsk to check out the dead men Robin found on *Prometheus* was the sudden death of the Prosecutor General, his boss. He went back to Moscow. He was tipped to take over the whole shooting match but he simply refused the offer. Didn't want to be tied down, apparently. It was Yagula who nominated the man who got the job in the end, though.'

'So,' said Colin. 'This Yagula. He's effectively his boss's boss?'

'That's what the gossip suggests. Or that's what Felix says the gossip suggests.'

'You keep a pretty close eye on this guy then?'

'Oh yes. If I'm ever coming anywhere near the Russian Federation – even as far out in the backwaters as this – I make damn sure I know where Yagula is. And what he's up to, if possible. And I always pack a long spoon in case our paths cross and I find myself dining with the Devil after all.'

'Have you any idea,' asked Colin as he swiped his key card and opened the door to their suite, 'just how bloody scary that is?'

'It needn't worry you,' said Richard decisively. 'He's just a bogeyman that Felix is using to keep a lid on things. He doesn't want anyone leaping to the conclusion that there's some kind of saboteur on board with us. Though that thought is scary enough in itself. But to be quite frank, the scariest thing I've come across in this little adventure so far is that bloody great ice-barrier piled along the coast to the south of us. No. You just keep planning how we can use your experience and know-how to open up a channel in that and get *Zemlya* safely into Leningradskiy Bay – if we can get her anywhere near there in the first place.'

Tension

The first course was borscht, which suited Richard's thoughts. As he looked into the blood-red depths of the clarified, beet-coloured beef bouillon, with its little white clouds of sour cream, his mind slipped far away from the carefully prepared speech Captain Sholokhov was delivering. He spooned a mouthful of the soup and savoured its rich, faintly metallic flavour, some part of him surprised at how ravenously hungry he suddenly seemed to be. The prospect of Stroganoff next was almost dizzying.

The last time he had eaten borscht, Richard was thinking, was in Arkangelsk. In a restaurant with Robin. They had sneaked away from Felix and his overpowering *biznizzmen* ship-breaker associates and tried a little tourist exploring on their own, behaving more like young lovers than responsible company executives. But their romantic interlude had had almost fatal consequences as things turned out. Certainly for Robin, who plunged into a nightmare of death and near-death aboard a rotting, derelict ghost-ship of a supertanker.

And it had been no picnic for Richard either, largely because of the overpowering presence of Federal Prosecutor Yagula. Who was, if anything, even more scary than Colin imagined him to be. But to be fair, the man got things done. Problems seemed to vanish as soon as the Federal Prosecutor appeared. The trouble was, so did people. In an earlier adventure, aboard the first Titan 10 submarine oil tanker, one of the crew had fallen foul of Yagula. As far as Richard knew she had never come to trial – she had vanished into the Butyrka remand prison in Moscow and had simply rotted there until she died. And much the same fate had begun to befall people in Arkangelsk. Even Felix had been lucky to walk away a free man.

While Richard was lost in his dark memories, the borscht had almost magically disappeared. As had the black bread and butter. Then, as Richard's soup bowl was replaced by a plate piled with pink creamy Stroganoff, the waiter quietly enquired what he preferred to accompany it – there was rice, noodles or twice-fried crispy potatoes. And a side salad. He decided on rice, then shook himself and began to look around the room, his fork rising and falling as he chewed the combination of tender steak, woody mushroom, paprika and sour cream almost ecstatically.

Sholokhov had finished his speech and was seated, silently sipping his soup in a vain attempt to catch up with his guests and the silver service. Felix was back in command of the room. He was seated at the head of the captain's table with Sholokhov, displaced – almost demoted – on his left. Richard was on his right. Colin beyond Richard, and an officer – presumably the first lieutenant – on Sholokhov's left. The tables were set out in a big inverted U. The legs were filled with people on both sides but the exclusive top was open opposite the exalted beings seated there. So it was easy for Richard to see everyone else once his attention travelled beyond his wonderful green salad.

The exclusive little planning-group from Sholokhov's

dayroom was augmented by the next echelon down the command chain, thought Richard, and the next rank in the social pecking order. Karchenko's senior officers; Sholokhov's deck officers – except for Lieutenant Brodsky who held the token bridge watch. Marina's top people – Nana Potemkin was back, accompanied, he supposed, by the senior member of each of the four reactor teams – and whoever was in charge of the turbine room below.

And the guests were there of course – the speech had been aimed at them, after all. Joan Rudd. Mick the cameraman and Al the sound engineer. Tom O'Neill. Mohammed Yamin. Then there was the chopper pilot, his co-pilot and engineer. Richard looked for Anna and found her staring back at him from the furthest table-end. He looked down, his face tingling with unexpected shock as their eyes met. All in all there were the better part of twenty people in the dining room, thought Richard. And a couple of places rather tellingly empty – Vengerov's of course. And Dr Mussorgsky's. But a surprising number of the faces were now quite familiar to him. He had been aboard for little more than six hours and yet he had met and begun to get to know half the people here. He had made a fair start on Felix's secret mission. But if he was going to get a fuller flavour of what was going on beneath the surface, he was going to have to get to know several more – and soon.

If only, thought Richard, if only there was some way to supersede Sholokhov and take over responsibility for the enquiry himself. Then he could really cut to the chase. And, if there was anything suspicious going on, get himself in a position to stop it before things got further out of hand and Federal Prosecutor Yagula – or one of his minions from the Prosecutor General's Office – really did show up.

It was at this point in Richard's thoughts that everything changed again. As changes go, this was an apparently inconspicuous one. Richard looked up as he felt the vessel hesitate, his senses alert at once. As with a supertanker, anything big enough to cause even a tiny faltering of the Ice Station's massive progress must be quite considerable. All the sailors, like Richard, were looking around, frowning. The rest of the diners just stilled the tinkling of their silverware, picked up their trembling glasses and proceeded with their meal.

Sholokhov turned to the man at his left and said something in a low voice. The officer rose and walked towards the exit, pulling a cell phone out of his pocket as he went. Cell phones augmented walkie-talkies aboard *Zemlya* and the signal was miraculously good. As it was for laptops. Lieutenant Brodski on the bridge was just about to get a call. But before the officer had even made connection as far as Richard could see, the captain's own cell phone began to ring. He put it to his ear. Said nothing. Gave a frowning nod and pulled himself erect. 'Excuse me, ladies and gentlemen,' he said. 'Duty calls. Mr Kulibin, would you mind coming with me?'

'Who's Kulibin?' Richard asked Felix as one of the men nearest Nana Potemkin rose weightily to his feet.

'He's the man in charge of the turbine hall,' answered Felix shortly, clearly unsettled by what was going on. Or rather, thought Richard, by the fact that he didn't know what was going on.

'Why would the captain want him?' wondered Colin as the two men followed the First Officer out.

'I'd say Mr Kulibin is probably the best engineer they have aboard,' said Richard.

'But I thought there weren't any engines on *Zemlya*.' Colin frowned.

'There aren't,' answered Richard. 'All the forward propulsion and manoeuvring comes from the four tugs that are working with her. And all of the tugs certainly have engineers of their own. So Captain Sholokhov wants engineer Kulibin to look at equipment, not propulsion or manoeuvring.' He found himself standing up as he spoke. 'And, as things seemed to begin with that little lurch, then it's logical to suppose the captain wants the engineer to check on the only other motorized kit aboard that could be involved. The capstans, windlasses and towing arrangements.'

'Why are you standing up?' asked Felix. 'Thinking of going to help?'

'No. I'm certainly not going out on to the weather deck dressed like this. But I might just pop up on to the bridge and have a look at what's going on.'

'Your decision,' said Felix dismissively. 'But pudding's on the way. Everything from *babka* to *zapekanka*.'

'I've never been a pudding lover, thanks Felix. I'll just

pop up and have a look from the bridge. Probably be back for coffee.'

'OK,' shrugged Felix, showing no sign of getting up himself.

As Richard turned to go, he heard Colin ask, 'Felix, what is *zapekanka*?'

'It's a kind of baked lemon cheesecake. One of Chef's specialities.'

Richard knew Colin's sweet tooth of old. And just the tone of Felix's voice told him he was on his own here.

The clear-view in front of the helmsman was opaque with driving sleet and rain. Richard crossed to stand by Brodski. The exterior cameras showed at once what the main problem was. The tug *Ilya*'s cable had fouled. The pool of light on the foredeck showed the port side towing capstan snarled with cable. And down on the distant after deck of the labouring tug, it was just possible to see that their double capstans were equally fouled. To make matters worse, the seaward edge of the pictures on the screen showed several blocks of ice – growlers – large enough to threaten *Ilya* if not *Zemlya*. And the tug was dancing this way and that, only just under control in the stormy water, clearly taking increasingly desperate measures to stay clear of the dangerous little chunks of ice. The inexperience of whoever had replaced the missing captain was beginning to have serious consequences by the look of things.

As Richard stood at Brodski's shoulder, two teams of oil-skinned men appeared on the monitors. A team of half a dozen, led by Sholokhov and his first officer, advised by engineer Kulibin no doubt, headed up a team of three deck-hands who hoped to clear the mess from this end. In the vaguer distance down on *Ilya*'s after deck, a similar team of waterlogged ghosts set about doing the same to the tug's twin capstans down there.

But the source of Brodski's worry – an emotion shared by Richard's older, wiser and far more experienced head at once, was the tension on the massive tow rope between the vessels. The line to *Ivan*, controlled by the tensioning devices in the capstans that were working properly, sagged in an easy but effective parabola. A parabola that tautened and loosened easily depending on how the hulls of the two vessels were disposed in the wild water. The line to the labouring *Ilya*'s snarled-up stern was almost bar-straight. It was running with water in any case – with rain and spray – but it looked to Richard unsettlingly as though at least some of the liquid spurting out of it like blood from severed arteries was being squeezed out because the weft of the hawser was being wrung out like a flannel in the fists of a bathing giant. The tension must be almost incalculable, he thought.

'Brodski,' said Richard in the calm, carrying voice he reserved for crises, 'you have to get everyone to ease off a bit. The tension on that line looks dangerously high to me. *Ilya* has to cut power. *Ivan* has to do the same. *Erebus* and *Terror* have to push ahead. We have to ease the tension on that line. Can you get *Ilya*'s bridge on your intercom?'

Brodski obligingly hit a button and a babble of hysterical Russian filled the air. 'What's he saying?' asked Richard.

'He says there's more ice ahead. He's going to have to go left to avoid it.'

'Tell him to calm down and ease back!' snapped Richard. 'He's got ice-strengthened bows hasn't he? These are growlers for God's sake, not bergs!'

A heated exchange followed, which became louder moment by moment.

'What?' asked Richard.

'He says who am I to give him orders? I must go and make love to my mother. The lieutenant – acting captain – told him to look after the ship at all costs before he went back to look at the towing rig and that's what he will do.'

Stymied, his mind racing, Richard looked down at the outside monitors. Sholokhov's little group had gathered round the fouled capstan, bunched in tightly because of the howling gloom, under the beam of the foredeck lighting. Down on *Ilya*'s aft deck, torch-beams showed the acting captain and his little group equally tightly packed.

Richard went cold. 'Brodski, can you contact Captain Sholokhov?' he asked.

'He has a walkie-talkie,' answered Brodski.

'Call him. Tell him to split that group up. Put it on speaker so I can talk to him. Drive the point home. If that cable snaps . . .'

Brodski did as ordered. One of the blurred yellow figures reached into his oilskins for the walkie-talkie. 'Captain here,' came Sholokhov's voice.

Ilya's bows snapped left. The voice of her helmsman rose in a shout over the grating impact of ice on the strengthened cutwater. Then both were drowned as he gunned the motors to maximum. The tug surged forward on full power. There was no give left in the overstretched hawser. It snapped exactly in its centre, halfway between the two vessels.

Ilya leaped forward, battering the growler aside, knocking its shattered bits into the stormy foam. Twenty metres of cable, half as thick as a man, whipped back on to the tug's aft deck with the speed of a cracking whip. Even had it not been moving at the speed of sound, the simple weight of it would have done some damage. As it was, it took the whole work-team, acting captain, engineer and whoever else he had with him and smeared them across the back of the bridge house above the mare's nest of the tangled capstans, ripping the right one out like a rotten tooth.

And much the same happened on *Zemlya*. Twenty metres of tightly woven steel and Kevlar cable whipped back on to the foredeck with the speed of a striking cobra. Anchored as it was to the tangle on the left-side capstan, it whirled around that fixed point like the scimitar of an attacking Saracen. Writhing and heaving as though it were some kind of dragon come to terrible life.

The figure which had straightened to answer the walkie-talkie was chopped in half and hurled away like a broken doll. The three men closest to him were stamped out of existence too, flung across the deck then tossed into the icy, floe-flecked water. And the rest of the team, throwing themselves on to the deck, scrabbled wildly away towards the bridge as the monstrous hawser writhed reluctantly to stillness behind them.

Richard was in motion. He had whirled and was out through the command bridge door and on his way down in the lift almost before he took his first great shuddering breath. He hammered the lift button so hard he took the skin off his knuckle. All his mind said on the swift ride down was *Shit, shit, shit* . . .

Then he was out of the lift door and pounding past the

security section towards the A Deck bulkhead out on to the weather deck itself. As he went past the port side lift it opened and Karchenko stepped out. Marina was a pale shape behind him. 'Get some men and follow me, Captain,' ordered Richard, every inch the master and commander here. 'We've got trouble.'

Post-mortem

Brodski was distraught. And terrified. His eyes were wide and tearful with shock. He had brown, soulful eyes, Richard observed coldly. Very coldly, as a matter of fact. Like the security team who had carried the wounded below to the doctor, Richard was drenched to the skin and frozen to the bone. Had anyone other than Gieves & Hawkes made his suit he would have despaired of it. Anna was below, trying to scare up something warm. Felix would be here any moment. But, apart from Brodski there was apparently no one left alive aboard capable of commanding a ship. So Richard had command of the bridge, and he was staring into his de facto First Officer's eyes trying to get the measure of the man as he tried to get a grip on the new situation.

'If we hadn't called him on the walkie-talkie he would never have straightened up . . .' whispered the young lieutenant, apparently on the verge of tears. 'It was only because he straightened up that he was chopped. Chopped . . .' he turned away and Richard thought he was going to be sick.

To be fair, the mess he and Karchenko had found on the streaming foredeck would have turned anybody's stomach. Though Brodski, of course, had been safe up here on the bridge, observing matters distantly through the monitors.

'That's bullshit,' growled engineer Kulibin, one of the three survivors quick-thinking enough to throw himself flat and crawl out of trouble. 'He was as good as dead long before you called to warn him. We all were. He was asking for trouble, bunching us up together like that under the circumstances. He made one mistake after another and that tosser Oblomov was no better. They asked for it, they got it. No one to blame but themselves. Though I would like to get my hands on the little fornicator who took *Ilya* away like that.' The helmsman seemed to nod his head in silent agreement. The Security guard, of course, behaved as though he was carved out of granite. Neither man showed any sign of having heard the conversation beyond that.

Oblomov, apparently, had been the first officer's name, thought Richard. No one knew the name of *Ilya*'s helmsman. Though the instant he learned what it was, there was going to be trouble.

'That particular fornicator is long gone,' said Richard. 'As is *Ilya*. Out of sight, out of radio contact and, I'd guess, running for safe haven out of this squall. If he can find one on that godforsaken coast. We'll have to make do with *Ivan* up front alone for the time being. Which means, I'm afraid, that you have more work to do, Mr Kulibin. Though your first task had better be to rig storm lines from the A Deck doors to every point on the weather deck we're likely to need to reach during the next couple of days. Then the tow has to be rigged round both capstans now and fed out over the forepeak or *Erebus* and *Terror* will never be able to keep us running straight and true on course. Mr Brodski, ask the helmsman for our current heading please.'

'We're already running three degrees south of our charted course,' warned Brodski after a momentary conversation in Russian – which explained why the helmsman hadn't reacted to the conversation in English at any rate.

'We don't have much sea room anyway,' said Richard. 'And from what I can see the squalls and the current are both pushing us further south towards the coast. Where, I can tell you, we do not want to go! Tell the helmsman to correct as far as he can. Six degrees to port. Warn the tugs – and ask *Ivan* if he can shift over until he's dead ahead of us without putting undue tension on his tow rope. We'll be lucky not to bump into Cape Billings at this rate. Or the ice-barrier that's probably piled up on top of it.'

'It could be worse than that,' said Brodski dully. 'The weather predictor says there's a force ten storm coming out of the west behind us.'

Richard nodded. He knew about this. Weathercity had warned him. And in any case, the way the squalls were being sucked westwards into some great meteorological vacuum behind them would have alerted him in any case. 'Where is it?' he asked. 'And when can we expect it?'

'It's somewhere over the North Land islands now,' answered Brodski. 'It'll be up with us tomorrow or the next day at the latest and if it spins north of us then we'll have northerlies blowing at a steady one hundred miles an hour all along its leading edge and gusting to one fifty, pushing us southeast into the bargain.'

'And pulling everything north of us south along with it,' added Richard thoughtfully. 'Like the southern edge of the pack, for instance. Still, if we can get to Wrangel Island, that will give us some protection from both storm and ice. It's not a bloody great mountain like Kerguelen Island in the Antarctic, but it'll still have a lee that would protect us.'

'Protect us from what?' demanded Felix arriving on the bridge with Anna in tow. He carried a huge woollen blanket and she carried a steaming mug of filter coffee.

'Brodski says there may be a bit of a blow coming,' said Richard reaching for the coffee. As he cradled it in his massive hands and watched its fragrant black surface becoming dangerously agitated as he shivered, Felix handed Anna the blanket and she stood on tiptoe to wrap it round Richard's shaking shoulders. Her fingers lingered against his cheek but the dark-stubbled flesh was too chilled to feel anything.

'*A bit of a blow?*' Felix's gaze lighted on the frightened Lieutenant like the point of a duelling foil. He was all too well aware of Richard's peculiarly British mastery of understatement.

'A force ten storm. Maybe worse. Early in the season, but . . .' Brodski hesitated. Mr Makarov looked to him like a man who might confuse the message with the messenger.

'I understand. Possibly hurricane force winds. Due to arrive?' Felix asked.

'Tomorrow . . .' Brodski faltered fearing for the safety of the messenger.

'Stop frightening the boy,' said Richard abruptly. 'I need him functioning at the optimum. I need everyone on top form if we're going to get through this.'

'You need . . .' snapped Felix, unused to being spoken to as though he were a junior rating. '*You* need . . .'

'Get a grip, Felix. Who else? Apart from Brodski here I'm all you've got as far as I can see. Even leaving aside whatever's going on with Vengerov. Even taking no account of the publicity machine you have aboard just ravening to get their twopence worth out to Indonesian Oil, all your other competitors, Newscorp and the documentary-watching world. You are heading into a hurricane in a barge full of nuclear reactors on a lee shore piled with shipkilling ice in the high arctic with twenty-five per cent of your power and manoeuvring gone. Brodski, give me the names of the deck officers. *Zemlya*'s full complement. Now, please!'

Brodski looked a little more confident. He knew this and he could see no unpleasant comebacks from sharing the knowledge. He started at the top and worked his way down. 'Captain Third Rank Sholokhov. Deceased. First Officer Senior Lieutenant Oblomov, also deceased. Second officer Lieutenant Brodski . . . That's me,' he added modestly. 'And Junior Officer Junior Lieutenant Kuznetsov.'

'Where is Kuznetsov?' asked Richard.

'If I know Kuznetsov,' said Brodski bitterly, 'he'll still be in the dining room stuffing his fat face with bloody *babkas*.'

Richard looked at Felix. 'It's possible,' said the Russian. 'It's less than half an hour since you left and Captain Karchenko came in and took a team. I was the only one who followed them out. I think even Dr Ross was too engrossed in his lemon cheesecake to suspect that anything much was wrong. They'll have finished pudding and be on to cheese. There's coffee, as you know. And sweets. I'm still trying to keep the lid on this.'

'Well I don't think that's the best alternative,' said Richard decisively. 'Everyone who counts – everyone still alive at any rate – is in the dining salon now. If I didn't look like a drowned rat I'd go in there and lay it all out for them. All we're certain of at any rate. No pointless speculation. No easy fabrication. And I'd give them some kind of plan to get us through the next few days. Keeping people in the dark is rarely the best option in my experience. Especially if they're bound to find out the truth in any case – and you're going to be asking them to help and trust you in the meantime.'

'They'll panic,' said Felix cynically.

'They won't if we pitch it right,' Richard assured him with more confidence than he felt.

'There'll be a stampede for the chopper,' sneered Felix.

With you in the lead, my friend, thought Richard.

'No there won't,' interrupted Anna suddenly. 'The captain says the Mil won't fly in this weather as it is. And if it's just going to get worse then there's no way he'll do anything other than lock her in the hangar for the duration.'

'That's it then! We're all stuck in this together for better or worse,' said Richard at his most forceful and decisive. 'Looks like the only way we avoid panic – now or later – is to lay it out fair and square for everyone as soon as we can.'

Felix stood silently for a moment. 'OK,' he said. He turned to the Security guard. 'You go and tell Captain Karchenko to keep his deck team out of the dining area – they shouldn't have gone back in without contacting me in any case.' He turned as the guard marched off as though across the Red Square parade ground. 'Mr Kulibin, I suggest you get something warm from the galley and get ready to go out to do what Captain Mariner wants you to do with the winches, storm lines and the towline. Put together whatever team you want but don't go into the dining salon. In the meantime, I'll go down and schmooze our honoured. You get changed as fast as you can, Richard. As you observe, we need a captain not a drowned rat to take charge of the situation.'

'I agree. You go. And Anna, you go with him. Ooze calm and confidence. And pray Karchenko and his men have stayed out of sight.' He put his coffee cup down on a control surface in a manner that would have earned a reprimand if any of his own junior officers had done it and turned to the only junior officer he had immediately to hand.

'Brodski, stay on duty. You've done an outstanding job so far. It's a relief to have a man I can rely on in charge of the bridge. I'll send Lieutenant Kuznetsov out with the engineer's team. He should know the anchor points for those storm lines if he's been properly trained – and if he earned his Lieutenant's papers rather than simply buying them.'

Richard swiped his key card and threw the door to his suite wide. He dropped the blanket like a cloak behind him, tore off his tie as he strode in and shrugged off his sopping jacket. He had pulled his shirt-tails free of his belt and unbuttoned it before he turned to find Anna there immediately behind him.

'Anna!' he almost shouted in surprise and frustration. So much for his first set of orders as acting captain of this floating disaster, he thought bitterly.

'Hush!' she commanded. 'I am not here to pleasure you, I am here to help. You must be quick and I can speed things up.' She swept the blanket off the floor and stooped to retrieve his jacket and tie. She slung them on the sofa and pushed him through into his cabin. 'You must almost be out of clothes.' She swung open his wardrobe. 'Ah. Thank heaven the laundry has pressed your blazer already. That will do. White shirt. Nice restful blue tie. Give me that belt. I will put it through the loops of the trousers for you. Change in the bathroom if you must. But I would not look, I assure you!'

'I'm so cold that there wouldn't be much to see in any case. *I* assure *you*!' said Richard, beginning to relax as she started sorting his outer clothing.

'Ah!' she riposted easily. 'More of your famous British understatement.' But at least her eyes remained fixed on the belt she was threading into his fresh-pressed, hopefully decontaminated trousers as she spoke.

'So,' the spruce, dynamic, square-jawed natural leader in his fresh-pressed blazer, starched white shirt and navy silk tie summed up twenty minutes later, 'accidents of this sort are tragic but sadly by no means unusual aboard working vessels in conditions such as this. *Ilya*'s inexperienced helmsman turned too fast and applied too much power trying to break through a small ice floe. The sort of thing we call a growler because trapped air makes it sound as though there are angry bears hiding inside it.

'Because the lines were tangled, the safety features in the power capstans both here and on the tug failed. The rope parted under the unexpected extra strain and the deck-parties on each vessel were injured or killed when the broken ends whipped back. *Ilya* has perfectly understandably run for cover. We have lost twenty-five per cent of our propulsion and fifty per cent of our watch officers. But the latter loss, although tragic, can be made up at once. I will assume command – as I have been trained and employed to do on many occasions in the past. I have Lieutenant Brodski – currently up on bridge watch – and Junior Lieutenant Kuznetsov – rigging safety lines on the deck outside – as able back-up. And Mr Makarov, my long-time associate, has agreed to aid in any way he can. So has Dr Ross, one of the world's most expert ice masters. Both men are widely experienced in a variety of vessels and a wide range of Arctic conditions. I will be contacting all three tugs remaining to us, to see if we can poach any of their more experienced officers into the bargain. Unfortunately as the weather is stormy and likely to be worsening, we will almost certainly be unable to fly anyone on or off *Zemlya* during the next few hours, so our other options are a little limited.

'As acting captain it will be my primary concern to bring *Zemlya* and all aboard her to safe haven. And, should the opportunity arise, to complete the enquiry into Mr Vengerov's unfortunate accident. But the first thing I will be doing – as soon as I have taken any questions from the floor – will be to assist Engineer Kulibin and his team as they centralize our forward tow to the tug *Ivan*, and adjust the positions, if necessary, of my own Heritage Mariner tugs *Erebus* and *Terror* so that we are in the best possible position to face any deterioration in the weather if the storm does in fact get worse.'

Given the fact that the dining salon contained several media people and a good number of men who counted themselves as rivals – if not as enemies – of the *Zemlya* enterprise, there were surprisingly few questions. Either to Richard or, when he returned, to Felix.

Felix appeared just at the end of Richard's bracing talk and simply took his position at Richard's shoulder and beamed as though this were a wedding rather than something akin to a wake. And Richard could see why at once. Karchenko and his men were suddenly dotted around the room, at the exits and – no doubt – at important points right throughout the vessel. If anyone did panic, as Felix feared, they would soon find themselves faced with a Security guard armed with a machine pistol asking them to calm down. And, suspected Richard more acutely still, there would be several such men between here and the helicopter on the topmost deck, just in case. With orders to use lethal force if necessary to stop anyone going aboard. Anyone except Mr Makarov, of course.

Richard might have assumed command of Ice Station *Zemlya*. But Felix had assumed command of Karchenko and his twenty unquestioningly obedient Spetsnaz security men, armed with more than enough state of the art hardware to fight a considerable little war.

Gear

Immediately after his speech, Richard got changed again. 'Colin,' he asked, 'you wouldn't go to the ship's stores would you? Ask any of the crew who speaks English and they'll tell you where to go. Get me a set of wet weather gear that would fit you and bring them up to our suite.'

'Going on deck?' asked Colin suspiciously.

'Yes. As soon as I can. To help and oversee Engineer Kulibin and his team.'

'On my way,' said Colin equably. 'I'll maybe come on out with you. Seems like things can get a bit risky on this vessel.'

'If you like but it'll be nasty. The weather at least.'

'Nasty's where I live, remember,' growled Colin, 'weather-wise at least.' And he heaved himself up out of his seat. But then, on the way out of the dining salon, Colin stopped at the one logical person he knew who could translate for him – Anna. They left together and Richard watched with a sinking heart.

As good as his word, Colin was waiting up in the suite when Richard arrived. As he had feared, Anna was there beside him. And Richard really felt that he had better things to do than to waste time getting rid of her. Especially as she was laden with a full set of the cold-weather gear he had requested – and all too willing to sort it out for him.

This was a mistake, he soon realized. For, in spite of the

fact that he was no longer ravenous, he was still almost light-headed with exhaustion. Still disorientated from three full days of restless travelling. So that every now and then as she turned to show him some new wonder unpacked from the pile she looked so much like Robin that his breath caught in his throat.

'This is all a bit *nouveau* for me,' Colin grumbled at his most Calvinist, sweeping a disapproving look over the clothing and – perhaps – the girl holding it as she looked expectantly towards Richard's bedroom. 'A bit upmarket,' he added before vanishing into his own cabin to change. 'But I got the full monty,' he threw over his shoulder as he closed his bedroom door firmly behind him.

'Full monty, what is this?' asked Anna. 'I saw an English film called *Full Monty* – about *male strippers* . . .' Her eyes were huge. They had picked up that grey tinge from the colour of the weather that was pressing against the windows like a rabid wolf trying to break in.

As Richard took stock of the clothing – much of it still in its wrapping – he took Colin's point. And answered Anna's question as briefly and impersonally as possible. '*Full Monty* means he brought everything he could think of.'

It certainly seemed that nothing had been left out here, he thought. But this was less what a working ice master would actually wear on a rainy sub-zero afternoon and more what some designer in Moscow or New York *supposed* an ice master might want to wear. But he had to admit that it looked the business.

Richard was unwrapping the Itaca Thousand Gram Arctic Boots, pulling them out of their box as he recognized one of the half-dozen Cyrillic words overprinted on it, thinking that this pair really put his Timberlands in the shade.

'Does that say "Archangel"?' he asked, pointing to Аркангелск.

'Arkangelsk, yes,' she answered. She made the familiar word sound strange and seductive.

'OK, that's it, thank you. Off you go now and let me get changed.' He was careful to use the tone of voice he saved for his daughter Mary – not the one that Robin would have recognized.

Anna surveyed the bed, her nose in the air, then turned on

her heel and departed without a fuss. But with a toss of those distracting curls. And her perfume lingered. And enough of her presence to disturb him as he stripped and stepped into the red thermals. But little by little the new-clothes smell drove the perfume out. And his mind became distracted by the simple quality – and colossal cost – of the clothing he was pulling on.

So that when Felix came in unannounced as he was lacing the boots up and said, 'Hey! Where did you get my emergency supply of cold-weather gear from?' he wasn't really surprised. He wasn't surprised, either, to find that Anna had only got as far as his stateroom on her way out and was, apparently innocently, deep in conversation with Colin; discussing the difference between what the ice master was wearing and what Richard had just put on.

Nor was he surprised to find, as he finally stepped out through the A Deck bulkhead door into the raving squall, that the outfit kept him as snug and warm as a roaring fire in Felix's palatial Black Sea dacha.

But stepping out through the door on to the weather deck cleared his mind of everything – as though he had been instantaneously transported from one planet on to another. And he was reminded – not that he needed reminding – why this was called the *weather* deck. He had strapped one of the safety harnesses hanging inside the door round his waist and he secured himself to the storm lines and gestured Colin to do the same as soon as he stepped into the storm. Then the pair of them leaned sideways into the howling northern blast and ran forward.

At least the deck beneath their feet was steady – for it was icy and slippery with a combination of sleety rain and freezing spume. But Colin's sealskin boots had soles that gripped as efficiently as Richard's moulded Itacas, and so they were able to make good progress. Like Cook and Peary racing for the Pole, they ran down the foredeck in an almost total white-out, each isolated by the screaming cocoon of gale and sleet. Richard had taken the lead because he was used to ships and this was now his command – but the conditions were those that Colin was used to, so the ice master had no trouble keeping up with his friend. Thus they arrived at the port side foredeck capstan almost shoulder by shoulder.

What they found there impressed Richard even more than the efficiently strung safety lines had done. Five metres behind the vertical capstan there lay a horizontal slave winch. The practical engineer, Richard assumed, had rigged a little three-legged gantry with a pulley at the top and was using the slave winch to hoist the heavy tow rope using a lighter line. Every time they got ten feet or so of the massive tow rope free, they would lay it on the deck, reattach the lighter line and start to heave again.

'This is good work!' bellowed Richard to Kulibin.

'It was the boy's idea,' bellowed the engineer in reply. 'Young Kuznetsov has a head on his shoulders. But the weather's a bit much for him. Keeps fogging up his glasses. I've sent him below to get the biggest rope clamps and securing plates we have aboard. I've given him details but I trust him to use his initiative. It'll take a little longer, but it'll give us time to clear away the last of the blood and guts.' He gestured down. The last of the water washing away was a disturbingly delicate salmon flecked with clots of beetroot.

'Good job,' Richard added to Kulibin. 'This is a good deal cleaner than it was the last time I was up here,' he bellowed to Colin.

'Don't tell me! I don't want to know,' answered the Scot shortly.

Richard grimaced and continued to look around. He had been too overcome and preoccupied on his last visit here. Too cold and wet to take any leisure. There were three spaces in the wall of the safety rail that reached from the scuppers to the wooden railing, where the banister was hinged to fold back. These were the port and starboard hawseholes – where tow rope or anchor chain attached to the capstans could go over the side. They were bedded, not by the sharp edge of the scupper but by pulley wheels set in the ship's side, designed to ease the passage of ropes or chains – and to protect them from undue damage and wear. And, right at the point of the bow itself there was a third, central hawsehole, floored with the biggest pulley wheel of all.

A rarity on the kind of ships Richard was used to dealing with, perhaps, but a logical addition to the design of a vessel destined to spend the majority of her working life anchored.

Furthermore, he thought, walking forward to the limit of
the safety line, straining to check on some unusual deck
furniture there, this must be the point at which the power
lines came up from the turbine hall two decks down. If it
wasn't occupied by an anchor chain, the hawsehole would
be a convenient exit for a power line to run ashore.. Or was
that too simplistic a concept? He remembered a phrase
someone had used to describe how Ice Station *Zemlya* was
fundamentally designed to work: *Turn it on and plug it in.*
So maybe not. 'Think that's where they put the power line
ashore?' he yelled at Colin, pointing with his mittened hand.

'Turn up, turn on, plug in,' bellowed Colin. 'Looks like it.'

To Richard's experienced eye, the measurements on the
foredeck seemed to be fine. So it was just a case of the
unexpectedly capable Lieutenant Kuznetsov and his initiative. Which, as it turned out, proved to be very well placed
indeed. The young lieutenant returned with a small but
willing team in tow. He would need to be a very popular
young officer indeed to get men out in this weather, thought
Richard admiringly. They were laden with ironwork and
tools which they laid out cheerfully enough for Richard's
inspection.

Kuznetsov was as Brodski's description had led Richard
to expect, physically at least. He was a round-faced, red-
cheeked, earnest-looking boy with slicked back black hair
visible whenever the wind inflated his hood like a waterproof
balloon and threatened to strangle him with the drawstrings.
It was difficult to tell whether it was the wind or his natural
shape that made the rest of his yellow Parka seem to bulge
so markedly around the waist. And, almost inevitably, he
wore thick round glasses whose lenses kept on misting up.
Neither circumstance, however, seemed to dull his indefatig-
able enthusiasm.

'I expect the first thing you plan to do is to put a loop
on the broken tow rope,' said Richard. 'How do you expect
to do that?'

'Engineer Kulibin and his men are freeing the rope from the
capstan, sir,' Kuznetsov explained earnestly, too well focused
on his plan to be nervous of his overpowering audience. 'I
believe I can begin soon. My plan is to take the broken end,
which as you see has begun to unravel, but which is quite solid

from this point a little further back . . .' Kuznetsov led Richard
to the mid-point of the first loop of rope on the deck. The
end was indeed frayed and needed to be tidied – but the boy
had chosen the first reliably solid section well. And it was near
the loop which already existed because of the way Kulibin's
men had laid it on the deck.

'I will bed a steel eye into the curve here. Then I propose
to secure the end of the rope to the section it is hard against
with these clamps to make the strongest possible loop. The
broken end will then resemble the eye of a needle. If I get
the chance I will further secure the ragged end. It might even
be possible to fother the loose strands into a cut splice on
the main line, thus tightening the whole thing more securely
the more pressure is put upon it.'

Spanner

'I have explained it well?' asked Kuznetsov anxiously. 'The
idea is good?'

'Good enough,' said Richard, making no attempt at all
to hide the admiration in his voice. 'What do you propose
to do with it then?'

The junior lieutenant seemed to glow under the effect of
the unaccustomed praise. 'I propose to bring it over to this
curved steel plate here.' Kuznetsov led Richard and Colin
along the safety line towards a large arrowhead of metal
pointing at the forepeak. The inner surface was hooked and
pierced by the uprights of half a dozen heavy-looking bolts.
It was obviously designed to accept two ropes at the wide
end but emit only one strand at the point.

'We will have to coordinate things carefully and make
full use of the gantry and a good deal of seamanship, while
hoping for a short period of calm in the weather,' explained
Kuznetsov a little breathlessly. 'But what I propose to do is
to lift *Ivan*'s tow rope out of its current hawsehole and drop
it through the forepeak hawsehole. At the same time we will

lie *Ivan*'s tow rope in the bottom of the plate so that it comes in on the right, here, and round out through the front, there. My men will drag the clamped end of *Ilya*'s broken tow rope and put it on the bottom plate here, you see there is an extra hook for it to catch on to. Then we will place the upper plate on top and bolt the whole device closed as tightly as we can.'

Kuznetsov looked up with a frown of concentration, pulled the misted glasses off his snub nose and polished them as he continued, again for Colin's benefit, 'Imagine a metal pair of bikini-bottoms lying on a beach. The legs come out of the leg-holes and reach towards the two capstans. The body comes out of the waistband and reaches for the forepeak through which it will join with tugboat *Ivan* dead ahead. I calculate that when *Ivan* takes up the strain again, the two ropes coming in from the two capstans can be adjusted to balance the strain from port and starboard, putting *Zemlya* back on a direct forward heading. And I am also certain that the tow can be resumed quite effectively without running any risk of the arrowhead plate going anywhere near the forepeak.'

Kulibin appeared at Richard's shoulder. 'He thought it all up off the top of his own head,' said the engineer. 'He's a bright lad.'

'Very good, Mr Kuznetsov. Carry on,' said Richard, feeling Kulibin hesitating; clearly wanting to say more, but in private. 'He'll go far,' he concluded as the lieutenant hurried off towards his waiting team.

'If he survives,' said Kulibin. 'If any of us do.'

'What do you mean?' asked Richard, suddenly feeling as though Felix's down-lined Parka had sprung a leak and ice water was running down the nape of his neck.

Kulibin glanced up at Colin, then looked back at Richard. 'I mean this kind of thing,' he said. He held up a long-handled metal spanner. There was more than a metre of it – the length of Richard's arm. It was just the kind that Kuznetsov's team would need to tighten the bolts in the arrowhead bikini-bottom plate. But this one wouldn't be much use to them Richard thought grimly. It was scarred and buckled, twisted out of shape.

'Don't tell me . . .' he said.

'Someone shoved it into the capstan motor,' spat the sturdy engineer, his voice trembling with outrage. He looked around the deck, as though fearing eavesdroppers. His team was dismantling the gantry. A couple of team members carrying the block and tackle towards the lieutenant's men who were already hard at work on *Ilya*'s broken tow rope. Kuznetsov was hovering anxiously between them, straining the safety line in his eagerness to get closer to the work.

'It's not the kind of thing that can happen by accident!' hissed Kulibin angrily. 'It is sabotage! It has to be. There must be someone aboard trying to . . .' He ran out of words if not of outrage. 'Trying to . . .'

'. . . throw a spanner in the works,' suggested Richard helpfully.

And there was a sound like a pistol shot followed by a whip-crack. Richard knew what had happened and tensed himself, grabbing at Colin with one hand and at his safety clip with the other. A black squall hit them instantly as though the whole thing had been choreographed. The wind was strong enough to make *Zemlya* give that telltale little heave. A wall of water came over the port side and washed knee deep across the deck. With the pressure of the wind, it was more than enough to send them all staggering across the suddenly restless deck, blown south almost as helplessly as the snowflakes cartwheeling though the dark storm. The safety line, which had been their saviour up until now, turned as treacherous as the serpent in Eden, twisting and slithering, tripping their slipping feet. Whipping down the wind, seeking to pull them towards the places and dangers it had been keeping them safe from until a moment ago.

Kulibin cannoned into the solid wall of flesh that Richard and Colin presented. He dropped the spanner and hung on for dear life. Colin was holding on to Richard now. And Richard was holding on to the loop of the safety line in his carabiner clip. Had he not been wearing the mittens and the gloves, the line would have cut his hands. He hung on grimly as the three of them staggered across the deck, past the disassembled bikini-bottom of the arrowhead plate, and into the starboard capstan before the line tightened and they were able to swing to a stumbling halt. 'Hold on to your lines!

Tight as you can. Don't let them slip!' Richard yelled. 'The men further down may be relying on us.'

Richard himself held on like grim death as the squall eased, the wave washed away, the snow cleared and their vision extended to the running scuppers and the safety rails once again. Everything on the foredeck was chaotic. There were bodies and bits of equipment everywhere, most of them tangled in the safety wires like fish in a snarled line. Richard blinked and shook his head, trying to make out who was where and who – if anyone – was missing. 'Kulibin! How many were in your engineering team?'

'Five. Six counting me.'

'Colin! Did you see how many the lieutenant brought with him?'

'Four. I'm certain.'

'So, we're looking for nine more apart from us. How many can you see?'

'Eight,' called Colin.

'Someone's missing. They'll have gone over the starboard side. But their lines and clips might well have held. We have to secure the line we're holding here to this capstan. Make sure it isn't going to give. Then we can unclip and go look. But unless Kuznetsov put retainers at every anchor point, once it starts to slip it'll all go,' warned Richard.

'He wanted to,' admitted Kulibin bitterly. 'But I told him not to. There wasn't time. I couldn't see the point.'

'That's why you're an engineer and he's a deck officer,' said Richard. 'But it's good you told us. Now we know where we stand. Colin, if I pull you some slack, can you loop it round the capstan? I'll tie it off.'

'Better hurry,' called Kulibin. 'Looks like Security's on their way and I think they've got wire clippers.'

'Shit!' said Richard roundly. 'Kulibin, you'd better unclip and go talk to Captain Karchenko. Tell him I want him off the deck for the moment.' As the solid engineer hurried off, leaving the twisted spanner on the deck – probably wisely – Richard heaved at the line with all his massive strength. He and Colin looped it round the top of the capstan and Richard heaved again, freeing enough slack to allow him to tie it off in the closest he could come to a buntline hitch. They unclipped gingerly, side by side, and straightened, both of them keeping their mittened hands on the lines in case they began to slip once again.

'Right,' said Richard as soon as they were satisfied. 'Colin. Go and tell the guys on the deck to unclip and go back to the bridge house. As soon as you get to a walkie-talkie, tell Karchenko he can come back down and help; and I'll do the same – but no wire cutters under any circumstances. My main target will be to see who's gone overboard and see how we're going to get them safely back, if we can – and if they're still in a condition to make it worthwhile.'

Moving carefully on spread feet, Richard walked towards the starboard side with the full power of the north wind battering on his shoulders and the back of his head. As he moved, he heard a dolorous howling, as though there was an army of damned souls gathering around his ankles. It was the wind in the tautened safety lines.

The blinkers of the hood gave Richard a weird fur-lined tunnel vision, and he followed this, step by careful step, towards the starboard safety rail. It was fortunate that there were no men on the deck between him and his goal, for he would have been lucky to see them once he started walking. Even had he done so, he would have been hard-put to stop, with the wind like a couple of men at his shoulders shoving him forward.

The safety rail hit him across the hips, and he leaned forward, looking down. For a vertiginous moment he felt as though he too might topple forward and he felt himself grasping the wooden rail with almost manic power. Immediately below him he saw a great tangle of safety wires hanging against *Zemlya*'s side, swinging restlessly in the wind-shadow of the hull, inundated with the waterfall of wavewash from the deck. And there, away on his left, a figure, plump and once bespectacled, wrapped bodily around the heaving line between *Zemlya* and the tug *Ivan*, swinging wildly above the black, freezing, ice-spattered water of the Arctic Ocean, riding the big black rope like a city boy astride his first bucking bronco.

Junior Lieutenant Kuznetsov. With his hood blown back. With his hair wild. With his glasses long gone. With a couple of minutes left to live.

Catch

'Hang on, Kuznetsov,' bellowed Richard in his quarter-deck voice. 'I'll get you up in a jiffy!' At least the boy's detailed explanation of his plans for the tow rope assured Richard he would understand the words. The next problem was likely to be finding someone else who would understand English and obey in turn. He looked down for an instant longer, waiting for Kuznetsov to react.

The boy on the tow rope looked up blindly. Even had his glasses been in place they would have been misted – and in any case, the squall was driving rain and the last of the wavewash straight down into his scarlet face. But he nodded. The boy and his would-be rescuer were in contact.

Richard staggered the few metres across to the hawsehole itself and dropped to his knees. The safety lines reached rigidly across the deck and then vanished into the little gaps on either side of the massive pulley-wheel that held the tow rope clear of the sharp-edged scupper before vanishing over the side. In spite of his apparent pudginess, the poor boy had obviously been swept bodily through the hole itself. Then he had slid down the tow rope until his safety lines brought him up short.

Richard tried to force his mittened fingers under the lines at once – with no success at all. No chance of simply pulling him up that way, then. He looked back across the deck. Kuznetsov's team were just beginning to pick themselves up. 'You men,' bellowed Richard. 'Come here!'

But they showed no sign of hearing – or of understanding. None of them spoke English, thought Richard. Colin had already gestured to them that they should get to safety as fast as they could. One by one, like geriatric robots, they unclipped themselves from the tangle of singing wires and began to stagger aft towards the bridge house.

'Right,' said Richard to himself. 'Looks like we're on our

own, Mr Kuznetsov. So let's get on with it.' And, paying no further attention to the departing crewmen or his distant friends, he started looking for something close at hand that would help.

Richard went scrambling across the deck. The first thing he found was a walkie-talkie. He grabbed it, thumbed transmit and bellowed, 'Bridge. Brodski! Get down on to the forepeak as fast as you can. Bring help.'

Richard grabbed the light messenger line that Kulibin had been using to lift the broken tow rope free of the fouled capstan. It had a solid hook on the end of it. Richard took a firm grip of this. He rolled over to the winch round which the messenger line was still whipped and kicked the gear into neutral. Then, with a gargantuan heave, he started to pull the line free of the drum. As soon as he had half a dozen metres free he slung it over his shoulder with the hook banging insistently against his chest, lurched to his feet and let the wind help him reel forward, unreeling the line behind him as he went. With the force of the squall at his shoulders, he picked up speed and so he made it back to the starboard rail in less than a minute. But what he saw and heard when he got there made him fear he was too late after all.

He could see at once that the safety lines were beginning to slip. The tone of the demonic music shifted down another key. Increasingly wildly, he started heaving at the rope, but the added weight of the soaking length of it made it almost impossible to turn the winch's cylinder at this distance.

As he heaved again, he looked down. Kuznetsov was beginning to slip as his lines loosened. The next squall arrived, battering Richard against the open edge of the safety wall, threatening to pitch him out through the gaping hawsehole too. More importantly, it hit the distant tug with a cross-sea that made her pitch and yaw. The tow rope swung and bucked with fresh venom. The young lieutenant's blind face looked up, as red as Richard's bowl of borscht at dinner, disconcertingly speckled with ice and salt instead of sour cream. There was concentration on the streaming countenance. A gritty determination to battle to the end.

Richard heaved again, his heart pounding painfully enough to bring tears burning into his eyes. And suddenly the lines were screaming high and clear as though they understood the agony of the situation afresh. Richard registered the change but came nowhere near to understanding it. He was too preoccupied by the fact that the rope was suddenly running freely through his hands, its hooked end swinging swiftly down towards the boy.

The labouring tug *Ivan* reared back off the last departing squall wave. She slid backwards towards the Ice Station. The tow rope sagged almost to vertical. Kuznetsov swung in against *Zemlya*'s side and hit like the clapper on a bell. He lost his grip, fell free and dangled helplessly, secured only by the howling safety line. But the boy wouldn't give up. Dangling at death's door he might be, but he still tried for another chance. The starboard anchor was hanging just beside him and as his line twisted, striving to come apart, he reached for the massive metal hook, wrapping his left arm round it and hanging on with grim determination.

'KUZNETSOV! Catch!' yelled Richard, so loudly that he tore his throat and seemed to taste blood on the back of his tongue. He swung the hook towards the young officer with a wrench that ripped half the tendons in his shoulder. The metal swung in lazily to thump the dangling lieutenant in the side.

Kuznetsov sprang into frenetic action in a heartbeat. His eyes sprang wide. His arms and legs convulsed. The massive anchor itself seemed to dance as the boy writhed. Richard saw the first bright strand of woven wire spring back beside the pulley wheel as the safety line began to give way just as *Ilya*'s tow rope had done. The anchor must weigh the better part of a hundred thousand pounds – it was just too massive for the boy to get a proper grip on.

Richard swung the hook in again and the lieutenant saw it coming this time. He grabbed at it, missed, grabbed again. But Kuznetsov's quick thinking didn't let him down. He had a hook. He had a carabiner clip on the front of a strong safety harness. One-handed, he pulled the hook down to his waist and jerked his legs in a kind of mid-air frog hop, fighting to bring the two together. The safety line snapped, its frayed end whipping back at Richard. It would have hit him, too, and opened up the side of his face as likely as not – adding another set of scars to the one white line along the sharp crest of his cheekbone. But Kuznetsov had got the hook in place even as he slipped off the anchor and his weight slammed Richard forward so that the line hissed venomously past the back of his head. Richard's side crunched into the edge of the hawsehole, almost jarring his grip free. But then he heaved back, rearing up to employ all the strength of his entire body, from shoulder to thigh. The lieutenant seemed to fly up the side of the vessel, bouncing off the anchor as he came, and Richard threw the rope back, hand over hand, preparing to heave again. But there was no need.

The messenger suddenly took on a life of its own, snaking back across the deck so suddenly and forcefully that Richard was thrown aside. He looked back, and there were two figures beside the port-side winch. A square one and a slighter one, both in the yellow oilskins all the crew were wearing. And, further back but nearer at hand, two big figures towered beside *Ivan*'s towing capstan. One in sealskins and the other in waterproof camos. The first pair had engaged the winch. The second had re-secured the slipping lines. Both sets playing crucial back-up, their quick-thinking giving Richard a chance, and saving Kuznetsov's life.

Richard swung back again, reaching down as the junior lieutenant came level with the deck. His hands met the boy's and their icy mittens gripped each other's wrists like men on the flying trapeze. One last heave and the intrepid young officer came over the top of the tow rope like a big yellowfin tuna and flopped down on to the deck, huffing and puffing, rolling over at last to stare up blindly at the low dark sky.

'Are you all right?' asked Richard, his voice breathless with exertion, deepened by concern.

'Thank you, Captain,' wheezed Kuznetsov in reply. 'Yes, I am very fine. And very pleased to be back aboard. Very pleased indeed.' He pulled the hook out of his carabiner and let it drop to the deck with a watery clang. He lay for a moment, gasping. He was a mess, thought Richard. His face and clothes were covered in a thick, rust-red grime; something that had come off the anchor, he supposed. Then, after a moment more, Kuznetsov blinked myopically and reached into the pocket of his filthy oilskin even as he lay there on his back, fighting to regain his breath, the rusty filth washing off him under the weight of the downpour. He brought out a twisted pair of spectacles and sat them at a crazy angle on the bright red button of his snub nose. Then he sat up gingerly and began to look around. '*B'lyad*'!' he swore. 'This is one big mess! Where is my work team? We have a hell of a lot of work to do!'

The two figures from the winch arrived then and Richard was not particularly surprised to see Kulibin and Brodski. 'You went through the hawsehole, Kuznetsov!' said Brodski in theatrical wonder. 'And came back in! *Through* it! Without even touching the sides. I would never have believed it if I hadn't seen it with my own eyes!'

'*Idi na xuy husesos*,' said the junior lieutenant equably. He began to pick himself up.

'That's not very nice,' said Brodski, wounded. He struck a pose of injured innocence. 'I winched you up the side, after all. Though it's a miracle the messenger held.'

Kuznetsov suggested something even more offensive, stretching luxuriously, apparently finding even the gusty downpour something wonderful to be enjoyed.

'Enough, you two,' snapped the engineer, who understood the insults better than Richard did. He stooped and picked up the walkie-talkie Richard had used to summon Brodski off the bridge. He put it in Kuznetsov's outstretched hand. 'You'd better call your men back out, lieutenant, or the pair of you will end up putting this all to rights on your own.' As he spoke, the wind dropped. And rain came sheeting down out of the low, black sky as though an Arctic monsoon had started.

'You boys work on the winches, capstans and cables,' said Richard, pulling himself fully erect as well, slightly less ecstatic to be alive than Kuznetsov seemed to be. 'I'd be grateful if you'd help them Mr Kulibin, to begin with at least.' He looked back at the two tall men in earnest conversation over the capstan, then turned back. 'I'll get the safety lines re-rigged. We want this all finished, if possible by the start of the first night watch. Which, Mr Kuznetsov, you will be taking. I'll take the middle watch and you'll relieve me at four, Mr Brodski, for the morning watch. Not, I realize, that there will actually *be* night – or morning – for a while longer yet. If you need me after I've finished rigging the safety lines, I'll be finishing the current watch, trying to get this lot logged as accurately as I can – which will take a series of meetings at the very least and probably a working dinner into the bargain – and trying to alert the authorities to our position without bringing the whole sodding Prosecutor General's Office down on our pointy little heads! And then, God willing, I'm going to get some uninterrupted sleep. Before I get very, *very* grouchy indeed.'

Even had the junior officers' English not been fluent enough to understand all of this – which it was – just the tone in which it was said would have had a considerable effect. When Richard turned and began to pull himself back over the wire-strewn battlefield of the foredeck towards the earnest conversation at the capstan, the two youngsters exchanged awed looks and began to follow his orders very seriously and very, very precisely.

'What is it?' asked Richard as he arrived at the capstan and pushed himself into the conversation Colin was having with Captain Karchenko. 'Go on. Tell me all about it. Make my day.'

'Your buntline hitch slipped,' began Colin. 'The whole of the aft section of the safety line all but slipped through it.'

'So it's back to knot-tying class for me, then,' said Richard gruffly.

'That's not the point. The point is that it pulled the section that broke down here. This is where we found it, though the break itself must have happened up by the A Deck door.'

'No shit, Sherlock,' said Richard. He swung round on Karchenko. 'Break it to me gently, Captain.'

Karchenko silently held up the offending end of the wire. It was the third break Richard had seen today. The tow rope and Kuznetsov's safety wire had both unravelled into a mare's nest of fibres at the point of failure. This one was bevelled, neat and precise. The point of failure was as sharp and shiny as a chisel blade.

'Oh that's great,' said Richard. 'There can no longer be any doubt. We have a saboteur aboard. At least one. As I believe Auric Goldfinger observed to James Bond in the sort of books you do not read: "Once is happenstance. Twice is coincidence. But three times is enemy action." We need to watch our backs at all times, and make it the highest possible priority to work out who it is and what they have planned.'

'And how to stop them,' rumbled Colin.

'When we find out who it is,' said Karchenko quietly, 'I don't think that stopping them will be a problem.' His hand went pointedly to his holster.

'In the meantime,' said Richard, 'we need to get the safety lines restrung and double tied at each securing point. So that if there's any more of this murderous foolishness, we'll only lose a dozen metres of line at the most. Then, Captain, I'd be grateful if you'd arrange a rotor of guard patrols for every area in the bridge house twenty-four seven for the duration; and, when we're working out here, on the weather deck as well.'

Karchenko nodded once, then turned and marched off towards the bridge house.

'You think he's going to check with Felix?' asked Colin.

'Of course he is! But Felix had better tell him to follow my orders or one of two things will happen.' Richard pulled back the hood of Felix's thousand dollar parka so that Colin could see the cold rage on his exhausted face. 'Either I'll be taking the chopper up again and flying it back to Pevek myself, whether the pilot says I can or not,' he grated. 'Or Felix will suddenly find himself in the Arctic bloody Ocean swimming home alone!'

Calm

Richard sat calmly in the captain's chair looking thoughtfully across *Zemlya*'s command bridge over the shoulder of the solid helmsman out through the clearview. Richard was used to being pitchforked into challenging situations. He had a mental checklist that he knew he needed to work through. A set of procedures that experience had told him it was best to follow in order to establish his command and to find out whom he could rely on. But he was hesitating before he began the practised routine for several vital reasons. To begin with, he was not about to do anything that would interfere with the re-rigging of the tow rope. Next, he was well aware that there was a mixture of people, professions, motives and motivations aboard that really needed thinking through before he went into any accepted routine like a lifeboat drill. Thirdly, he had work that needed his immediate attention – he had mentioned the ship's logs to Colin, and the need to report the mounting toll of deaths and near-deaths to the relevant authorities – incidents that no longer looked so accidental. And in Russia, there was a wide range of authorities – local and federal, civil and criminal.

But here, as in a widening range of circumstances aboard, Richard was being stymied by the fact that he did not read Cyrillic or speak Russian. Within the next few minutes, by the look of things, he was going to have to do some nifty ship-handling – involving three tugs as well as the barge he now commanded – to allow his young lieutenants to swing the tow rope into its new position. But he couldn't communicate adequately with his own helmsman – let alone *Ivan*'s. Nor the tug's captain, as far as he was aware.

At least the skippers of *Erebus* and *Terror* would speak English, even if their crews were local – they were Heritage Mariner men after all. Though to be fair he had never met them. All he knew about them was that *Erebus* came from the Eden and *Terror* from the Tyne. The towns of Cargo and South Shields respectively. They went by the names of Bill Beaumont and George Hebburn.

As Richard sat thinking, the foredeck CCTV showed the two lieutenants with their teams working smoothly under the engineer's advice. As Richard watched, they were actually preparing to swing the tow rope out of the starboard hawsehole – *Kuznetsov's Exit*, Brodski had christened it and into the cradle on the forepeak. *Kuznetsov's Exit* was the Bowdlerized version that had been translated for him – though he rather thought the Russian '*mud'ak*' had a more scatological meaning.

Richard pulled himself erect and strolled across to the control panel. There was a range of communication equipment there, a microphone stalk, a walkie-talkie in a retaining clip and an old-fashioned telephone connected to the ship's address system. At least the phone was obvious – it couldn't be anything else. And the All Hail button was marked in the

usual colour. Richard put the handset to his cheek and pressed
the button. Chimes echoed distantly but satisfyingly, calling
everyone's attention for the captain's announcement. 'Would
Mr Makarov kindly come to the bridge. I say again, Mr
Makarov . . .'

'Nice pullover . . .' spat a cold voice, five minutes later.
Felix was clearly not in the best of moods. Richard decided
to tread warily. 'It's very comfortable, thank you. I'll return
it in good condition. Or replace it if you prefer. Same for
the complete outfit. It's the best cold-weather gear I've ever
come across.'

'Not very suitable as a captain's uniform, though,' observed
Felix, only a little mollified. 'We have to keep our standards
up. You'll be going on worldwide television. I don't want
you looking like one of those Mediterranean tanker captains
who spend most of their time in flip-flops, shorts and T shirts.'

'Point taken,' allowed Richard easily. 'If I can find something more formal I'll put it on. But I fear poor old Sholokhov
was too small. Even if I could wear the uniform of the Russian
merchant marine with a clear conscience. I can go through
his wardrobe, though, as soon as the opportunity arises.'

'His quarters have been cleared out. We've moved you into
the captain's accommodation as you're doing the captain's
job.' Felix held out a key card and Richard took it without
thinking. 'You should have seen the bustle on the CCTV,'
said Felix. 'All his stuff has been stored below already,' he
concluded.

'OK.' Richard took a deep breath, shocked by the realization
that he must have been watching the foredeck too closely to
see anything else. Even a certain amount of coming-and-going
in and out of his cabin. Then he let the breath out again in a
long, controlled, silent sigh. Striving to get his head round
what Felix had done – and what possible motivation he might
have for doing it. A kind of tit-for-tat in the alpha male contest
of who was actually running things here, probably. He shoved
the key card into his trouser pocket. 'I'll see what I can find
before I do my next interview with Joan Rudd,' he said eventually, through gritted teeth. 'In the meantime I need your help.
I need someone to translate my orders for me until we get the
tow line sorted out. Then I need your advice on who would

be best to help me long-term. I need to read and write Russian. I need someone who can pass on my orders accurately and swiftly. Under pressure if need be.'

'You have two bilingual lieutenants,' observed Felix coldly. 'They should do.'

'They have to keep watch themselves. We're running a standard three watch rotation – eight hours on and sixteen hours off. But the eight hours on in two four hour shifts. One in the forenoon and one in the afternoon. I'll be doing the two twelve-to-four watches and they'll be fitting in. I'll use them in emergencies. But while they're awake they'll have other duties. So long-term I need someone else. Someone with no immediate duties aboard who can help out when I'm on watch. Help out more generally. A multilingual Miss Moneypenny, in fact. Maybe two. There's a hell of a lot of paperwork – even under normal circumstances.'

'And these are not normal circumstances. Point taken. I'll think it over. See what names I can come up with.' Felix frowned, his eyes narrow and veiled. He was having one or two ideas already by the look of things. Ideas which, like the removal of Richard's kit, would be double-edged as likely as not. 'In the meantime,' said Felix, looking up innocently, his brown gaze suddenly lambent, 'what orders do you want me to pass along?'

Richard reached for the walkie-talkie. 'Mr Kuznetsov?'

The figures on the forepeak CCTV screen stirred. The plumpest one reached into his pocket. Put something to the side of his head. There was a hiss of static, then, 'Captain?'

'Are you ready to proceed?' demanded Richard.

There was a muffled conversation. The figures on the screen gestured and nodded to each other. Nodded again, with certainty. 'Affirmative, Captain.'

'Right,' said Richard, turning back. 'Felix, what I want you to do is . . .'

An hour later it was finished. Richard was back in the captain's chair finishing his out-of-step watch and Felix was long gone. *Zemlya* was steadily on course through calm waters that at last began to resemble the restful picture in the dining salon. *Ivan* sat squarely ahead of her, ploughing through a gently steaming sea, the tow rope reaching down into its parabola through the forecastle; two legs on the foredeck stretching back through Kuznetsov's bikini-bottom arrowhead clamp to the pair of capstans. Which were in turn, set to monitor and automatically adjust to the stresses put upon the whole rig. *Erebus* and *Terror* were snuggly secured to port and starboard. Captains Beaumont on *Erebus* and Hebburn on *Terror* had responded well to Richard's orders and proved themselves able, quick-thinking tug skippers.

The current course was laid in for the time being, taking them towards Leningradskiy with all possible dispatch. Especially as Richard knew that the current calm was illusory. Brodski's Force Ten storm was out there somewhere behind them and coming fast. If the storm chasing them across the Arctic Ocean proved to be as bad as he had been led to expect, Richard planned to overshoot Leningradskiy both in longitude – by heading further east – and by latitude – by heading much further north. Leningradskiy Bay was closed to them by the ice-barrier in any case. Even if Colin came up with a plan to get through it, it would require the kind of careful manoeuvring that was out of the question in a storm. It would be much safer in the mid-term to put the solid bulk of Wrangel Island to windward of them rather than risk the unwieldy and underpowered *Zemlya* against a lee shore; especially a lee shore palisaded with the shipkilling barrier of ice that Colin Ross had taken the chopper down to look at so closely on their flight down towards Leningradskiy.

Richard closed his eyes briefly, consulting the chart he kept in his head. At these latitudes, it was a rough chart, true enough. But he was planning, not plotting; so that hardly mattered. He saw *Zemlya*'s present position as properly plotted most recently. 69.9 degrees north latitude, -175.5 east longitude. Approaching Cape Billings. Running north to keep well clear of it too. Their target, at the end of the voyage, the butterfly-blue bay ten miles north of Leningradskiy about 69.4 north and -178.3 east. Just short of the 180 degree line where the eastings reverse into negative register because they lie in the western hemisphere. And that was important, because in the meantime, if the storm hit hard, he would be running for 71.0 north, -178 east, in the wind-shadow of Wrangel Island.

Richard stirred, his eyes still shut, calculating. If he continued to push hard, the little interlinked flotilla might make eight knots; say ten miles an hour. Leningradskiy was about ten hours' sailing away, therefore, with no safe haven offered, quite the reverse. The thought of *Zemlya* being driven helplessly on to the jagged ice-cliff of the shore and starting to come to pieces in the teeth of near-hurricane northerlies armed with further hammers and rams of ice from the southern edge of the pack was chilling enough even before you added in the reactors and the chance of precipitating another Chernobyl.

Wrangel was nearly twice as far, but still reachable within the next twenty-four hours, wind and weather allowing. But there would be miles and miles of sea room if anything went wrong. And, given *Zemlya*'s recent history and current position, something disastrously unexpected seemed a likely bet for the immediate future. Likely enough to be a necessary part of the equation in any event. This was an instance of the lesser of two evils, it seemed to Richard. Though he could hardly believe he was wrestling with the kind of problems of windage and lee shores that had preoccupied his youthful naval heroes, C.S. Forrester's Horatio Hornblower and Patrick O'Brien's Jack Aubrey.

'Yes?'

Richard's thoughts were interrupted by a quiet voice. He opened his eyes and caught his breath. With the light from the clear-view behind her – the whole view tinged with gold as the low sun shone through the restless filigree of steam on the water – it really could have been Robin standing there just in front of him. Her wide eyes grey with shadow. Her hair a riot of gold, like the contents of a pirate's treasure chest. His whole body convulsed with longing for her. His huge hands reached towards her automatically. It took him an agonizing instant to remember that this was Anna, not Robin. But the realization didn't help much.

'Yes?' she said again.

'What do you want?' he demanded, much more rudely than he intended.

'Mr Makarov said you wanted me to be your secretary,' she said softly. 'Your Miss Moneypenny. Like in James Bond, is it not? I said I would be happy to be your secretary. Your Moneypenny.'

'Did he? Did you? Why?'

'Mr Makarov said as I am multilingual and as I trained in secretarial work at School 1060 in Kuntsevo before I ran away to become an air hostess,' she explained with disarming frankness, 'he thought I would be just the person you need. Especially as I have no duties aboard currently. I said I would be honoured to assist you. In any way I can.' She smiled, suddenly. 'Though I think I would like to be your Pussy Galore. No? Your *From Russia With Love . . .*'

He simply had to get away from her. Get her away from him.

Damn you, Felix, he thought. Damn you and your little games.

'The first thing I need you to do for me,' he said, fighting to make his voice less brutal than his thoughts and keep his tone professional, 'is to go down to the ship's stores and get captain Sholokhov's stuff. Have it taken back to the captain's quarters. I'll be there soon myself.'

She frowned. He could see the argument fighting to get to the tip of her tongue. But then she changed her mind. 'At once, Captain.' She smiled dazzlingly. 'What is it we say? Now that I am at your command? *Aye aye!*'

As she bustled away, Richard heaved himself up and strode across to the console. He pulled the walkie-talkie from its clip. 'Mr Kuznetsov?' he called.

'Yes, Captain?' came the youthful voice at once.

Richard could hear half familiar sounds behind it. It took him an instant to recognize the chiming of cutlery and the clatter of plates. The conversation of feeding people. He looked up at the bridge chronometer above the helmsman's head. 20.30. Dinner time, even though lunch had been held back until 16.00. 'Mr Kuznetsov, I'd be obliged if you would come on watch at once. Bring your dinner. No. Have the galley send your dinner up here please.'

'On my way, Captain. *Steward . . .*' The contact went dead.

Kuznetsov was up surprisingly quickly. Richard had only seen him in his oilskins so far – and was pleasantly surprised to see that his uniform did not appear to bulge or strain unduly. 'What's for dinner?' he asked paternally.

'Russian salad, with eggs, potatoes, carrots, pickles and

sausage. Then Piermani, beef-stuffed dumplings with noodles and . . .'

'Enough already,' laughed Richard.

'I was part way through my salad but I ordered a fresh one sent up. The first one tasted strange to me,' explained the lieutenant, looking a little worried, the circular lenses of his glasses glinting like gold doubloons in the evening sun.

'That's fine. Are you OK making up the log of current conditions for me? I'll be filling the report of recent events later.'

'Will you want me to help with that? Captain Sholokhov often got me to keep the logs all together.'

'No, that won't be necessary. I already have all the help I can use.'

'Oh?' Was there a trace of jealousy in the boy's question. He had found a commander he liked and didn't want to share him yet. The youthful face folded into a frown.

'You'll have many new duties. Don't worry. You're effectively Second Officer. Quite a promotion. Now, you have the bridge, Lieutenant Kuznetsov.'

Richard left the boy glowing once again, and stepped back to allow a breathless steward carrying an enormous tray come in on his way out through the door. Sholokhov's cabin was immediately behind the bridge. The door yielded to the key card and Richard stepped in to what seemed to be the twin of the suite he shared with Colin. But the second cabin behind the big open plan reception area doubled as the day room and office. He had already been in there, with the carefully limited group who had discussed Safety Inspector Vengerov's irradiation. He popped his head round the door and looked at the table, now empty, which had held the laptop and Mick's camera. Glanced into the bathroom that seemed identical to the one he had shared with Colin, except that it boasted a sizeable bath instead of the shower stall. He went through into Sholokhov's cabin, shaking his head at the indulgence, and already thinking of having a good soak at the earliest opportunity.

This was strikingly different to the one he had just unknowingly vacated. Although the wardrobes seemed identically placed and similarly sized, it contained only a single bed – where his contained a king-sized double. The extra space

was filled by a big desk. It was an unwieldy, old-fashioned
mahogany desk, so massive that it was difficult to imagine
how it had been forced in through the doors. The desk top
boasted a big blotter – big enough to be framing his briefcase,
at least three inches larger than the case on all sides. Intrigued,
Richard crossed towards it, thinking that it could have been
Joseph Conrad's desk – the nautical writer and one-time
ship's officer, famously always facing the wall when he wrote.
Fearful of being distracted by the breathtaking locations he
was writing about – sometimes even writing in.

Richard took the handle of his briefcase and pulled it
towards him, wanting nothing more than to see the desk
itself. Wondering aimlessly whether Sholokhov had sat here
like Conrad. Or whether Richard himself might try putting
some words on paper. As the case came, so the blotter beneath
it came too. It fell on to the chair and then cartwheeled down
on to the deck. Richard put his briefcase on the bed and bent
to retrieve and return the blotter. But as he did so, he noticed
that a piece of paper was sticking out of the side. He took
the corner of it and pulled it out from under the big A2
blotting sheet.

It was a piece of A4 paper covered in jottings and calculations. The notes were all in Russian – a combination of
western and Cyrillic scripts. Richard was about to put the
paper down, its scrawled notes having no meaning for him
whatsoever, but then he stopped, frowning. For, independently
of the impenetrable letters, there were a series of figures.
And the figures did make sense to him. For at least some of
them were the figures he had himself been considering so
recently. He recognized the latitude and longitude for
Archangel, where the vessel had begun its journey. He saw
a line or two further down the page 69.44,-178.36 which
were the coordinates of the anchorage at Leningradskiy. But
then, a couple of lines down again, there were the figures
71.38, -156.45. The last set of figures were underlined and
boxed in red.

Richard sat back, staring, his mind racing wildly. There
might be an innocent explanation. He might well have got
hold of the wrong end of the stick. But still, his breath was
short and his heart was thundering. His pulse like a drumbeat
in his ears. For the last set of figures, highlighted as they

were, 71.38 degrees north, -156.45 degrees east, was the
exact location of Point Barrow in Alaska. Barrow: gateway
to the North Slope oilfields.

Command

I t took Anna longer to get back to the captain's quarters
than she had calculated because the crewman in charge
of the ship's stores insisted on checking with Mr Makarov
before he released the late captain's artefacts to her. And
when he got the OK, he simply handed over everything, so
she had to round up a couple of helpful crewmen to carry
some of it up for her.

Richard answered the door, calling 'Just coming!' on her
first knock. But it took a moment or two for him to open it.
She heard the bolt being turned back and the security chain
rattling. She therefore had the leisure to wonder what on
earth a man like this could possibly be scared of. She decided
he was probably wise to be so careful. Look what had
happened to Captain Sholokhov after all. And to Nuclear
Safety Inspector Vengerov. But in all her momentary whirl
of speculation it never occurred to her that he was securing
his door so carefully to make sure that *she* could not sneak
in unannounced.

Richard had changed his clothes once more, and Anna
took the opportunity to give him a covert once-over as he
gestured her and the laden crewmen in, directing them silently
to pile everything they were carrying on the table in the day
room, then waved them out again. He now wore his beautifully tailored double breasted blazer with gold-coloured
buttons. His shirt had the finest blue pinstripe. His trousers
were grey, with creases that looked sharp enough to slice
bread. She had never seen shoes with such a shine. They
looked like black mirrors. His silk tie was a deeper blue even
than his blazer and it was patterned with a design she recognized as crowns and anchors. It was only when she looked

closely that she saw the same crown and anchor design etched on his buttons.

'What do I look like to you?' he asked quietly as she was about to follow the last crewman out. The depth of his voice started the goosebumps down the insides of her thighs again.

She turned, then paused, inspecting him more openly, calculating the true meaning of the question. He seemed to her to be a plain-spoken man; one who said what he meant and meant what he said. The opposite, for instance, of Mr Makarov. She answered plainly. 'You look like an off-duty officer.'

'Got it in one,' he said obscurely. But he was apparently pleased with her answer. 'I'm going down to dinner,' he said.

She waited a heartbeat for him to add, '*Would you like to come with me?*' But when he did not, she just shrugged. 'Me too,' she said, turning away again.

And if he heard the disappointment in her voice he gave no sign.

As Richard rode down in the lift with Anna far too close beside him, he took refuge in the piece of paper Sholokhov had left beneath the blotter on his desk. The writing still made no sense to him at all, but the figures did. Especially the figures in the box. Perhaps the impenetrable notes said, 'If *Zemlya* gets swept too far east, take care at this point.' Or 'This is the point you must avoid at all costs.' He was tempted to show the writing to Anna, but thought better of it. She was Felix's creature after all. And he did not yet know exactly what Felix was up to – if Felix was up to anything. But the fact that his Russian partner was in any kind of contact with Satang Sittart of Luzon Logging and Indonesian Oil had to give him pause. So he did not know whether he could trust either Felix or Anna. And of course, there was the other aspect. If he did begin to trust Anna enough to show her the paper, to what uncalculated dangers might he be exposing her? These thoughts were sufficient to take Richard down. As the lift hissed to a stop, he folded the paper and slipped it into his pocket, then he held the door open for Anna, standing well back so that she did not have to squeeze past him to exit. Like him, she seemed preoccupied and she hurried away with little more than a nod of thanks.

Richard stepped out, squared his shoulders and strode off towards the dining salon. He was aware of the faintest air of tension as he entered. Precisely why, or where it came from he did not pause to assess. Instead, his gaze swept across the seating at the top table. Felix as usual was taking his ease in the captain's chair, though it appeared that he had not yet started his meal. He had certainly started a bottle of vodka. Colin was sitting beside him, clearly uneasy. Yet another challenge, thought Richard. Yet another test. Much as he had expected.

He caught a passing waiter. 'Get the Chief Steward, please,' he said, emphasizing the universal term in the hope that even a Russian speaker would understand it.

A tall dapper man in a perfect short white jacket appeared almost at once. 'I am the Chief Steward, sir,' he said in passable English. 'My name is *Andrei*.'

'And I am the new captain,' Richard answered shortly. 'My name is *Captain*. Mr Makarov is in my seat. Ask him to move.' And on that he pushed the IN door and strode past Andrei into the galley. Here a squad of sous-chefs and kitchen hands were producing Russian salad and meat dumplings at an impressive rate, and boiling noodles in a huge steel cauldron. A small, plump balding man was taking his ease in an open-fronted office with a notepad and a cup of coffee in front of him. Richard crossed to him so swiftly that he was already towering over him when he looked up. 'Chef?'

'*Dobry vecher.*' The pencil hovered above the notepad. Richard read, upside down, MENU written on the top of the page in curly print.

'English please, Chef,' he asked.

'Good evening,' obliged the Chef in a thick, French-flavoured accent. 'And you are . . . ?'

'*Bonsoir.* I am the captain. The new captain. Your food is wonderful. *Formidable.* But I was wondering whether I could agree the day's menus on a regular basis.'

'Captain Sholokhov never . . .' the chef's Gallic moustache seemed to bristle with outrage. But Richard noted that the pencil point did not waver. The bluster was for show. More territory marking. It was common practice for the captain to agree the menu.

'I have relieved him and I do things differently. Send the menu for each day to my cabin at eight o'clock each morning please.' Richard paused. He could play alpha male games as well as anyone. 'Now, tonight's dinner. Do you have a steak?'

'Of course! But . . .'

'Thank you. Eight ounces cooked weight. No starter or soup – it's not the Russian way I know, but it's *my* way. One steak, medium rare, green salad, and do you have any of the crispy twice-fried potatoes from lunch? Good. That'll be perfect then. I'll be in the captain's chair.'

'*D'accord*,' said the Chef, with no noticeable irony in his tone. More to the point, with no appreciable resentment either.

Richard turned away. Then turned back. 'Perhaps you would be good enough to give me a sheet of that paper,' he said. 'And a pencil if you have one. What with one thing and another, I think I'd better update the top table seating plan so the Chief Steward knows where everyone should be seated in future.'

The chef's eyebrows rose so high that they would have vanished into his hairline if he had possessed one. He tore a sheet off the menu pad and passed it up with the pencil he had been using himself.

'*Merci beaucoup*,' said Richard cheerfully in his brutal French.

Richard pushed the OUT door and strode back into the dining salon. There was a much more palpable atmosphere of tension now, but he paid no attention to it. As though preoccupied with far more important matters, he walked up to the top table without even a glance towards the captain's seat. So that it was a nice surprise – and something of a relief – to find it empty as he came past Colin. The rest of the top table, indeed, was vacant.

'Felix finished his dinner?' he asked as he sat down.

'Felix,' answered Colin, his voice rich with amusement, 'suddenly took a fancy to eat up in his suite.'

'Did he?' said Richard. 'I wonder why.' He leaned back in the warm chair, unconsciously mimicking Felix's easy attitude for an instant. Then he straightened and moved the silverware to one side, placing the menu sheet on the table.

'Colin,' he said, apparently apropos of nothing, 'which of the Russian speakers aboard would you trust most?'

'Dr Leonskaya,' he said without a second's hesitation.

'Me too, I think.'

'Not Anna?' asked Colin.

Richard shot a glance down the table to where she was seated at the far foot. She met his gaze, then looked down. He realized she had been watching him. 'Not Anna,' he said.

'And Dr Potemkin. She seems pretty straight to me. What about Felix? He's your business partner after all.'

'He's playing mind games. He may be up to something else. I trust him with my business, but I would hesitate to trust him with this until I have his position and motivation clearer in my mind.'

'Trust him with what?'

'I'll tell you later,' said Richard decisively, changing gear once again. 'Now. The new seating plan.' His pencil made a rough sketch of the top table on the sheet of paper. 'Captain here, as it should be. Honoured guests to left and right. Senior officers – or as close as we've got to senior officers – here and here.'

He was still making notes ten minutes later when the Chief Steward himself made something of an entrance, bearing an oval platter laden with a steak that looked to be at least twelve ounces – even after it had been seared to perfection. Behind him came three more stewards in procession, carrying a bowl of salad, a bowl of twice-fried crispy potatoes, and a cruet with dressings and mustards, sauces, salt and pepper. Everyone in the dining salon, either covertly like Tom O'Neill, or blatantly like Anna, watched the procession going to the top table chair. Watched the exclusive little à la carte meal being presented to *Zemlya*'s new commanding officer.

'Good Lord,' said Colin, after the Chief Steward had served the food to Richard's satisfaction and wafted away again. 'How on earth did you manage to get a steak like that one?'

'First,' said Richard, reaching for his knife and fork, 'you have to be the captain. And then, you have to take command.'

Weather

What Richard hadn't said to Colin – and what he pondered silently all through his calculatedly leisurely dinner – was that taking command would bring a mountain of responsibilities with it, as well as a few minor rights. Were he taking over the captaincy of one of the stricken tankers or container vessels to which he had been called over the years, he would be filling the next few hours checking on the condition of the vessel itself, then double-checking on work done by the officers around him.

Things were different aboard *Zemlya*, thought Richard. He had fewer deck officers to check up on – but it looked as though he would have to train up the ones he did have. There were no engineering areas to check per se. He would have to rely on Bill Beaumont and George Hebburn on *Erebus* and *Terror* – as well as *Ivan*'s nameless skipper – to run their own vessels and provide propulsion and steerage as and when.

He certainly was in no way competent to check up on Marina Leonskaya and her reactors. Nor, indeed, Kulibin and his as yet unvisited turbines. There was no need to double-check the Security contingent. He might want to keep an eye on Mohammed Yamin as a potential problem – but Yamin was really down to Felix to look after. As was Yamin's boss at Indonesian Oil, Professor Satang S. Sittart. They would all almost certainly turn into bitter business rivals if things went wrong and Yamin thought Indonesian Incorporated would be better going after the Akademik Losmonosov series. Or even that the complex of Sino-Indonesian companies he represented could build a better floating reactor themselves. But they might well become golden geese if all went well and they just wanted to buy more Ice Stations like *Zemlya*. The same was true for Joan Rudd and Mick; and true in spades for Tom O'Neill. Out of nowhere came the hope that Felix had been keeping some kind of an eye on the copy

O'Neill had been sending back to Newscorp. One really negative report from him could conjure up a storm of a completely different – but no less dangerous – type.

By the time Richard had masticated his way through the huge steak Chef had sent him, he had ordered his immediate priorities. He had a set of plans designed to get him through the next few hours – a kind of course calculated to guide him through the oncoming storm of work and out into calm waters beyond. And, as it happened, the first thing he needed to get clear in his mind was the progress of the actual storm that was tearing up the ocean increasingly close behind.

'Anything you want me to do?' rumbled Colin as Richard pulled himself erect. 'I feel like a bit of a spare part here and I'm keen to get on with planning to get through that ice-barrier if it can be done.'

'Yes.' Richard paused. He had been so deep in his study that he had all but forgotten Colin was still sitting beside him. 'Get Felix to come to the bridge would you? I need to discuss what we're going to put in our initial reports to the authorities. And I need to know what's gone into any reports he's seen so far – including news reports. Felix won't have liked being ordered around. So smooth any ruffled feathers, will you? There's a good chap.'

He turned away, then, as the full import of Colin's own words struck him, he turned back, frowning. 'And you're not a spare part by any means, even though I'm going to have to ask you to put your close examination of the ice-barrier on hold for the moment. Because when this ice storm arrives, I'm going to need an iceman of your experience to keep my ice station afloat, otherwise we'll never make it to the barrier – let alone into Leningradskiy Bay!'

Kuznetsov was on the bridge, very much on watch and in charge, bouncing around from the helmsman to the security guard to the radio room, his glasses gleaming determinedly. 'The first thing we need,' Richard informed him, 'is an accurate weather update. Can you get me one please Second Officer?'

'I have one! This is just off the printer!' announced the junior lieutenant enthusiastically. He guided Richard over to the work area where he had spread the colour printout of the weather chart. Spread it out, but clearly hadn't looked at it very closely, thought Richard, his blood running cold. He pored over the bright, apparently innocuous flimsy. 'Get me Bill Beaumont on *Erebus*,' he directed.

All unaware, Kuznetsov toddled off to the communications section and pushed the button that would get the tug's current watch officer up on screen. As he did so, Richard scrutinized the weather chart. For what he was looking at was not a simple force ten storm system, but a tight little northern hemisphere depression with pressure gradients, isobars and estimated wind-speeds that seemed to settle the question of whether there were actually hurricanes in the polar regions once and for all.

'Captain Beaumont will be available in five minutes,' announced Kuznetsov.

'OK. Come here. What do you see?' Richard gestured to the weather chart.

Kuznetsov obeyed, frowning. In the pale light, he looked a little green around the gills. 'Well, it's a weather chart. It looks like a really tightly constructed northern hemisphere depression. That's about all I can say with any certainty. I did a long section on nautical meteorology at the academy. I wasn't very good at it.'

Kuznetsov had a vague look of panic in his usually cheery face. It might be a reaction to the impromptu meteorology lesson or it might be something else, thought Richard. Was the boy becoming seasick?

'Do you remember what these markings tell us?' prompted Richard gently.

'I think so.' Kuznetsov dragged one hand down his suddenly sweating face.

'This one, just under the one thousand and twenty millibar reading. What does it tell you?' Richard prompted, his frown deepening.

'The sky is obscured because the blunt end is all blacked out and there is a steady wind of twenty miles an hour from the south. Those feathers on the other end of the arrow tell me that.' Kuznetsov readjusted his glasses. Much more stressful memory work like this, thought Richard, and they'd start fogging up again.

'And this one further in, nearer the front line?' he asked gently.

'The sky is obscured. The wind has swung round to the southeast. There are no feathers. What's that V-shape instead?'

'That tells us the wind has gone up to sixty miles an hour,' Richard explained. 'What about here?'

'That's right at the top, where the two front lines meet. The eye of the storm. The sky is clearer. The wind is due east. There is one of those V things as well as three feathers now.'

'Winds of ninety miles an hour. And what about these arrows in behind the front lines, where the isobars are almost on top of one another?' Richard's voice was at its calmest now. Had Kuznetsov known him better he would have realized that this was the voice Richard reserved for the most dangerous of situations, where what was needed was calm and the greatest enemy was panic.

'Winds due north, swinging northwest back here. Two Vs. Two Vs with a plus sign. That's bad, isn't it?'

'Two Vs is hurricane force – in excess of one hundred and twenty miles an hour. The plus sign there means it's actually off the scale,' Richard explained. Then he let a little more steel into the velvet of his deep and reassuring voice. So that Kuznetsov would never forget his next words. 'You'll probably never see another chart like this, but if you ever do, the first thing you do is get the captain on to the bridge as fast as ever you can. And the navigating officer, unless you are the navigating officer.'

Kuznetsov's face was white as the implication of Richard's words sank in. 'So it's not just a northern hemisphere depression. It really is a hurricane.'

'Except that some purists insist that hurricanes only exist in the Atlantic – just as typhoons only exist in the Pacific and Indian Oceans. But yes. We have to batten down for northerly winds blowing steadily between one hundred and one hundred and twenty miles per hour but gusting right off the scale – whether you call it a hurricane or not. And they're likely to hit in the next twenty four hours.'

'We're in trouble, aren't we? When that thing catches up with us . . .' Kuznetsov really did look sick now. Sick or terrified.

'Not if I can help it,' Richard said. 'Not now that we have a chance to do something about it. Now, how was your navigation at the academy?'

'Better than my meteorology,' said Kuznetsov dully.

'Good,' said Richard, hoping to distract the lad with a little responsibility. 'I'm going to need you to monitor the weather with me soon, but while I'm talking to Captain Beaumont, I want you to get the chart and the navigating equipment and see if you can work out a course that will take us to Wrangel Island. Say to 70.875 north latitude, minus 179.80 east longitude. I seem to remember a nice safe-looking bay on the chart there. Can you do that?'

Captain Beaumont's face appeared on the communication screen then. Richard turned away without waiting for his trainee navigator's reply. Instead, he took the flimsy over and held it up to the camera above the screen that allowed the two-way video-link to work. 'Bill, have you seen this?'

Storm

Ten fairly intense minutes later, Richard had talked to both Bill Beaumont and George Hebburn. There would be a longer and more detailed conference soon enough, but the basis of his plans were on the table, and *Erebus* and *Terror* at least were beginning to prepare for the worst. There was still no sign of Colin and Felix, however, so Richard took Kuznetsov out on to the covered bridge wing where he could see the sky through the thick glass cladding. Together they observed and discussed the telltale cloud formations that predicted the onset of the storm.. They were already directly beneath the lower, thicker layers of altostratus, which blotted out the sky above and threatened to unleash more snow and hail.

Richard led the young lieutenant to the aft section of the bridge wing so that they could look over the top of *Erebus,* away into the white wake their little flotilla was leaving across the leaden Arctic Ocean. Here the great storm clouds, the nimbostratus and stratus, sat like a black wall seemingly closing down on the obsidian water in the distance. Then, suddenly it seemed, a low layer of stratocumulus reached out immediately above them, like the fingers of a grasping demon, even as the first great gust of the storm wind roared up from the south. For an instant, the whole of the terrifying vision astern seemed to lighten, leap out of focus. A wall of sleet hissed over them with sudden, shocking violence.

'That's it,' yelled Richard. 'The pressure just went off a cliff. You can almost feel it tumbling. Let's go check – and see whether there's anyone in Chersky with their head far enough above the bunker to give us a weather update from the black heart of the thing!'

Felix was waiting for them as they ran into the command bridge, but he was not worried about the weather chart, the air pressure, the approaching cataclysm, or whether there was anyone in Chersky willing – or able – to give them a meteorological update. Instead he was clutching a printout of his own.

'Look at *this*!' he howled. 'It is O'Neill! It has to be!'

'Go out on to the starboard bridge wing,' Richard told Kuznetsov. Now was not the time to expose a sick boy to an enraged Felix Makarov. 'Give me a report on what's happening to the south of us. Take some binoculars. See if you can make out the coast. I particularly want to know about any ice piled along the shoreline if you can make anything out. I want to know what we can expect if the worst comes to the worst and the wind takes us down on to the lee shore.'

As Kuznetsov hurried across the bridge and out on to the starboard bridge wing, Richard turned towards Felix. Colin, towering behind the outraged Russian, caught Richard's eye and shook his head. Rolling his eyes up in a gesture of weary hopelessness. 'Now,' said Richard. 'What's this all about?'

It was the front page of the London *Times* Internet edition, dated today. There was a photograph of *Zemlya* at her launch ceremony. Beside it a headline which read:

ZEMLYA: Experimental Ice Station or Nuclear Death Ship?

Richard started scanning the article, checking for the byline – *Staff Reporter* – and then for the main facts that the story sought to deal with. But he only got snatches.

Since the launch pictured here there have been nine deaths, near deaths or unexplained disappearances . . .

Professor Vladimir Kirienkho in an unexplained accident on Mozhayskoye Shosse, inbound from the MKAD ringroad towards the suburb of Kuntsevo . . .

At least one other officer before the vessel set sail . . . Captain Gagarin of tug *Ivan*, reportedly lost overboard . . .

Vasily Vengerov of the Nuclear Safety Directorate . . . First Officer and engineer, tug *Ivan* . . .

Captain Sholokhov and First Officer Oblomov from Ice Station *Zemlya* herself . . . Death toll mounting . . .

What are the authorities doing?

Then, under that, the next chilling sub-head:

Zemlya: Chernobyl afloat?

'This doesn't look good,' said Richard, with masterly understatement.

'Doesn't look *good*?' snarled Felix. 'It's a *disaster*. What I've got to do is . . .'

But they had to wait to find out what Felix had to do, because just at that moment two things happened almost at once.

Kuznetsov came panting in off the starboard bridge wing, pale as a snowflake and shaking. 'Captain!' he called. 'Captain, there's a helicopter approaching!'

And just as he said this, the radio officer stuck his head out of the radio room. 'Captain!' he called. 'I have helicopter Kamov Ka-32T inbound from the airbase at Mys Shmidta. He says he will be landing on the helipad in five minutes' time.'

'*Chto za huy?*' spat Felix, clearly being pushed beyond some kind of boundary here.

Richard glanced across at Kuznetsov, and was so surprised by the shock on the boy's face that he raised his eyebrows.

Kuznetsov, supposing his captain was enquiring as to the English translation mouthed *what the fuck*? He turned away, apparently heaving with nausea.

'Let's go up and see, then, shall we?' suggested Richard. 'Second officer, you have the bridge. I'll want an accurate pressure reading when I get back, please. And start making up the logs.' Then he hurried aft through the bridge door with Felix and Colin close behind him.

The three big men crushed into the lift.

'What in hell's name does the Air Force want with us?' fumed Felix.

'Perhaps they're having another revolution at the airbase,' suggested Richard. 'Maybe they've decided to invade us. Maybe *Zemlya*'s going to be their battleship *Potemkin* this time round.'

'*Chyort voz'mi!*' gasped Felix. 'Maybe we should have Karchenko and his security men with us!'

'I'd be surprised if they're not on their way up in the other lift as we speak,' said Richard. 'I'll bet his lookouts saw the chopper long before Kuznetsov.'

'And he monitors all radio traffic anyway,' said Felix, completely unaware of the speaking look that Richard and Colin exchanged on hearing the information he so thoughtlessly let slip.

'The captain certainly won't want to miss out on anything like this,' nodded Colin in agreement.

'Spetsnaz are Navy special forces, like Marines, Commandos . . .' said Richard, bringing the conversation to an end. 'They'll not want to let the Air Force steal a march on them. Not on Karchenko's watch.'

The last observation was enough to take the three men up one level to the top weather deck. The Kamov appeared suddenly, heaving itself up over the left-hand edge of the deck-house, so close that another gust of the southerly gale might have driven it into the wall of the bridgehouse itself. The winged Air Force emblem in its gold wreath caught the last of the light, as the undercarriage swung dangerously towards the helipad. A cannonade of hail swept like grapeshot across the deck as it settled, its four tyres screaming and its four legs flexing. It juddered sideways, then came to rest, facing them, seeming to glare down at them like a fantastical monstrous beast.

As soon as it was down, the side door slid open and a set of steps folded out and down. A huge man unfolded himself out of the space inside and stepped down on to the deck. His black Astrakhan hat was matched by a black Astrakhan coat so long its tails seemed to sweep the dancing hail off the deck. He turned, reached back into the cavernous fuselage and grasped a pair of cases. He swung back towards them, nostrils pinched, thin shark's mouth turned down grimly.

'This looks like trouble,' muttered Colin to Richard as the stranger strode forward, apparently lucky not to be beheaded by the Kamov's lower rotor.

'He *is* trouble,' said Richard. 'Trouble personified!' And Felix shot a glance at captain Karchenko that brought the whole of the provisional little Spetsnaz honour guard crashing to full attention as he strode forward to meet his most unwelcome guest, stuffing into his pocket the news article that had almost certainly brought him down upon them, holding his hand out in courteous greeting as though he were glad to see him come aboard. 'Federal Prosecutor,' he called as though this visitation was his most cherished dream come true. 'A pleasure. A privilege.'

'Federal Prosecutor?' asked Colin in a stage whisper. 'Is this who I think it is?'

'Yes,' said Richard grimly. 'Federal Prosecutor Yagula. This is where everything hits the fan with a vengeance.'

Yagula

'**W**ho's in charge here?' demanded Yagula as he strode out from beneath the Kamov's double blades.

'Federal Prosecutor . . .' said Felix again, holding out his hands as though greeting an old friend.

'Ah. Makarov. Have these taken to my quarters,' said Yagula handing him the cases. 'Then arrange for my associates. They will bunk in together.'

Behind him, a pair of identical twins was climbing out of the Kamov. Identical in every respect except that one was a man and the other a woman. Both Teutonically blond, ice-eyed and dressed in the uniforms of the MVD Militsiya. Both as disturbingly unsmiling as their fearsome leader. At the sight of them, a kind of stirring went through Captain Karchenko's men, like a breath of wind through a field of barley. A roll of thunder rumbled quietly in the distance, just loud enough to be audible over the Kamov's pounding rotors.

Richard had an instantaneous, irreverent thought that Yagula had outmanoeuvred Felix in the power game by check-mating his Spetsnaz command with a couple of officers who could have stepped straight out of a WWII history book: Nazi Gestapo SS officers. Their epaulettes bore the double red stripes and single stars that declared their rank as Major. Even Karchenko would have to follow their orders. 'Who is in command here?' demanded Yagula again as Felix gaped at the suitcases dangling from his welcoming fists. He was having a really bad day, chuckled Richard to himself sympathetically.

'I'm acting captain,' he said easily, stepping forward. After Felix's humiliating experience he did not offer to shake hands. And he had no intention of being wrong-footed, outmanoeuvred or intimidated.

'Ah. Captain Mariner,' nodded Yagula. 'Of course. Well, I will start with you when my associates and I have settled in.'

Behind him, the Kamov lifted off and thundered away, low across the writhing sky, apparently just above the restlessly heaving sea. The black plume of its exhaust whipped away downwind instantly.

'Just send an associate to find me when you're ready,' said Richard, with a shrug that bordered on the dismissive. 'And I'll come as soon as my duties permit.' He turned on his heel and led Colin off the helideck, leaving Felix and the others to take care of their unwelcome visitors.

'Was that wise?' asked Colin as soon as they were in the upper corridor. 'If he's as powerful as you say, he won't have liked being treated like that.'

'By the time he gets himself sorted out,' said Richard as they arrived at the lift doors and he pressed the button, 'we'll be in the early stages of a hurricane and even the Federal Prosecutor's priorities may get reordered when the winds go over one hundred knots.' The doors opened. They stepped in, side by side.

'How so?' demanded Colin as the lift doors hissed closed behind them.

Richard looked his friend straight in the eye, wondering whether even Colin Ross had any idea what mayhem was coming down on them. 'He'll find he's less worried about finding out how people died and more concerned about keeping himself alive.'

As the doors hissed open on the bridge deck a couple of seconds later, Richard turned to his friend. 'Get Ivana to move your kit into the captain's cabin with me,' he said decisively. 'The office doubles as a second berth and looks to be quite comfortable. Felix is going to want to put Yagula in our old quarters anyway and we might as well get on with it. Stay ahead of whatever games the two of them are playing. On the one hand, there's the only proper bath aboard, which has to be something of a temptation. On the other hand, and talking of temptation, you can chaperone me if Anna goes into her *From Russia With Love* act.'

'I'll get it myself,' rumbled Colin amenably. 'Though it's the bath that makes the difference – after the better part of a year on the ice.' He strode off along the corridor then slowed and turned back. 'Though thank God we're not politicians, eh?' he threw over his shoulder. 'Heaven alone knows what the newspapers would make of all this bunking in together!'

Richard went through into the captain's quarters with a wry chuckle, and was confronted at once with yet another problem: all of the late Captain Sholokhov's kit was piled in the middle of the day room, and there was a surprising amount of it. A couple of sizeable suitcases, an overnight kitbag and a briefcase all in a neat pile with the case for a laptop standing on the luxuriously carpeted deck beside it. Sidetracked, Richard opened the briefcase, and there, beside bundles of papers, trade journals and whatnot, was a square, solid Geiger counter.

Richard picked the brown and yellow box up and switched it on without a second thought. At once the red warning light began to glow while the telltale clicking started to warn him of elevated radioactivity nearby. His experience with the unfortunate Inspector Vengerov made him think to check himself first. Holding the noisy little machine in his right hand, he brought it towards his chest, then up to his head and shoulders. There was no intensification. It was not until he scanned it down his left arm towards his left hand that the clicking grew louder and more rapid. He reversed his grip and checked his right hand. The same thing occurred. Frowning, he put the machine down and crossed to the bathroom, his immediate thought to wash his hands carefully at once, just as Mussorgsky's nurses had washed Karchenko and himself. As he did so, the clicking quietened. By the time he reached the bathroom door, the light had changed from red to green.

Richard stood there lost in thought, his radioactive hands held away from his body like a pianist standing at an invisible keyboard. He had touched something radioactive. What could it be? When could he have done it? Where? He had been out on the foredeck, pulling young Kuznetsov aboard. Apart from that, he had only been here changing his kit, on the bridge giving the decidedly green-looking boy his lesson in reading weather maps, in the lift with Felix and Colin and up on the helideck with Yagula and his matched pair of Nazi stormtroopers.

The penny dropped then. Richard had an instantaneous vision of the intrepid junior lieutenant rolling back on to the foredeck, smeared with the thick rust-red filth from the massive anchor. The boy wasn't seasick or terrified: he had managed to get himself poisoned somehow. Judging from the rapidity and the intensity of the sickness, severely poisoned. He might well be dying!

Without a second more of hesitation, Richard returned to the Geiger counter, snatched it up and strode across to the door. He tore it open and stepped out. Only to freeze. The female twin of Yagula's associates was standing immediately in front of him with Colin hovering a little nervously behind her.

'Captain,' she said crisply. 'Colonel General Yagula . . .'

'Later,' said Richard, brushing past her. 'Colin. Come with me. I need you on the bridge. Now.' He strode forward and Colin fell in obediently at his shoulder. After a moment, the rigid major turned and followed suit.

With Colin and the MVD officer in tow, Richard slammed on to the bridge. At once the Geiger counter's already elevated clicking rose a notch. If the boy had got himself irradiated, thought Richard, then everything he had touched would likely need decontamination. He glanced at the junior officer who was slumped in the watch chair, semi-comatose. He put the Geiger counter to the bridge phone. The clicking eased. Untouched. 'Colin,' he ordered crisply. 'Use the all hail channel – that button there. I need Brodski and Mussorgsky up here now. And Anna. They all speak English. They'll react to their names. At the double, I hope!'

As he crossed to Junior Lieutenant Kuznetsov, the clicking intensified again, becoming that almost continuous buzzing that had warned Vengerov that he had been poisoned. It was easily loud enough to overpower Colin's voice as it boomed through *Zemlya*'s communications system. The source of the radioactivity was clear.

Even so, the MVD Major inserted herself between Richard and the radioactive boy once again. She was frowning, more with concentration than concern or anger. Clearly she had been told to invite rather than to order his presence. 'The Colonel General—' she repeated.

'I thought he was Federal Prosecutor,' snapped Richard pushing past her once again, careful not to touch her with his radioactive hands.

'The Federal Prosecutor holds military rank in MVD and Army equivalence,' she persisted, pushing back in front of him. 'And he wishes that you—'

'Look, Major. I am radioactive. The young officer immediately behind you is radioactive – and likely to be poisoned. That's why this counter is going mad. I'm not going anywhere until we have both been decontaminated and my bridge has been decontaminated too. Tell General Yagula – or whatever he calls himself nowadays – that if he wants to talk to me I'll be here or in decontamination three decks down. But he'd better be wearing lead underpants if he wants to keep up his reputation with the ladies.'

Dr Mussorgsky arrived then and Richard simply dismissed the major and her boss from his mind. She crossed to the bridge door and exited as though she was heading for a firing squad. 'We need to get Lieutenant Kuznetsov to decontamination,' he said to the doctor. 'Have you got anything that would tell us how many Gray units he's being exposed to? This Geiger counter is all very well but it's either red or green with no gradations in between as far as I can see.'

Mussorgsky shook his head. 'Not on me,' he said.

'OK,' said Richard. 'We'll check when we get him down to the sickbay. Then you'll need to send a decontamination team up here to clean the bridge and check anything that he or I have touched.'

Brodski arrived. 'You have bridge watch,' said Richard. 'But don't touch anything until the whole place has been decontaminated. Get the helmsman to tell you where Kuznetsov went and what he touched.'

Anna arrived with Captain Karchenko in tow as Richard was saying this. 'Captain, get your man watching the CCTV monitors to do the same. It'll help the decontamination teams to work faster. Anna stay close to me – but not too close – I may want you to translate my orders, but I don't want you getting irradiated. Right, Doctor, I'm irradiated already, and I have as many children as I want. I'll carry the boy down to decontamination. Let's move!'

Chainlocker

Colonel General Federal Prosecutor Yagula clearly had not thought to pack lead underpants, thought Richard wryly some time later as he was declared decontaminated for the second time on board *Zemlya*. He saw nothing of the man during the time that he and Lieutenant Kuznetsov had undergone the ministrations of Mussorgsky and his team. The weak and sickly Kuznetsov was consigned to the temporary isolation ward which he now shared with the sedated but recovering Vengerov. The weather had closed in so fast – and was worsening with every passing minute – meaning that the Mil was in its hangar and there was no way to get the lieutenant off *Zemlya*. Besides, nowhere nearby could serve him better than the specialist facilities aboard the Ice Station.

'I should give you some of this too,' said Mussorgsky as he injected a sedative into the lieutenant's bicep. 'You look as though you really need some rest.'

'I do,' answered Richard roundly. 'And when I get my head down, I won't need any narcotics to see me off. But I have things to do. People to see.'

'"The woods are lovely, dark and deep",' quoted the doctor. '"But you have promises to keep . . ."'

'"And miles to go before I sleep",' acknowledged Richard. 'Or the length of the foredeck at any rate. What I need from you is some sort of protective outfit, a receptacle for radio-active samples and your most sensitive and accurate Geiger counter. Have you anyone who could accompany me on a little expedition to the foredeck looking for the source of Kuznetsov's poisoning? It's the sort of thing that, as your acting captain, I feel I ought to know about.'

'I can come with you myself once these two are safely asleep. Indeed, I can go myself without you if you tell me what you're looking for – and let you get some rest.'

'Thanks for the offer and I'm tempted. But I need to check on several things on the foredeck personally, and this is the last chance I'll get to do so for a while. Frankly, I really haven't got an absolutely solid idea as to what we're looking for yet. But if you could help me with whatever samples I manage to come up with, then that would be excellent.'

'Samples of what?' asked Mussorgsky as the pair of them, clothed in white, gloved, hooded and masked like soldiers on snow patrol, stepped out on to the weather deck and clipped themselves to the re-rigged safety lines. But the question was whipped away by a vicious gust of snow-laden wind, and he found he had to crank up the volume and bellow the question again. Especially in the face of the unnervingly eerie howling sound that reminded the good doctor most forcibly of the werewolf movies that had scared him most in childhood.

Richard turned, little more than a hulking white shape already almost invisible in the gusting blizzard. 'That red stuff for a start. I have no idea what it is or whether it has anything to do with anything at all. But Kuznetsov was covered in it when I pulled him aboard.'

'Where did it come from?' demanded the doctor, frowning.

'Off the anchor. I didn't see anything on him before he grabbed that.' As Richard answered, the squall eased, running away to the north. The air cleared and the werewolf wires stopped howling. Mussorgsky found himself halfway along the foredeck towards the winches, with the safety wires in a web at waist height all around him. Gaining confidence, he released his death-grip on the safety rig and eased the weighty lead-lined sample box on his chafing shoulder. The snow wall fell back to reveal the one great hawser reaching forward from the pair of upright capstans reaching away through the point of the bow towards the stern of the labouring tug ahead.

Richard stopped at each of the capstans, checking them minutely, double-checking the hawser both here and, from the forepeak, all along its sagging line to the aft of the tug. Then, apparently satisfied, he crossed to the starboard side of the foredeck. Mussorgsky followed him through all of this little journey, entranced by the dangerous novelty of being out on deck so late and so close to such a massive storm, but feeling a bit like a spare wheel. However, as soon as the pair of them reached the starboard section above the main anchor point, the doctor became a much more active member of the little team. 'There's some of the red stuff on the deck there,' said Richard grimly, easing himself down on one knee and gesturing Mussorgsky to join him. 'It looks like some sort of oil grease contaminated with rust. Most of it's been washed away. Do you think there's enough to get a reading from? And maybe a sample?'

Mussorgsky leaned forward, pointing his Geiger counter at the red smear on the deck. The moment he pressed the button the little machine sprang to life. 'That's a very active sample,' said the doctor, his voice rising with worry. 'I could take a smear of it back and see if I could get some sort of an idea what it actually is. But if you're right about it, then perhaps we should try and get some of the original.' He looked up at the frowning Englishman. 'I mean, if this has been wiped off the anchor on to Kuznetsov and then washed off him on to the deck – then all but washed off the deck into the bargain, it could be hundreds of times weaker than the original. Maybe thousands. It'll only give us the vaguest idea of what we might be dealing with.'

'I take your point,' said Richard. 'But I'm not going down to get a smear from the anchor. And neither are you.' He hesitated for an instant. Then continued. 'However, I think I have an alternative. Whatever was on the anchor might well be on parts of the anchor chain and that I can get at with relative ease.'

Inboard from the hawsehole nearest the anchor – the hole Brodski had christened *Kuznetsov's exit* – there was a plate in the deck with hinges at the forward end of it and a recessed handle nearest the bridge. On every vessel Richard had served on, this would have been the access to the chainlocker, and Richard saw no reason to suspect that *Zemlya*'s architect would change that aspect of maritime tradition at least. On closer inspection, while Mussorgsky was scraping the tiny sample left on the deck into a kind of test-tube from a lead-lined box, Richard soon worked out that there was a double-hatch. A small one, light enough to be opened by hand by the looks of it; but that was only a small section of a much larger hatch designed to open the entire chain-locker itself. A hatch that would need power of some sort.

Richard reached down and twisted the handle on the small hatch, pulling it upwards with surprisingly little effort. Sure enough, a shallow, black-throated hole was floored with a lazy steel and rust-coloured anaconda of anchor-chain links. Immediately at his feet there was a set of steps – little more than a ladder allowing immediate access. He stepped down without thinking and stooped. There was a little toolkit clipped to the makeshift banister – just where he would have put one. It held a few tools and a rubberized torch. He pulled the torch free and turned it on, preparing to go on into the locker itself.

Mussorgsky's hand on his shoulder stopped him. The doctor pushed in beside him, holding the Geiger counter exactly as he himself was holding the torch. No sooner did the sensitive machine get below deck-level than it was flashing red and clicking like a football rattle.

'Take very great care,' advised the doctor, more than a little redundantly.

Richard nodded, flashing his torch around. It seemed that most of the huge links just beneath his feet were liberally smeared with the thick red slime that had covered Kuznetsov. He had no intention of getting closer to them than absolutely necessary. He had heard of sailors slipping into chainlockers and being swallowed as though by quicksand. A strange shift in the cloud cover above and behind him let some lambent light in here seeming to make the red stuff glow eerily. A side-wave made the metal stir infinitesimally but infinitely threateningly.

Mussorgsky crouched further forward, pulling another test-tube out of his lead-lined box. Richard stepped down at his side, flashing the torch around. The chainlocker was surprisingly cavernous, even though it was all-but full of the great links of serpentine metal. Each link was an oval more than eighteen inches long, its central section closed with a cross-piece. Each crosspiece was stamped with a half-familiar symbol that made Richard frown as he searched his capacious, near-photographic memory. Then he remembered. The character was Chinese. He had seen it the year before London Olympic year when he had been in Shanghai soon after the 2010 Expo. It was the mark of the Jiangsu Iron Foundry in Jingjiang, China. China again, he thought, with a mental shake of his head. What was the matter with Sholler, Narodny or Profain, of Petersburg and Moscow, all good Russian chain makers? Price, he supposed. But Felix seemed to be looking for a world of pain with his Chinese preferences.

Each central section of the Chinese chain almost closed the massive link, leaving an aperture perhaps five inches wide at each end for the next links to fit through. Most of these were clear, but one nearby, Richard saw, was blocked. There was something pale trapped in it. Something vaguely familiar yet disturbingly out of place. It was not until the torch-beam glinted off the gold of a signet ring that Richard realized that what was wedged in the chain link was a man's fist. It was marble-white for the most part. But smeared with the rust-red slime as well. Skin on knuckles at top and bottom bashed and bruised away to show a flash of tendon and bone. Wiry black hairs agonizingly human against the stony pallor of the thing. No body, as far as Richard could see. Just the severed fist wedged in the chain link.

Fascinated, Richard stepped down deeper. 'Do you see that, Doctor?' he asked.

'What?' Mussorgsky looked up. Followed the steady gold finger of Richard's torch beam. 'Oh! My God!'

'Could we fit it into your sample box if I can somehow get it free?'

'Of course! My God. That's . . . That's . . .'

Richard returned to the tool rack and unclipped a screw-driver. He handed the torch to the doctor who kept it pointing at the strangely severed fist, then, clearing his mind of the horror-stories he had just been remembering, he stepped on to the chain itself, trusting it not to swallow him after all.

It was by no means an easy task. The chain was slippery and if it didn't actually swallow him, neither did it lie still and leave him to work in peace. When he reached the fist itself he found it to be every bit as rock-hard and tightly wedged as it had seemed when he first saw it. Unyielding in every sense of the word. Moreover, he kept moving into the torch-beam and almost blinding himself as he sought to use the screw-driver to lever it free without doing it yet more damage. Then, part way through the delicate operation, the daylight thickened to near darkness, the safety lines took up their werewolf chorus once again and the heavens opened.

But at last it was done. Richard turned towards Mussorgsky holding the fist between his hands. Even through the protective gloves it felt ice-cold and rock hard. Like the marble it seemed to be made from. The doctor put the torch on the step above him and held out the lead-lined box, open. Understanding the medical man's reluctance to touch the strange object, Richard simply dropped it in among the test-tubes Mussorgsky had filled with his various sorts of rusty slime. The signet ring chimed unsettlingly against the glass tubes. Mussorgsky closed the top. 'We go back now?' he begged.

And Richard nodded wearily. 'Yes, Doctor,' he said. 'We go back now. Hand in hand.'

Fist

Even Richard's massive strength had limits. Just as there were things his muscles could not lift, move or achieve, so there were things that his will could not enforce. And on the way back along *Zemlya*'s foredeck he reached his absolute limit, physically, emotionally, spiritually. As the bliz-zard returned on a dangerous southerly gale punching his side, shoulder and head like a robber determined to mug him, he stumbled, even though the deck beneath his staggering feet remained as steady as Southend Pier. He fumbled almost drunkenly with the clip as he tried to detach himself from the safety wire outside the A deck door. And as he sought to enter the sudden, almost disorientating calm of the bridge house, he failed to raise his right foot high enough to clear the step over the bulkhead and he went sprawling into the corridor.

Mussorgsky solicitously helped him to his feet and stayed close by his side as they went on down to the doctor's domain. They pulled off their soaking protective clothing, and Richard slumped into a chair, looking vacantly across the neat little surgery. The Russian medic, like most of his age, had done his stint in the army and he knew the look of a man at the end of his strength. Suddenly all business, he crossed to his dispensary and returned with two tablets. 'Take these pills and go straight up to bed,' he ordered.

Richard looked down at little white discs in his broad palm. 'There's a hurricane that's going to hit us within the next eight to twelve hours,' he rumbled.

'Then you need to sleep now so that you're at the top of your game when it arrives. If you can't even coordinate well enough to step through a doorway in the middle of an Arctic Ocean hurricane then you're going to kill us all. Take the pills. You can bunk down in here if you want or you can go back to your cabin. Either way, I'll ensure you rest well and wake up refreshed when you're needed.'

Richard nodded. Nodded slowly, as though his head were suddenly made out of lead. The sudden relief from respon-sibility was as tempting as a Siren's call. And yet there was still so much to do. *Miles to go before I sleep*, he thought, and closed his fist over the little white tempters.

There was a sharp rap at the sickbay door and the little portal swung wide to reveal both of Yagula's neat blond stormtroopers. 'The Federal Prosecutor insists . . .' snarled the masculine major.

Richard opened his hand again at once, tossed the pills into the back of his throat and swallowed.

*   *   *

Anna was naked. Almost – but not quite – stark naked. Showered, towelled, powdered and perfumed, she was lying beneath a single sheet dreaming sensuous dreams of Richard, when the door to her cabin was thrown open and three brisk footsteps brought a dark figure across her tiny cabin. Light blazed. She sat up, disorientated, bashing her forehead on the ceiling above her bunk. She looked around, dazed, the last wisps of her erotic dream dispersing like smoke. Ivana in the bunk below her rolled over, snoring like a Ukrainian tractor starting up on a cold morning. The cabin light was on. A blonde woman with icy eyes was standing startlingly close, her face level with Anna's bunk. She was wearing the uniform of an MVD major. 'Get dressed,' she ordered brusquely. 'Federal Prosecutor Yagula wants you. Now.'

The first cabin Richard and Colin had shared had been changed even in the short time the Federal Prosecutor had been in occupation of it. The sofas were pulled back against the walls. There was no sign of the fruit bowls or the magazines. A desk had been conjured up from somewhere and it sat in front of the long window that looked north into the blizzard which was blowing up towards the pack in the teeth of the southerly storm.

Behind the desk sat the massive, fearsome Colonel General Yagula himself. At the end of the desk with his back to the cabin doors sat Felix Makarov. Between them stood a pair of vodka bottles. Jewel Of Russia Elite, a bowl of ice, a pile of *vobla* whose fishy smell hung heavily in the air, and two shot glasses. Anna stood in front of the desk and the twin majors stood at her shoulders.

'You are right, my dear Makarov,' rumbled Yagula. 'The likeness is remarkable. And he did not see it himself you say?'

'Not at first,' answered Felix. 'But later . . .'

'Ah, yes. Later.' Yagula's fearsome gaze settled back on Anna, whose heart was beating all too loudly. This time not with lust, but with terror.

'Of course, he has *had* you?' It took her a moment to realize the Federal Prosecutor was addressing her. And what he was asking.

'No, Federal Prosecutor,' she managed.

'You *refused* him?' That was Felix Makarov, outraged.

'No,' she answered, her chin coming up defiantly. 'He refused me.'

'Ah . . .' mused Yagula. There was silence for a heartbeat as he mulled the information over. 'Well he is bunking in with Dr Ross . . .' He let the suggestion hang.

'No!' snapped Anna. 'He is a man! He is not *goluboi*! He is happily married, and faithful to this witch who looks like me.'

'Of course he is,' rumbled Yagula, uncharacteristically accommodating. Or seemingly so. Then his voice cracked like a whip. 'And you are a clean, pure country virgin; not a *Shluha vokzal'naja* train station whore at all!' Suddenly he surged to his feet. He strode round the end of the desk like a bear going into the attack, stopping only when he was towering above her, face to face. '*Na kaleni, suka!*' he snarled. '*Sosi moi hui sooka!*' He gestured down at his trouser-front. Even in the midst of her horror and terror, Anna saw how beautifully tailored the cloth was.

'No, Federal Prosecutor!' she said, even as the majors on either side of her grasped her arms with one hand and began to push her shoulders down with the other in a smoothly practised motion. 'You can get this bitch down on her knees, perhaps. But unless you are going to tear my teeth out, you'd better hope that anything you want me to suck is made of solid steel!'

Yagula stepped back. Half sat on the front of the desk, looking down at her speculatively. The pressure on her shoulders eased. She remained defiantly upright after all, though her knees, so stiff a moment ago, suddenly seemed treacherously weak. Felix Makarov simply gaped at her. Then the Federal Prosecutor gave a roar of brutal laughter. 'Yes!' he said. 'Parts of me have been compared to steel on more than one occasion. But today is not the day I want to put them to any test. And I'm afraid your teeth are far too pretty to spoil. So they will remain where they are. For the time being. And so will you. At Mr Makarov's command, and of course, at mine. Now, my officers will escort you back to bed. But they will not – I repeat *not* – tuck you in. Goodnight!'

As the door closed behind the three, Felix Makarov looked across at Yagula who had straightened, turned and reached for the nearest vodka bottle. 'You see, Lavrenty Michaelovich?' he said, slipping into the familiar patronymic form now that they were relaxed, like a Frenchman moving from *vous* to *tu*. 'It is just as I said. The stupid little *sooka* is more than half in love with him, even though he has not yet touched her.'

'And less than half in love with either of us, Felix Edmundovich. But it's all the same to me. Hate, love, friendship and fear – I can use them all equally. Even full of hatred and fear for us, her feelings for him still make her a useful pawn, perhaps more than a pawn, who knows? She will definitely have her uses.'

'And your beautiful blond assistants. Have you used either of them yet?'

'Ah. My hunting hounds; my matched *Ovcharkas*, *Alisa* and *Dmitri*. No. They are for each other alone, unless they choose to hunt as a pair elsewhere.'

'Hence the warning about putting Anna to bed . . .'

'Precisely. She is our meat for the time being. But when they hunt new flesh it is always their choice; never mine. And I like to be in control of these matters as well as all the others, as you know. Which brings us back to Richard Mariner, does it not? We cannot control him. He has outmanoeuvred you as far as I can see. The delectable but high-minded Anna has proved that. And he simply refused to obey any of my summonses; even to the extent of knocking himself out with a sleeping draught and putting himself in the doctor's care for the next few hours. He knows he holds the whip hand while he is aboard and *Zemlya* is stormbound. We must trust him to keep the vessel safe when he awakes to face this hurricane – or we will all die, which is of course not part of the plan. And therefore, even sleeping, he extends his protection to the doctor who is tending him and the silly bitch who is half in love with him. It is extraordinary how he works is it not? But on the other hand he has always been inquisitive. Even in the most extreme of situations, I have seen him questing. More like a bloodhound than a Borzoi, perhaps. But even so, he is unstoppable when he gets the scent.'

'That's to the good, Lavrenty Michaelovich.' Felix assured him earnestly. The pair of them tossed back their vodkas, then Felix continued, 'There are matters here I want him to investigate – some of which have caused even you to come aboard. But there are other things I do not want him to discover.' He swept his hand up over his forehead and across the top of his shaven skull, then reached for the bottle once more. 'It is a delicate balance.'

'A delicate situation, Felix Edmundovich. Perhaps even dangerous. But nowhere near as dangerous as the situation you will find yourself in if I discover that you have been anything less than absolutely and utterly honest, full and frank in all your dealings with me!'

Even as Felix Edmundovich and Lavrenty Michaelovich, rendered almost friendly by the vodka, were draining their bottles and beginning to think of sleep, so the two they had been discussing, both unknowingly under the protection of the sleeping Richard Mariner, were wide awake and all alone. Anna was lying rigid in her bunk, feeling as isolated as a newcomer in a Gulag, in spite of the fact that Ivana was still performing her tractor impressions in the lower bunk. The ex-air hostess lay wide-eyed in the darkness, going over in her mind what the federal prosecutor had so nearly made her do. After about fifteen minutes she suddenly hurled herself out of the bunk and out of the cabin, down to the nearest toilet where she was violently sick.

Dr Mussorgsky also felt a little nauseous. His speciality had been general medicine before he began to focus on the assessment and treatment of radiation sickness and this was too close to post-mortem work for him. Although he himself had been born and raised in Chernigov before his education in Kiev, he had been fascinated by tales of the disaster at nearby Chernobyl, and had even met men and women who had been involved – or knew of those who had. There were men and women all over Ukraine who were still suffering from the fallout.

The region around the nuclear power station was generally off-limits during his youth, but his inability to get at the heart of his obsession had simply fired his desire. The medical study of radiation effects had been a very well-supported course at the University of Kiev's Faculty of Medical Radiophysics. When he was older and things relaxed, he joined other tourists and stood in the shadow of Reactor number four with his Geiger counter reading over 800 micro-Roentgens instead of the more usual Russian background reading of 10. But he had his doctorate by then and knew precisely how long he could risk such dosages for.

Now, at well after two a.m., he was looking at the complex of readings from his Geiger counter as it showed him how many Roentgens were being emitted by the red slime he had scraped from the anchor chain while Captain Mariner had been retrieving the severed hand. He was mentally trying to calculate how many Gray units they represented. Roentgens being radioactive output; Gray units being how much of the radioactivity human flesh was likely to absorb.

The calculation from one form of measurement to the other was important in two ways. Firstly, how dangerous the red slime was to Kuznetsov – and anyone else getting too close to it. Secondly, how many Gray units must have been absorbed by whoever had left their flesh and blood smeared all over the anchor chain in the first place. For he had suspected, with increasing certainty, that the red slime was blood rather than rust even before Captain Mariner found the severed fist.

The fist in fact lay before him now, giving off almost as much radioactivity as the red slime. It was the right fist. The wrist had been crushed rather than cut and the arm had most likely been crushed to red slime by the weight of chain falling around the anchor. For Mussorgsky knew that the fist must have belonged to the second lieutenant. The officer who had been crushed to death on the St Petersburg slipway two nights after the Professor was killed in the crash on the Moscow Ring Road.

That was one of the reasons he was frowning so deeply now. There had been no doubt in the reports. Crushed to death. Accidentally. Not irradiated. Like the nuclear inspector next door. And yet, the victim of that apparently routine, if unfortunate, accident was here – in part at least – giving off almost as much radioactivity as Reactor number 4 at Chernobyl.

During the hours since Captain Mariner had taken his sleeping pills, he had tested the radiation to see if he could isolate the main radioactive particle – it was better to know your enemy if nothing else. His spectrometer equipment had shown at last the telltale signature of Uranium 235; the same dust that had poisoned Vengerov. But he had talked to Marina Leonskaya at length and he knew as well as she did that the reactors on *Zemlya* used a different type of uranium dioxide within their gadolinium safety nets. That U235 was old-fashioned, Chernobyl-type RBMK 1000 reactor fuel. What on earth was it doing aboard *Zemlya*? And whom should he tell? Captain Mariner, of course, as soon as he woke up – if they were not in the grip of the hurricane by then. But in the meantime – who? He did not trust Makarov. Nor did he wish to become involved with Yagula. Marina, then. Except that it was an open secret that she was being bedded by captain Karchenko – who stood somewhere between Makarov and Yagula in terms of being untrustworthy and just plain frightening. So, who, therefore? Nana Potemkin, perhaps?

As Mussorgsky pondered, so he continued to work. The clenched fist with its crushed wrist and skinned knuckles was in a radiation-proof tank, and the doctor was examining it with remote control pincers. Turning the resolutely inflexible appendage first one way and then another, with no real thought at first of doing anything other than looking at it as closely as possible. But then the ring caught his attention, just as it had caught Richard's, and he began to examine that. Began to wonder if, perhaps, he might take it off. But to do that, he would have to try and straighten the ring finger at least.

And it was as he tried to straighten the fingers that he managed to open the fist altogether. The whole hand sprang wide suddenly and utterly unexpectedly, like a kind of monster in a horror movie shockingly springing to life. Mussorgsky swore with surprise and dropped it.

But not before he realized that something had fallen out of it. The thing it had been clenched around all along.

A computer memory stick.

Memory

Richard sprang awake. Wide awake, every nerve thrilling. He seemed to leap from the deepest sleep to the fullest alertness in the blink of an eye. *That's better*, he thought. *Back on form.* He sat up, staring around in the gloom. He had no doubt as to where he was or as to what was happening. He glanced down at his battered old Rolex's luminous face, wondering inconsequentially how many micro-Roentgens it was pumping out. He had been asleep for six hours. Just what the doctor ordered. Though poor old Brodski would have pulled a watch and a half. Better relieve him immediately. A seven hour watch was more than Richard liked to expect from anyone except himself, independently of the state of vessel and weather. A soft rustling alerted him to the fact that someone else was moving about in the shadowed room. He assumed that the figure moving quietly about on the far side of the little ward was Mussorgsky, so he said, 'That was just the job, Doctor. Thanks.'

But a youthful voice answered him, 'It is not the doctor, Captain. It is Second Lieutenant Kuznetsov.'

'Kuznetsov! How are you feeling?'

'I am well, thank you, Captain. I was about to return to my duties on the bridge. Have you become contaminated too? I hope I did not wake you!'

'I'm fine. Just a little tired. But that was six hours ago, when I brought you down from the bridge and went out to check on the chainlocker. I'm back on form now. We'll both go up on to the bridge if you're feeling well enough. Though we'd better check with Doc Mussorgsky first.' But the doctor was not in his office or the dispensary beside it. Richard spent only the briefest time prowling around, his attention caught by the splayed hand in the glass-sided examination vessel like a starfish at the bottom of an aquarium. The jars and phials full of Potassium Iodide, DTPA and Prussian Blue vibrating gently on their racks and shelves.

The corridor outside was empty – at six a.m. on a stormy day bound to be exhausting and dangerous, that was hardly surprising, thought Richard wryly. But as the pair of them hurried towards the lifts, the chiming of cutlery in the dining salon made them turn aside.

Andrei the chief steward and his team were hard at work. Silverware lay trembling gently on snowy linen. Cups and glasses chimed against each other like little bells. The air was already heavy with breakfast smells. Richard bustled through the room and into the galley itself. 'What's for breakfast?' he asked Chef. Chef looked up from above a cauldron that seemed to be full of seething milk. His hand steadied a big jar of orangey-coloured grains. The balding head swivelled towards Richard. '*Zavtrak* today is a selection of omelettes, sandwiches made of different types of bread and filled with eggs, meats and fish. Milk and millet *kasha*. Tea or coffee. It is not yet eight, but I have the day's menu ready.'

'It'll be fine as long as it's all hot and substantial,' said Richard. 'We're in for a bit of a blow and I want everyone as warm and well fed as possible.'

'*Obed* is *schti* of red cabbage soup, a selection of meats and *Zakushka* salads. *Uzhin* is *pelmeni* dumplings with a range of fillings accompanied with mashed potato and mixed vegetables.'

'*Schti* and *kashka* are all we need,' enthused Kuznetsov in a proverb Richard half-remembered from previous visits to Russia. It meant soup and porridge are all we need. He rubbed his hands. Chef smiled a little indulgently.

'Excellent,' said Richard. 'Please send up an omelette, a bacon sandwich and a cup of coffee to me on the bridge. Mr Kuznetsov, place your order.'

'*Kashka*, thick, in a big bowl with extra butter, please,' ordered the young lieutenant. 'And a pile of sandwiches. Egg and fish on black bread. You have smoked eel?'

'I have smoked eel, smoked cod and cod roe; I have smoked sturgeon and I have smoked salmon fresh from Lake Baikal. I have anchovies, sardines, sprats, rollmop herrings and pickled mackerel. Shall I go on?'

'Salmon, then. Perhaps anchovies with the boiled egg. And

lots of *kashka* please. With extra butter. I am exceedingly hungry.'

'I could never get over the idea of putting butter in porridge,' said Richard a couple of minutes later as the pair of them waited for the lift.

'*Kashka* is not porridge!' answered Kuznetsov, mightily offended. 'Porridge is just *govno* . . . ah . . . *mud* in comparison!'

Richard smiled, sensing a lively discussion to be engineered when Kuznetsov next crossed Colin Ross's path.

The lights flickered. The deck gave a tiny heave. There was the sound of breaking crockery from the dining salon. The lift doors hissed open. Richard stepped in with Kuznetsov at his heels like a faithful puppy. The lift car hissed upwards out of the cocooned levels below the weather deck and into the bridge house proper. As it did so, the light flickered once again – though the powerful lift motor did not hesitate. Richard was abruptly aware of chilly drafts of restless air. And, because the walls, floor and ceiling of the little car were so close at hand, he felt quite acutely that the whole of the lift shaft was wavering away from the vertical.

Richard's almost subconscious recording of the unsettling situation around him – gathering evidence of extremely nasty weather in his experience – was not enough to distract him from a brief but exacting examination of Kuznetsov. The last time he had seen the young lieutenant, he had seemed very ill indeed. Whether Dr Mussorgsky had treated him with the Potassium Iodide or the Prussian Blue after decontamination, Richard had no way of knowing. But the boy seemed to have made a remarkable recovery. He was bouncing with energy and keen to get on with the job.

'Mr Brodski, you are relieved,' bellowed Richard, striding forward on to the bridge. 'Go to the galley and get something to eat. Mr Kuznetsov recommends the *kashka* I believe, but there are omelettes and sandwiches as well. Then get your head down. You have four hours until I call you again. Six at the most. And I need you bright. Have you anything to report before you go?'

As Brodski made his brief report, his words conjured the weather chart into Richard's memory, with its blunt arrows and swirling lines. They were coming under the leading edge of the cold front now, and it looked as though the whole system had shifted south, spinning over the land. Which was bad for *Zemlya* – because it meant that the southerly storm would be tearing chunks of ice off that wall wedged against the coast and dragging them into the Ice Station's path. While, on the other hand, once the eye had passed, the full force of the hurricane would be dragging the southern section of the pack straight down at them. 'What's our current position?' Richard asked, substituting the weather map for a sea chart in his mind.

'Last reading was 70.34 north, minus 177.87 east,' said Brodski. 'That was about ten minutes ago at oh-six-hundred local time.'

Richard frowned. He would have to check on that. It was a fair bit further north than he would have expected. 'When did the southerly storm really start to take hold?' he asked.

'Oh-two-hundred local. It's all in the log, Captain,' answered Brodski.

'Quite right. One final thing. When was the helm watch last changed?'

'Two hours ago at the start of the morning watch. They're running normal watch rotas, sir. So are Security.' He nodded towards the Spetsnaz soldier watching the CCTV.

'And so are we now that Mr Kuznetsov and I are back in harness. I'll finish the morning watch and stay available for the forenoon watch. That'll give you the full six hours. You've earned it. But eat first. Now off you go.'

Richard watched the weary officer slouching off the bridge. He was impressed that the young man had kept on top of his watch duties so well, in spite of everything going on around him. He had the makings of a good, solid officer. 'I'd say we'll all need to be up and about and sharp as tacks from the start of the afternoon watch,' he said to Kuznetsov. 'Because what's going to hit us then will be about twice as strong as this. And it won't be coming up off the land. It'll be coming straight down from the Pole itself.'

'*Sookin syn!*' swore Kuznetsov. 'I thought this lot was bad!'

'It's bad enough to be going on with,' said Richard. 'We need to be in contact with our three tug captains to keep on top of the increasing strains on the tow. And to factor their readings in to our own – their equipment is better than ours in many regards because *Zemlya*'s designers have equipped her primarily with what she needs to stay safe at anchor pumping out power. I don't think they thought she'd ever need to navigate through an Arctic Ocean hurricane! We need to stay very precisely on top of our course and our position. We're far farther north than I thought we would be. We want to shelter in the lee of Wrangel but we don't want to bump into it! But most of all we'll need to keep an eye out for ice, and we are not blessed with Collision Alarm radar, like *Erebus*, *Terror*, and especially *Ivan* out in front there.'

As he spoke, Richard crossed to the watch area and began to check the GPS to see if there was any possibility of error in Brodski's northings. But no. The position looked accurate enough. 'Get on to *Ivan*'s captain,' he ordered Kuznetsov. 'What's his name?'

'Captain Zak. He is a very experienced man. An excellent captain.'

'He'll need to be. But he'll only be as good as his equipment. Talk to him about the need to watch out for ice. See if you can winkle out of him what sort of radar he has aboard, but don't alert him or upset him if you can help it.'

Ten minutes later, Kuznetsov returned with the news that the tugs had both been equipped with Huayang Electronic Technology's latest version of the American Raymarine E140W widescreen touch-screen Multifunction Display. And the Collision Alarm function was set to FULL with ranges of twenty, ten and five mile warnings. Richard frowned distractedly. He knew Huayang Electronic from his Hong Kong days, and from his more recent visits to Shanghai. Like *Zemlya*'s anchor chain, the tugs' navigation equipment was Chinese. How far was Beijing already involved in this project, he wondered.

But then he dismissed the thought until the next time he was talking to Felix. He had far more immediate concerns now that he knew that Captain Zak on his lead ship had equipment equal – if not superior – to the Kelvin Hughes radar systems that Bill Beaumont and George Hebburn on *Erebus* and *Terror* used.

Time for a little four-way conference, though, he decided. For now that he was confident they would get some kind of warning about what the southerly storm might be bringing up from the ice-bound coast, he needed to set their course a good deal further round into the face of it. Or, all joking aside, they might well be driven up on to the southern shore of Wrangel Island itself.

And if that happened, and the reactors went up as a result, there was very little doubt in his mind that, unless Dr Leonskaya's assurances of absolute safety were copper bottomed and iron clad, the plume of radioactivity would be carried south and east by the hurricane over the East Cape of Siberia, across the Bering Strait and on to the North Slope of Alaska. Round about Point Barrow, as likely as not. Just where the late lamented Captain Sholokhov had marked the odd northings and eastings in the red box in his impenetrable notes. Now there was a spooky coincidence. Perhaps he should take that suspicious little slip of paper to Nana Potemkin after all. As soon as he got a moment free.

In the end, Dr Mussorgsky took the memory stick to Nana Potemkin, for even after a couple of hours' effort, he could make no sense of it at all. He even began to wonder whether, like film stock, electronically stored memory could be corrupted by radioactivity. Nana was not only the closest thing aboard to a computer expert but everyone also agreed that she was the most solid and reliable of the nuclear people, with the possible exception of the engineer Kulibin. At least she wasn't sleeping with Karchenko. The problem was that she was sharing that suite with Marina Leonskaya, who was. But Mussorgsky knew Nana's routine as well as anyone aboard. At five thirty a.m., therefore, he checked on the three men sleeping soundly in his little isolation ward and picked up his laptop still with the memory stick in the side of it. He carried the slim machine down past the stirring galley and the still silent dining salon towards the recreation facilities.

He was a little concerned about taking a laptop into a swimming pool, but that was where he knew he would find Nana, the solid, square body clothed in a black one-piece costume. Powering up and down the pool with the same steady dedication as the greatest fitness freak among Karchenko's command. And, at this time in the morning, she would invariably be swimming alone. Which was why, he vaguely supposed, she chose this ungodly hour to do her exercise.

Sure enough, not only was she alone in the pool, the corridor beyond the glass wall and the observation platform it shared with the gym were empty as well. Mussorgsky put the machine on the wooden seat furthest from the pool's edge and went to the nearest set of steps. For a moment he watched her as she powered through the water, marvelling at the simple muscularity of her arms and shoulders, buttocks and legs. Her square body was so muscle-bound it was almost deformed. No wonder that in the hothouse sexual atmosphere aboard she seemed to stand aloof, he thought. She probably didn't have much choice, particularly surrounded by the bunch of bunny girls Mr Makarov had brought aboard to amuse his friends. Even Marina Leonskaya looked more like a centrefold than a scientist.

Then, he crouched and slapped the water until Nana registered that someone was there, and swam over. 'What?' she said, raising her square, muscular head covered in a black rubber swimming cap that clung so tightly it seemed to have made her hair vanish. She was by no means pleased at the interruption.

'I have something to show you,' he explained.

'It had better be something important if you expect me to break my morning routine,' she growled, flexing her shoulders.

'It is. I think it is. It's really strange in any case.'

'OK,' she said, pulling herself easily out of the water and on to the pool's side. 'Show me,' she ordered abruptly, springing erect, catching up a big black towel and beginning to dry herself as she walked beside him.

The minute Nana saw the laptop, she insisted that they take the machine out of the pool and into the dry safety of the gym. She slipped on a pair of flip-flops and a big black terry-towelling dressing-gown, but kept her black swimming cap in place. They sat side by side on one of the gym's long benches with the laptop resting on her thighs. But then, as he began to explain about the memory stick and where he had got it from, she decided that the gym was too public too.

They ended up in the big equipment cupboard at the rear

of the gym – at the forward end of the deck, below the big
Security area that was Karchenko's domain. Mussorgsky
thought nothing of it – Nana's suggestion seemed logical
enough, particularly in the face of his own growing paranoia.
They put the laptop on a waist-high pile of mats and the
computer expert opened the memory stick and began to sort
through the files it contained.

'Where did you say you got this?' she demanded after a
moment or two. He explained about the slime on the anchor.
About Kuznetsov, the chainlocker, the fist wedged in the
chain. As she listened, she shook her head in simple wonder.
'I'd never have believed it,' she said. 'Never in a million
years. Look at this!'

'What?' he said, straining his neck to see.

Straining the neck she broke with one crisp, utterly
unexpected movement.

Holding the dead doctor's head like a medicine ball, she
waited for his body to stop twitching, then she lowered it
gently to the deck. At the side of the room there was a big
wicker basket half full of assorted basketballs, medicine balls,
footballs. It only took her a moment to fold him into this
and conceal him for the time being underneath the balls.
Then, hardly even breathing heavily, she took the laptop and
carried it outside. There was more movement now, and the
distant sound of cutlery being laid out down in the dining
salon. She returned to her locker and grabbed her clothes,
using them to conceal the laptop. Last of all, she pulled off
her swimming cap and slipped a neat grey wig over the bald
dome of her head. Then she went out to the lift and ascended
one level.

As the lift door opened, Nana Potemkin glanced out into
the lateral corridor between the big A Deck bulkhead doors.
It was empty. The sound of the storm covered the scurry of
her flip-flops as she crossed to the door marked Security and
punched in the entry code. Then she paused for a moment
while the biometric scans confirmed who she was. The door
sprang open and she stepped in. She stood silently until she
was certain that she was alone except for Karchenko.

The captain was in his usual position facing the wall of
CCTV monitors that showed so much more than the carefully
filtered slaves so impressively manned on the bridge. That

showed the insides of the cabins as well as the corridors and common areas. Even of Makarov's cabin. Of Yagula's. Of the captain's. Of the strange matched pair of MVD Majors'. And in their centre, the one communication channel aboard that remained unmonitored. A screen currently filled with the gaunt face of a bald man of indeterminate years and mixed race. A man whose ears were completely concealed by disturbingly unsightly hearing aids.

'Good morning, Dr Potemkin,' said Professor Satang S. Sittart, although it was only two a.m. in Manila where he was. 'To what do the Captain and I owe the pleasure of this unexpected visit?'

Nana Potemkin moved forward then, to stand beside Karchenko. Out of sight of the camera that was putting them all on Skype, the Spetsnaz captain's hand slid under the black terry-towelling and up the sculpted marble of her thigh. And up. And up. 'It's the missing memory stick,' she said simply, suddenly breathless. 'The one that the second officer Vengerov stole from the captain's cabin the night we killed him with the anchor. Dr Mussorgsky's brought it back to us.' She glanced down at the top of Karchenko's thoughtfully bowed head as she moved her hips against his probing fingers. And her own hands moved fractionally, in a speaking echo of the killing stroke Karchenko had taught her – and which she had used on the doctor so recently. 'The *late* Dr Mussorgsky,' she added.

Southerly

'*L ED!*' Captain Zak on *Ivan* saw it first. Richard had been expecting the warning for so long that he hardly needed Kuznetsov to shout the translation; 'ICE!'

'Where away?' demanded Richard without thinking and his young lieutenant ran across from the GPS to the video screen, changing from navigator to translator. Richard looked at his watch. Coming up to eight. He'd call Anna in and let the boy concentrate on his bridge duties in a minute. Since the pair of them had consumed their bracing breakfast an hour and a half ago, the lieutenant had been busy keeping up the logs, checking their position and heading, and monitoring the weather reports as Richard had kept in contact with his tug captains. Apart from the food, only his occasional duties as translator had interrupted his concentrated and vital bridge work. Now, interrupted yet again, Kuznetsov was calling, 'The ice is ten miles south. On the heading we're swinging on to that's ten miles off the starboard bow. A bearing of maybe ten degrees, he says.'

'Can you see it yet, George?' Richard asked Captain Hebburn, joining his eager lieutenant at the video screen display, concentrating so completely that he shouldered the Spetsnaz observer aside without a second thought. *Terror* was on the southern side of *Zemlya*'s labouring hull, taking the full brunt of the southerly storm, even as they tried to complete the turn on to their new heading, her radar with the clearest view of conditions between here and the ice-bound coast after *Ivan*'s.

'Nothing yet,' came the answer, the Tynesider's accent drawn out by tension. But it had a gritty, determined ring to it. Richard nodded to himself, turning away from the video screens and walking purposefully out on to the starboard covered bridge wing. Stepping out through the bulkhead door on to the glass-sided, glass-roofed lozenge took him another couple of circles towards the heart of hell, he thought. Standing quite steadily in the face of *Zemlya*'s odd, truncated pitches and rolls, he looked back along her hull to where the big tug's running lights beamed in bright blades through the snow, foam and gathering ice. Directly to the south, there was nothing but that whirling darkness, seemingly trying to swallow the bridge wing, the entire vessel, indeed. A glance ahead showed only the most distant glimpse of *Ivan*'s riding lights – like one of the little space ships he remembered from the old film *Close Encounters of the Third Kind*. The noise was extraordinary.

After a moment, Kuznetsov joined him. 'Remember what this looks like, boy,' said Richard gruffly. 'And remember it's just a southerly storm. We won't be running out here quite so cheerfully when the hurricane arrives. Independently of whatever it brings in the way of spray and precipitation, ice floes and bergs, the wind will be twice as strong as this. I've known hurricanes to rip bridge wings off altogether.'

Kuznetsov shuddered and folded his face into a determined frown.

With Kuznetsov at his heels, Richard went back on to the bridge, checking all the bright displays automatically as he passed them, patting the helmsman on the shoulder, pausing in front of the four-way video display again. 'How are things on *Erebus*, Bill?' he asked.

'We have it easy over here in the wind-shadow,' came the Cumbrian's stolid answer. 'I'm relieving the men as often as I can so that we'll be on top form when the wind shifts. But at the moment, compared to *Terror*, we're on holiday.'

Richard gave a bark of laughter and crossed to the port bridge wing. Some holiday, he thought, as he stood there looking back along *Zemlya*'s length. The only real difference was that the wind-shadow of *Zemlya*'s massive hull made the air seem clearer. There was no white water breaking over the vessel as though she were a half submerged reef. But she was pitching and tossing, reeling and rolling as wildly as her twin on the starboard side. Smashing against the fenders as forcefully. Being jerked to heel as ruthlessly by the short-hauled tow ropes fore and aft. Thoughtfully, Richard turned to look ahead again. A flaw in the relentless southerly suddenly let him see the foredeck under the deck and running lights. Kuznetsov's ingenious single towline stood stark and straining as the one great hawser ran away forward to *Ivan*'s heaving stern.

'You did really good work there, boy. That foredeck towing rig was inspired!'

'Well,' temporized the young officer, all aglow at the unaccustomed praise. 'It was the engineer really. He thought it all up and told me what I needed and where to get it. It was kind of him to let me get the credit. But I don't really deserve it. The whole idea was Engineer Kalubin's really.'

Richard turned towards the boy, his face folding into a thoughtful frown. But just at that moment, George Hebburn's flat Tyneside voice called from the videolink, 'Ice. Ice at the ten mile line, bearing fifteen degrees relative.'

Richard and Kuznetsov stepped briskly out of the bridge

wing and on to the bridge proper. Richard's mind was
distracted from thoughts of the foredeck and the towing rig
by much more immediate problems. 'Do you know how fast
ice-floes can drift?' he asked.

'My meteorology, you remember,' answered the youth,
unhappily, 'is no better with ice than with storm charts.'

'They can move at more than ten knots with the wind
behind them on the back of a making tide. And we're heading
south to meet them. How soon will the ice *Ivan* can see hit
the five mile mark?'

'Twenty minutes?'

'Twenty minutes, give or take. That means we'll have to
do what?'

'Expect to hit the first floes in forty minutes. Keep an even
more careful ice-watch. Change our heading again, come
back round due east. Keep just south of Wrangel until we
can find a safe haven, and just north of the ice.'

'While praying all the time that the two don't come together
like a pair of jaws and catch us in between. Good. And will
the weather let us do that?'

'Ah . . .' Kuznetsov went bustling over to the chart table
and pored over the weather readouts and the calculations he
had been making when *Ivan*'s captain had interrupted him
with his first ice warning. And no sooner had he started his
vital calculations, with Richard at his shoulder, than Captain
Zak was back on line.

But *Ivan*'s skipper momentarily took second place to a
sudden bustle on the bridge. A pair of stewards appeared
with a fresh supply of coffee and tea, and a tray to clear the
breakfast things. Anna was following in their footsteps,
worried by the deteriorating situation and anxious to help.
And, if the truth be known, feeling that the safest place aboard
was as close as possible to Richard – as far from Yagula and
his disgusting suggestions as possible.

'Anna!' Richard greeted her with a wide grin of relief.
'You're the answer to a maiden's prayer! I was just about to
send for you. See what Captain Zak wants, would you? My
navigating officer is too busy trying to save our souls to be
doubling as a bilingual secretary. Mr Kuznetsov, your tea
will be over here, well away from all that electrical equipment. Don't let it get cold.'

'Thank you, Captain. But most of this stuff is redundant until the reactors start coming on line in any case.'

Anna crossed to the video screen and began to talk to Zak while Kuznetsov, a little grumpily, immersed himself in mathematics once again. After a while she came towards Richard. 'I am not sure I follow all the technical terms he uses or the navigational reasons he cites, but basically, Captain Zak wants to shorten the tow line between *Ivan* and *Zemlya*.'

'That would make sense once we get closer to the ice,' began Richard. 'But . . .'

Colin Ross came bustling on to the bridge. He was carrying Richard's laptop and a CD. 'Richard,' he said forcefully, 'I think you ought to look at this.'

Richard knew his old friend too well even to hesitate. 'Coming, Colin,' he said. 'Anna, tell Captain Zak that it's fine to shorten his cable. Mr Kuznetsov, you carry on with those calculations. Any problems, just ask me. Now, Colin; what is it?'

Colin put Richard's laptop on the chart table and flipped it open. 'Mick's backed the footage from his camera on to a couple of CDs. He's lent me this one and I've been looking at the stuff he shot over the ice-barrier across Leningradskiy Bay . . .' As he talked, Colin was slipping the disc into the side of the laptop and tapping both buttons and mouse pad in an expert manner. 'I can't get my head round your system, Richard. It's simply weird,' he continued as he worked.

'I didn't think so,' said Richard. 'How is it weird?'

'I don't know. It's like the computer has a mind of its own sometimes. Ah. Here we go. Now look at this.'

The aerial footage of the ice-barrier sprang across the screen as sharp and colourful as stained glass. 'The barrier looks solid,' said Colin. 'That seems inevitable, with the southward drift of the ocean simply piling ice along the edge of the land. But it isn't as simple as that. Look here.' His broad finger stabbed on to the soft surface of the screen. 'That river there. The one which flows through Leningradskiy itself. Look. You can follow the track of its current out from its estuary into the bay and then across the bay itself because it's a different colour.'

'I see,' said Richard, frowning. 'Though it's a bit difficult to be sure because there's some kind of a fault with the picture. Everything else is like cut glass, but that wavy line there is vaguer. Almost out of focus.'

'That's what I thought too, at first,' said Colin. 'Then I talked it over with Mick and he says the equipment is fine. That vagueness is something else. It's not a fault, it's really there. It's steam. Heat! The city of Leningradskiy is pouring heat into the river and the river is carrying it across the bay, all along that misty, wavy line to . . . here!' Colin's finger stabbed down again. And there, beneath it, extending the line of the city-heated current, was a broad grey line of darker coloured ice. A dark line stretching at an angle from one side of the barrier to the other. 'In my experience,' said the ice master, 'a dark line like that means the ice is melting, rotting, ready to fall apart.'

'Have we got any scale on this?' asked Richard.

'Yes,' answered Colin. 'As it is there in the picture we took yesterday, that passage of rotten ice would take *Zemlya* and the tugs through into the bay. But it gets better, doesn't it? Because the whole of Leningradskiy is underneath a southerly storm. As are the bay and the barrier. That barrier won't even be closed now. I'll lay you any odds you want that the barrier across the bay is splitting wide open, if it hasn't split already. And, when you can get back there safely I'll bet you anything you like that there'll be a way to get us safely into the bay before it closes up again.'

Richard looked up, his mind racing. But Kuznetsov interrupted his train of thought with something even more immediate. 'My calculations are completed and double-checked, Captain,' he said, pompously. 'The ice to the south of us will hit the five mile warning line on the collision alarm radar at any moment. As soon as it does so, we will have twenty minutes to turn away from it and come to a heading a little north of due east before it is actually upon us. Within an hour of that, we will begin to run along the lee shore of Wrangel Island which will still be more than fifty miles to the north of us. As we do so, the southerly storm will moderate to a calm – which is the eye of the depression. This brief respite will allow us just enough time to find a safe haven in the island's wind-shadow before the hurricane-force winds arrive from the north. Even were the seas to the south of us free of ice, we would never have time to reach Leningradskiy Bay before the hurricane caught up with us.'

'The boy's good,' rumbled Colin. 'No wonder he was able to design that rig on the foredeck.'

'He didn't,' said Richard shortly. 'Apparently that was the engineer – and he just let the boy take the credit. And you chose a good time to tell me that, Mr Kuznetsov, because I've just realized the flaw in the system. It means that only *Ivan* can adjust the length of the tow rope – we can't. We have no control over the length of the tow at all.'

'Is that important?' asked Kuznetsov anxiously.

'Probably not. Anna, has Captain Zak shortened the length of the tow line?'

'Yes, Captain. Though he says he may need to shorten it again sometime.'

'OK. I can't stop him anyway.' Richard turned back to Colin. 'Let's have a closer look at that river of rotten ice.' But Colin was having trouble with the laptop again. The pictures Mick had taken of the ice-barrier were gone. In their place was a head and shoulder shot of an earnest-looking officer wearing the badges of a second lieutenant. He was speaking rapidly and passionately, clearly upset by something. His face was vaguely familiar. His dark hair slicked and neatly parted. His brown eyes sparking with passion. On his uniform lapel there was a name tag that read: Лиеутенант В Венгеров. And that too was vaguely familiar.

But before Richard could even begin to think what all these conflicting experiences and observations might mean, they were overwhelmed by something utterly unexpected. One by one, all the dead banks of monitors came alive. Kuznetsov squawked and grabbed the teacup he had stood on them against his captain's orders. But then he froze. All of them stood unmoving for a moment as they realized what this must mean.

The reactors were coming on line.

Венгеров

Marina Leonskaya looked at Richard, her face blank with incomprehension. 'But of course we are bringing the reactors on line,' she said as though talking to a backward infant. 'It is what we are scheduled to do.' She tapped a clipboard very like the one Vengerov had carried on his doomed visit yesterday. But hers clearly held the schedule of works, not the list of possible safety concerns and breaches. They were in the little vestibule outside the reactor room. Through the glass top of the heavy door behind her, Richard could see the whole reactor team bustling about – both at this level and up among Nana Potemkin's computers high above.

'Scheduled,' said Richard, his voice blank, his mind whirling.

'Indeed.' Marina nodded emphatically, her face fixed and stubborn. 'We are working to a very strict timetable here. And this day, at this hour, we are scheduled to bring the reactors on line and begin to run the final tests. Tomorrow we are scheduled to be in Leningradskiy Bay and beginning the process of making power-contact with the local grid there, widening the test to the broader spectrum before everything finally goes on line. It is all as planned. And, I must observe, as specified in contracts at every level. I will do my part as contracted. It is up to you to do your part.'

'Tomorrow, Marina,' Richard explained, trying not to address her like a child, and failing, 'we are likely to be sheltering in a bay to the south of Wrangel Island trying to ride out a hurricane without being destroyed by huge great chunks of pack-ice skimming down into the Bering Strait at the better part of ten miles per hour! There is no chance of us being in Leningradskiy Bay, no matter what it says in anyone's contract. My part, as you call it, is simply to keep us all alive for the moment. I am suggesting to you that this is not the best time to be running tests on your nuclear reactors, no matter what your *part* may be!'

Marina glanced across at Nana, and the solid, reliable scientist gave her most thoughtful frown, nodding her grey head decisively. 'You must see the captain's point, Marina my dear. We will run a day or so behind schedule on our arrival time because of the weather. Could we not run a day behind schedule on our tests?'

'No! It is not so simple, Nana, and you know it. The computers are programmed – you programmed some of them yourself. If we switch them off, we could put ourselves weeks behind schedule, not days.'

'Of course!' Nana looked at Richard, her face puckered with concern. 'Is there not a middle way, Captain? If, as you say, you will find safe haven south of Wrangel Island, then there is no need to stop Marina's work, even if the weather worsens – we are in the grip of a severe storm now, for instance, and yet the effects are hardly noticeable down here. In the meantime, we could keep the closest possible eye on what we are doing and what you are doing and, if matters begin to deteriorate too badly, we will simply pull the plug.'

'But you can't just pull the plug on a nuclear reactor can you?' rumbled Colin. 'Isn't that what they tried to do in Chernobyl when they realized the emergency drill on Reactor 4 was going wrong? They hit the panic button. The graphite control rods went into the Uranium core too fast, wedged and then broke. The whole lot went critical and exploded.'

Nana's mouth opened to give a powerful reply. But before she could do so, Marina's nose went up into the air. 'As I have explained on more than one occasion, Dr Ross, this is not Chernobyl!' she snapped. 'Now, the simple facts are these, Captain Mariner. This is my station. I am the director and therefore in charge. You are the delivery man – no, indeed, you are the *replacement* delivery man. It is your job to get us to Leningradskiy and get us safely anchored there. It is my job to run the reactors according to the schedules I have been given. And that is just what I am doing and will continue to do. That is all.'

'She has a point,' said Felix ten minutes later as he sat easily on the sofa in his suite, with a cup of coffee waving airily in his hand, in almost lordly disregard of the weather battering against his picture window. In disregard also of his friend and associate's concern. 'We are on a tight schedule here, Richard, with a very clear contract. You don't want to know what the penalty sections in the Time of Performance Clauses specify. A day or two late is allowable. Weeks would cost a fortune. A month would likely ruin us.' He took a sip of the fragrant liquid.

Richard realized it was the first time on this trip he had seen Felix drink anything other than vodka. He wished Colin could have been here to see this particular miracle. But Colin was back on the bridge keeping an eye on Kuznetsov. 'Even so,' he snapped, angrily, 'having this lot go up like an atom bomb wouldn't do us too much good either, Felix!'

'But that's not going to happen is it?' schmoozed Felix expansively. 'You're going to keep us safe; hide us in your haven off Wrangel, and get us to Leningradskiy within the next seventy-two hours. If things get too dangerous then we'll have to shut the reactors down and hope for the best with the start-up and the contract next week. But even if things go wildly out of control, there won't be any explosion. The reactors are safe. Dr Leonskaya explained to you I know, just as Professor Kirienkho explained to me . . .'

Just for an instant Richard saw a slight shifting in Felix's earnest gaze.

'Professor Kirienkho?' he prompted.

'We had a full and frank discussion in St Petersburg before he went back to Moscow for the final time. He was happy with the whole thing. Excited. Keen to proceed. As with Dr Leonskaya and Dr Potemkin, this project was to be the making of him. Make his fortune. Put his name right up there.'

'Instead of which,' said Richard brutally, 'it put his name on a tombstone in the Kuntsevo graveyard! Which is more, now I come to think of it, than your second officer or that poor skipper of the tug *Ilya* got!'

Before Felix could answer, Anna pushed through the door without so much as a knock. 'Have you seen Dr Mussorgsky?' she asked breathlessly. 'The nurses say Inspector Vengerov is dead.'

Richard looked down into the late Vengerov's staring eyes, then, dispassionately, at his flared nostrils and gaping mouth.

The body under the tossed bedding had obviously writhed and convulsed during the final moments. Richard looked back up at the silently screaming face. The thing that shocked him most was Vengerov's hair. He remembered it as being black and slicked into gleaming perfection. Now it was almost all gone. It seemed strange to Richard that Kuznetsov and he could have been sleeping in the little ward next door and not have seen how Vengerov had worsened. But loss of hair and loss of life were by no means the same thing, he thought grimly. Not even when you're dealing with radiation poisoning. There was the faintest dusting of what looked like talcum. It had congealed in the spittle at the corners of the dead inspector's lips. On the rims of his nostrils. It clotted like sleep in his eyes. 'Get me a Geiger counter!' Richard ordered, without looking up. 'And stand well back, all of you.'

There was a rustle of movement behind him as the nurses, Anna, Felix, Yagula, the two majors, and Captain Karchenko all stepped back on his command. The nurses were competent to declare their charge dead, thought Richard. But that was only the beginning. Especially in the absence of the doctor. Someone with relatively high level accident and emergency skills needed to look at the matter as well. And, as a working captain, he kept his first aid certificate up to the highest level possible.

The Geiger counter arrived and the instant he switched it on it went to red, clicking deafeningly as it warned of high-level radiation. 'We'll have to clear and seal the room,' said Richard. On his way out, he ran the counter over the foot of the bed. No reaction. He caught up the patient's notes that hung in an old-fashioned clipboard hanging there. The name at the top of the first page read: Венгеров. 'Right,' he said as the little crowd lingered outside the closed door. 'I want the nurses to secure the area – tape the door shut if need be. Karchenko, send your best men to find the doctor. I want to know where he is. You I want on the bridge with me as soon as you can get up there. Felix, I need you on the bridge as well. You too, Federal Prosecutor – and you are welcome to being your MVD officers with you. Anna, I want you to go and find Joan Rudd and Mick. I want them on the bridge. Tell Mick to bring his camera and any CDs or memory sticks on to which he's burned the footage he's shot so far. Then go to my cabin and get my laptop so we can watch it all if we need to.'

'With all this fuss and upset, you'll probably get Tom O'Neill barging in, warned Felix. And he'll probably bring Mohammed Yamin in tow.'

'Why on the bridge?' demanded Yagula. 'If we have a large discussion, it would be better in my cabin. Because, in case it has escaped your notice, I am the senior official aboard.'

'It's got to be on the bridge because *I'm* calling it. I want some explanations given and some questions answered. And I can't afford to come and have them answered in your cabin, Federal Prosecutor, because – in case it's escaped *your* notice – I'm the one who's driving this bloody boat.'

The meeting in the chart room behind the main command bridge began with just six people. Richard and Colin, Yagula, his two officers and Felix. 'Right,' said Richard as soon as he closed the door behind him. 'Let's cut to the chase here and discuss some basics before the others all arrive. I'd have said offhand that Inspector Vengerov was murdered.' He was the only one of them still standing and, as he talked, he prowled restlessly across the room. Although his attention was on the conversation – and his thoughts were clearly centred on it – his gaze kept wandering to the glass panel in the top of the door and – through it – out on to the bridge. For, as he had pointed out to Yagula, it was he who was in charge of the barge. And if he got any part of that responsibility wrong, then the deaths that had occurred so far would just be the first of a long, long list. 'That last time I talked to Dr Mussorgsky,' he continued, 'it seemed as though Inspector Vengerov was on the mend. He had been comatose but once he came to he started to perk up pretty quickly. It looks to me as though someone's smothered him, probably with his pillow. But there's more to it than that. For some reason I can't fathom as yet, they sprinkled the pillow with that radioactive dust before they did it. Now who would do that – and why?'

'Anyone coming and going along that corridor would have been seen by the CCTV, surely,' said Felix. 'It should be easy enough to check up on who. Though we'll have to work harder to find out why.'

'It should. We will,' promised Richard tersely. 'But it seems to me that for all the apparent care Karchenko's taking with security, the patrols, the constant guard overseeing the screens on the bridge – there's still a lot going on aboard that's unobserved. And that leads me to ask the question first posed by Juvenal if I remember my prep-school Latin lessons. *Quis custodiet ipsos custodies?*'

'Who watches the watchers?' mused Yagula. He glanced at the MVD officers. 'Who guards the guards?' he repeated. Then he turned to Felix. 'Well, Felix Edmundovich? Who does oversee Karchenko and his men?'

Felix shrugged, coming as close as he was able to looking sheepish. 'They're security,' he said. 'I have no choice except to assume they're secure.'

'And you used to work for the FSB!' said Richard, shaking his head in wonder at such naivety.

Yagula nodded his agreement, frowning. 'Perhaps we need to pay a visit to the Security section,' he decided.

'I wouldn't rush into that, Federal Prosecutor,' warned Richard. 'You've seen how well they're armed.'

'It was amongst the first things I noticed about them,' answered Yagula. 'Well, let's leave our visit to Karchenko's lair until later, then. Especially as he should soon be on his way here himself. What do we need to consider more immediately?'

Richard put the patient's notes on the table and pointed to the name.

Венгеров

'That,' he said. 'I've seen it before. It's on the name badge of the second officer who was killed on the slipway at St Petersburg. The man whose fist we found wedged in a chain-link. They were both called Vengerov. Were they related?'

'Wait a minute,' said Colin suddenly. 'Vengerov. *Vengerov.* I knew there was something about that name! Wasn't it Victor Vengerov who was the shift manager at Chernobyl on the night of the explosion in April 1986?'

'That is correct,' answered Felix slowly, suddenly avoiding Richard's eye. 'The two men were brothers. And the shift manager at Chernobyl on the fatal night was their father.'

'I think that needs explaining.' Richard was looking at Felix, but it was Yagula who answered.

'Second Lieutenant Vengerov contacted the St Petersburg prosecutor's office on the day he died, making an assignation at which he promised to hand over some evidence that would support concerns he said he had about *Zemlya*. But it was at that meeting, before anything could be exchanged, that the accident with the anchor occurred. The man from the local Prosecutor's office withdrew, but naturally he made a report. Through my long association with Felix Edmundovich, I have taken a little financial interest in this project myself and so I heard about the accident at once. Rather than follow it up through official channels and further slow *Zemlya*'s progress . . .'

'We have mentioned the contract,' Felix inserted. 'The penalty clauses.'

'. . . I decided to send in someone to look around. As chance would have it, the dead officer's brother worked for the Nuclear Safety Inspectorate.'

'Motivated by his father's involvement in Chernobyl perhaps,' rumbled Colin.

'He was more than willing to investigate both his brother's concerns and his apparently accidental death.'

'And obviously he found something,' concluded Felix. 'Though we'll never be able to work out what it was now.'

'I'm not so certain,' said Richard thoughtfully.

'What do you mean?' asked Felix, genuinely puzzled.

'We can get an idea of the Second Lieutenant's worries at the very least.'

'Can we?' demanded Yagula. 'How will we do that? Necromancy?'

'No,' answered Richard. 'Technology.'

Bearing

Second Officer Vanya Vengerov stared earnestly out of Richard's computer screen. His long face and carefully parted hair made him look very much like his more recently deceased younger brother, which added to the unsettlingly ghostly effect. His uniform was spick and span. The badge on the lapel said:

Лиеутенант В Венгеров

He was speaking Russian but Anna was offering a running translation to Richard and Joan Rudd was making notes for the time when she and Mick would edit in the subtitles. The timbre was a little tinny, especially as the volume was on full against the raving of the southerly that still beat against the starboard of the bridge house, but Anna's translation was easily able to overcome the storm.

'Unlike my younger brother Vasily, I was not motivated by our notorious father's death at Chernobyl to study nuclear physics. Therefore I am not competent to comment on the reactors themselves beyond the fact that Professor Kirienkho himself has expressed to me some concerns which I do not fully comprehend. I should here like to reiterate some of the points we brought to the attention of Mr Makarov and his associate, Professor Sittart, forty-eight hours before Professor Kirienkho's death. As a serving ship's officer, I am used to dealing with computer controlled equipment and I should like to express my concerns about some of the equipment we have aboard. It may just be a question of style, but too many of the computers I see being installed are of the old-fashioned sort. They have dials and buttons instead of keys and mouse-pads. They have electrical displays – actual bulbs instead of LEDs – let alone LCDs. The only touch-screen equipment I have seen is on board the tug *Ivan* which has been supplied with Chinese computer hardware superior in every regard to the stuff I see being loaded on to *Zemlya*. I realize that *Zemlya*'s hardware is the very equipment with which many of our most modern nuclear facilities are controlled on land. But I had thought we were taking a great leap forward with *Zemlya*. It seems to me that there is an air of "make do" everywhere aboard. Everything is cost-driven – and that can undermine quality with fatal results. One only has to consider the questions about the quality of concrete involved in the Deepwater Horizon tragedy which did such damage to oil drilling in the Gulf of Mexico a couple of years ago. There are times when only the best quality will do, no matter what the cost. I mean, it seems ridiculous to me; why use the cheapest paint? It looks good now, but it is supposed to last for thirty years. Why bring aboard fuel that has been standing in barrels somewhere on the slipway for most of this millennium? The barrels are rusty and God alone knows what the actual fuel oil is contaminated with after so much time. Why is all the pipework and machinery in the turbine halls either battered or boxed up? Why cut corners on everything from crewing to anchor chain and then spend a fortune on guest suites, entertainment facilities, security and CCTV? It's beyond me. I can't see the logic of it. But it worries me. Gives me sleepless nights.'

'Is that it?' asked Felix. 'Is that all?'

'We were supposed to do another session,' said Joan. 'However, it was slated for the morning after the accident.'

'Well,' said Richard, his tone betraying his disappointment, 'there's nothing to go on there. Thanks Joan. Mick, can I hang on to that disc so I can go through it again? Just in case there's something we've missed. I mean it's really only of interest because of the accident.'

Mick and Joan left accommodatingly enough. 'Anna,' said Richard. 'Would you go and see what's holding Captain Karchenko up?'

As soon as the door closed, he took a deep breath. 'But of course Lieutenant Vengerov's death wasn't an accident,' he said. 'It was almost certainly murder. And in fact, there's a lot to worry about in that interview. If he'd been complaining in those terms around the vessel, then he may well have done enough to get himself in all sorts of trouble. And, like his unfortunate little brother, someone had already signed his death warrant with a massive dose of Uranium 235 before the anchor fell on him so conveniently – to stop him communicating further with the Federal Prosecutor's St Petersburg colleague. There's been almost no doubt in my mind for a while now that we have a murderer aboard. And I mean a real murderer. First degree stuff. With malice aforethought and all that legal jargon. Not just a saboteur too reckless to care whether someone gets hurt or killed on the side. Our immediate problem seems to be that we have a saboteur in place as well. And if the two of them are working together, then we're looking at a world of pain and trouble – independently of what the weather's planning to throw at us. But most immediately, Felix, we need to get clear exactly what Professor Kirienkho and Lieutenant Vengerov said to you and Sittart.'

'More or less exactly what you heard Vengerov say there. But he was addressing the wrong audience – to a certain extent at least. Sittart had almost nothing to do with things. He is a go-between, a facilitator with some deals we are trying to set up with Beijing. He was interested in the project. Offered money to back it and some supplies to help it along. He was even more hands off than I was. No. The man in charge of filling everything out was Captain Sholokhov. If I'd known then what I know now, I wouldn't have trusted him.'

'What do you know now, Felix Edmundovich?' rumbled Yagula dangerously.

'What? Oh only that he was inefficient enough to get bad equipment in and foolish enough to get himself killed by the tow rope. I must check his bank records – he must have been feathering his nest. Lining his pockets . . . *huesos*.'

Karchenko slammed into the chart room then. 'You sent for me?' he said accusingly, looking at no one in particular, as though it was he whom Felix had just called a cocksucker.

'I asked you to get up here as quickly as possible,' answered Richard shortly. 'We need to discuss security as a matter of urgency – and you're the man responsible for it!'

'I have been assigning search parties as you ordered, Captain,' the security man snapped back, clearly not used to being addressed like that. Especially in front of men as powerful and influential as Felix and Yagula, not to mention two MVD majors. 'And I have reviewed the CCTV footage of the corridor outside the medical facility. There is nothing to see.'

'I didn't see you on the bridge,' probed Richard, his voice suddenly gentle.

Karchenko frowned as he fought to understand what Richard was driving at. He glanced out and saw his Spetsnaz guard watching the bridge monitors. 'No,' he said airily. 'The bridge monitors are slaves. The monitors down in Security have the detailed records. I reviewed the footage down there.'

'I see,' said Richard, more quietly still. Quietly enough to earn a frowning glance from Felix who knew that Richard was at his most dangerous when his voice was at its gentlest.

Lieutenant Kuznetsov knocked and entered in one movement, too preoccupied to be aware of the cracking atmosphere in the room. 'The storm is moderating, Captain. It now looks more like a force eight gale to me. Captain Hebburn on *Terror* agrees, though I can't check with Captain Zak on *Ivan* because he's not answering at the moment. And Captain Beaumont from *Erebus* reports land at the ten mile limit on his radar. Land bearing . . .' He glanced down at the back of his hand, where he had written the figures. 'Three four zero relative.' He glanced up, proud of having delivered the report so professionally.

'And our heading is?' asked Richard, his voice growing louder and more decisive. And not a little amused.

'Zero nine zero true according to the gyro and the GPS. Due east.'

'Good. Now see if you can work out the true heading of Wrangel Island from our current position. Off you go then. Look it up if you need to. Call me when you have the bearing calculated and checked. I'll be in Mr Karchenko's Security area. I suspect all you'll have to do is look up and call "Captain!" and I'll hear and see you quite clearly from down there.'

Karchenko grunted and turned on his heel. 'I'll come too,' rumbled Yagula.

Karchenko gave a rigid salute. 'Of course, Colonel General,' he snapped.

Yagula nodded and gave a wave in reply. 'Have you seen this area Felix Edmundovich? No? Well, now's your chance. And now I think of it,' he turned to his matched pair of MVD *Ovcharka* hunting hounds, 'I would like a list of every security camera aboard with an estimate of what it is likely to observe. Be thorough, please. Be *very* thorough.'

As they all got up, Richard looked down at Colin. 'Colin, would you do me another favour please? Get Anna involved if you need to. But I would really like to know what Victor Vengerov's involvement in the Chernobyl disaster actually was; just in case it has a bearing on the deaths of his two sons.'

Yagula and Karchenko went down in one lift. Felix and Richard went down in the other. 'This is what I get for failing to carry out my usual routines,' fumed Richard unhappily. 'I should be on top of all this. And Security is by no means the only place aboard I have yet to inspect.'

'Give yourself a break, Richard! You've been working non-stop since you arrived. I know you got some shut-eye but that's, what, six hours in the better part of ninety since you left London?'

'Still not good enough,' grunted Richard, his voice heavy with frustration.

'If anyone's to blame . . .' began Felix. But the lift stopped and the doors opened before Richard could find out whom Felix blamed. Though he began to suspect acutely that the Russian was beginning to blame himself. But, thought Richard, there was likely to be far more going on here than even Felix suspected. Sittart was hardly likely to be sitting as quietly on the sidelines as the Sevmash men believed. Felix was like a fisherman who had gone out angling after tuna and hooked a Great White shark instead.

Karchenko and Yagula were already at the security door and as Richard and Felix joined them, the Spetsnaz captain completed the security procedure. He stepped back smartly. 'After you, Colonel General,' he said, and then swung in immediately behind Yagula as though trying to block Felix and Richard with his back. All four of them entered in a scrum. Richard, the tallest by a hair, scanned the place, frowning. His immediate impression was of a sort of TV studio or editing suite. A wall of monitors rose from desk level to deck-head, stretched from one side to the other across quite a sizeable room. More than twice as many as there were on the bridge. On the desk-level shelf there were a range of controls that made Richard at least suspect that what the screens showed could be further adapted in a range of ways. There were four black leather chairs on castors, designed to roll across the heavy-duty flooring, so that a team of security operatives could oversee the whole of the vessel with ease.

A number of questions sprang into Richard's mind as he looked around. But Yagula asked the first of them for him, so he was content to stay quiet and listen for the moment. 'And what does the CCTV system record. Precisely?' asked Yagula, prowling closer to the screen that showed his MVD officers examining one of the cameras – both in close up from the camera that was their immediate subject and in long shot from the next.

'All the common areas above decks and below, inside and out, Colonel General,' answered Karchenko guardedly. 'They, like we, are there in case of an attempt to overpower the facility and steal fissionable materiel. You remember what happened at the airforce base at Mys Shmidta only a few years ago.'

'The security of the reactors is paramount,' agreed Yagula easily.

'These ones here are showing the same pictures as the bridge monitors,' said Richard. 'But those ones over there . . .'

'Those ones are coming on line in parallel with the reactors, Captain. They are the security observation system for the secure areas. The Reactor Room, the computer control room, the Turbine Hall and so forth.'

'This all seems reasonable,' said Felix, relief beginning to creep into his voice.

Richard looked closely, fascinated by the simple vastness of the turbine halls he had not yet visited as the CCTV pictures presented them. And Lieutenant Vengerov's words came back into his memory. The equipment down there did look battered and still part boxed up. The Engineer and his team still had some work to do if they were going to get their end of the operation ready according to Marina Leonskaya's schedule, he thought.

A red light began to flash on the console over on Richard's left. 'Now, what's this?' he wondered aloud. And before Karchenko could prevent him, he pushed the flashing button. Immediately, the screen above it switched from a picture of the empty corridor outside his quarters to the picture of a Google Search Engine computer screen. Into which the words 'Victor Vengerov' were being typed. 'Well, I'll be damned,' said Richard. 'That's my laptop.'

'Of course we monitor all Internet business also,' said Karchenko, but this time his attempt to sound airily confident rang hollow. Frowning, Richard pushed the red button again and the Google page disappeared. But the picture of the empty hall was not restored. Instead, the interior of the captain's quarters came into view, showing Colin Ross hunched over the laptop in question while Anna prowled restlessly around in the background, busily going through the late Captain Sholokhov's possessions.

It took only an instant for the implication of what he was seeing to hit Yagula. He leaned forward and pushed a button at random. A stateroom replaced a corridor in the frame. He pushed again. A bedroom replaced the stateroom. He pushed again. A shower-room appeared. 'Now that,' snarled Yagula, 'is what I call a *secure* area!' He reached into his pocket and pulled out his cell, punching a number into the speed dial. Two things happened simultaneously. The MVD officers reached for their phones and a crackling channel opened up on a speaker below the screens. 'Come down to Security, both of you,' ordered the Federal Prosecutor, his voice echoing out of the speaker an instant after it left his lips. 'Your current assignment has been overtaken by events!'

In the echoing, static-filled silence after he broke the connection, he turned, his face thunderous. 'What's in there?' he demanded, gesturing to a solid-looking door on the right of the area.

'The armoury, Colonel General,' answered Karchenko grimly.

'And there?' Yagula gestured to the opposite door.

'Supplies and equipment.'

'Right! When my officers arrive, you will hand over your command to them and then you will conduct them through every detail of what this room contains and explain every element of what these machines have been programmed to do. If they are satisfied with your attitude and explanations, then I will cancel the reservation I am about to make for you of an isolation cell in the lowest level of Butyrka prison! And, if you are careful which of these infernal buttons you press, you will be able to listen while I do it! Do I make myself clear?'

Karchenko snapped to attention. 'Yes, Colonel General Yagula!'

'To you, Captain, I am *Federal Prosecutor* Yagula.'

And just at that moment, as Richard had predicted, Lieutenant Kuznetsov's voice came through loud and clear, summoning him back up to the bridge.

Ten minutes later, as the storm moderated sufficiently to reveal the shape of Wrangel Island in the distance off the port bow, Richard was sitting in the chart room, poring over the weather chart and trying to calculate when they would come out from under the calm eye and into the full force of the hurricane at last, when Colin appeared with his laptop and Anna in tow with a printout. Anna put the printout in front of Richard who picked it up and scanned it, frowning. 'It's part of an absolutely huge article about the disaster,' Colin said. 'We printed the bit that seemed most relevant, but there's extraneous information in there as well.'

'That's OK,' said Richard, his attention already gripped.

It is instructive in this context to parallel the experiences of two of the men most closely associated with the disaster. Victor Vengerov was the shift foreman on the night of the disaster. It was he who finally called the scram (the emergency shutdown) of Reactor Number 4. This procedure led to a further spike in energy output rather than cooling the core at once, with the results stated above. When the first explosion occurred, Vengerov made two 'phone calls. The enquiry later established the conflicting nature of these calls – a conflict which lies at the heart of Vengerov's damaged reputation. The first call was to the local fire station, where it was taken by watch commander Lieutenant Sergei Molokov. This call alerted the firemen to the existence of a serious fire at the reactor but made no mention at all of radioactivity.

*The second call was to Vengerov's wife at the family
residence in the nearest town, Pripyat. This call did
warn of the danger of radioactivity and as a result of
it Mrs Vengerov was able to get safely to her sister's
house in Kiev with her sons Ivan (Vanya) and Vasily.
In the meantime, Lieutenant Molokov assembled his best
team, which tragically included his own two sons. They
approached the blazing reactor twenty minutes after the
alarm call and proceeded to fight the fire as though it
were a normal blaze. Not even the lumps of burning
graphite with which the site was littered [note 150], the
'taste of metal'[note 151] on the air or the 'prickling
sensation on our skin'[note 152] warned them of the
danger. There are records of the Molokov brothers
playing football and 'catch' with the graphite blocks.
[note 153] Like Vengerov himself, all the firefighters in
the first team were dead of acute radiation sickness
(ARS) within the week.[note 154] While Vengerov's sons
went on to pursue successful careers in the merchant
marine and the nuclear safety inspectorate [note 155],
Molokov's family continued to suffer tragedy. His wife
committed suicide in May 1986 [note 156]. His daughter
Anoushka [note 157] was assigned to the state orphanage
where it was discovered she had contracted radiation
poisoning from the fallout. She married her childhood
sweetheart in April 2001, 15 years after the incident,
but he died of leukaemia within six months of the
wedding. On the night of the explosion they, like other
members of the local Komsomol youth movement, had
been assigned to help with clearing up and tending the
wounded.[note 158] It was only later that the authorities
learned how badly the young volunteers had been
exposed to radiation.[note 159]*

'Have you read footnote one fifty-seven?' asked Richard as
he looked up from the tragic little story.

'Didn't seem any point,' answered Colin. 'It was Vengerov
we were interested in, wasn't it?'

'I guess so,' said Richard. 'Anna, will you take this stuff
back to the cabin please?'

Ten minutes later, while one of the majors was in the

armoury checking everything against the Security manifest while the other was in the supply store doing the same, Karchenko suddenly leaned forward, reaching for a red button flashing silently beneath one of his screens. He pushed it, and a computer screen appeared, also silently. His eyes narrowed as he read what the search engine had called up off the Internet:

'*Footnote 157 . . .*'

Another click showed the Captain's cabin. Just for an instant before the MVD major returned. Karchenko got an almost instantaneous picture of a pile of documentation and a battered old briefcase beside the closing top of a laptop. And a flash of golden curls as Anna began to gather it all together.

Eye

The northern hemisphere depression that contained the hurricane winds was so tightly constructed that the calm heart of the monster, the eye, came upon them with almost supernatural speed – and then lingered for less than an hour. An hour packed with action on every level for almost everyone left alive aboard.

Richard had seen the chart – gone through it in extraordinary detail as part of Kuznetsov's meteorology lesson – so he knew what was happening with even more certainty than usual. Almost as soon as he had confirmed his young lieutenant's calculations and observations, he was able to report to Yagula and Felix, 'We'll be creeping along the southern shore of Wrangel searching for a safe haven for the next hour or so. The weather's moderating pretty fast so we'll be able to work by eye instead of radar soon. Within half an hour at most, I'd say, the eye of the storm will have caught up with us. Then there'll be an hour or so of calm seas and light airs. With any luck, Federal Prosecutor, that will allow you to get to Mys Shmidta airbase in the chopper – and you can take up to one third of the people aboard with you, if you want to. Though you'll have to decide now and work fast – and you'll have to pray for a bit of luck. There's an outside chance you could run into the storm wall over Leningradskiy – perhaps even over the ice-barrier. That would be very dangerous indeed.'

Felix perked up immediately, but Yagula frowned. 'I still have work to do here – independently of protecting my investment. And I have to tell you that I did not become the man I am, in the position I hold, by running away!'

Richard nodded. 'Nevertheless, there are people aboard who might want to go ashore, given the circumstances, while there is still a chance to do so with some safety.'

But Yagula was shaking his head again. 'Almost everyone aboard is caught up in my investigation now. We have proved to my satisfaction that the Vengerov brothers were murdered by someone aboard. That there have been several attempts to sabotage the ship – which may or may not have led to the deaths of several other people. No one leaves until I am satisfied that I have a clear idea of what is going on.'

'Very well,' Richard acquiesced. 'But I would suggest to you that if we do not employ the Mil during the calm in the storm's eye we are missing a chance to get a clearer idea of how we might get through this safe and sound.'

'How so?'

'The southerly storm we have just ridden out is likely to have broken up the ice-barrier; even have opened Leningradskiy Bay. Colin was certain that there was a channel of rotten ice through the heart of the barrier there. It could be of crucial importance to know if that's the case.'

'I agree,' snapped Yagula. 'I am willing to send the Mil to the ice-barrier with Dr Ross aboard – and anyone who wishes to accompany him; the reporter and documentary team, for instance; but only on condition that they keep in touch, give a detailed report – and come back aboard if humanly possible.'

'And only, I would suggest, if the pilot is willing to undertake the flight.'

'Right,' snapped Yagula. 'We need to see him and ask him! You get back on the bridge and I'll take care of that.'

*   *   *

Anna killed the Wikipedia page with footnote 157 on it and snapped the top of the laptop closed, her heart thundering loudly enough to drown the clatter of the printer. The implications of what she had found were limitless! She had to go and tell Richard at once. And she might as well take the stuff she had found in Sholokhov's kit – maybe he could make sense of that as well. It never occurred to her that she should tell anyone else. She shoved the laptop and the paperwork into Sholokhov's old briefcase and all but ran across the stateroom to the cabin door, tearing it open and tumbling out.

Almost literally into the arms of Federal Prosecutor Yagula. 'Ah,' he said. 'You'll do very well indeed. Go and find the helicopter's pilot and tell him to report to the bridge at once.'

'But Federal Prosecutor, I must see Captain Mariner at once.'

'Don't you dare argue with me, girl! The last female who dared do that died in Butyrka prison still waiting for her day in court. Died of AIDS I am informed, though I can state with absolute certainty that she had no such disease when she went in there. Apparently sexual favours are currency in such situations. She was very, very popular, apparently, for the short time she survived.'

'I will fetch the pilot at once, Federal Prosecutor. But may I return with him to talk to the captain?'

'Fetch the pilot, then talk to whoever you want to!' Yagula snarled. 'Tell him he's taking Dr Ross to the ice-barrier – and all of those fucking journalists along for the ride. That way if they do go down in the ocean it won't be a total loss!'

Anna had a fair idea where the pilot would be – up in the hangar with the chopper's engineer. They were both relentlessly careful of their machine – both a little nervous of having to fly it at such latitudes, she thought. An emergency landing outside their native St Petersburg was one thing; an emergency up here was quite another. She puffed into the hangar, still hauling Sholokhov's battered old suitcase, therefore, calling for the pilot at the top of her voice. And, sure enough, he climbed out of the Mil, at once. Breathlessly, she began to pass on a bowdlerized version of Yagula's terse message. The pilot shrugged, his face folding into a worried frown, as he strode off. Anna paused to catch her breath, then the urgency of her original mission drove her on once again.

By the time she reached the lift that had brought her up here, it was taking the pilot back down. Too impatient to wait for it, she simply ran across to the companionway and started pounding down the stairs. It was only one level down to the command bridge, after all.

The companionway opened on to the bridge deck at the starboard side, near the bulkhead door that led to the outer stairways. As Anna stepped off the lower step, she paused again, looking at one of the series of prints adorning the long panelled wall at the rear of the bridge itself. The picture showed a three-masted sailing ship framed against a much taller iceberg which stood like a floating mountain terrifyingly close behind it. Beneath it was written *The Final View of Terror. 1845.* She wasn't really looking at the picture, she was simply trying to collect her thoughts so that she could get the vital information to Richard as speedily and incisively as possible, for she knew how busy he would be.

When she turned and started towards the bridge door, she suddenly found Captain Karchenko standing in front of her. Without a word he grabbed her and bundled her back towards the lift. Before the stunned woman could even give a squawk of surprise she found herself in the lift car with him, plunging downwards. '*Chto za huy,*' she gasped.

'*Past' zakroi, blyadischa,*' he spat at her.

The door opened and he dragged her out, backing into the corridor outside Security with her. She sucked in a breath to scream, in spite of the fact that he had told her to shut up. But his gun was there, suddenly, pushing painfully into her face. 'Shut it, whore,' he snarled again.

Several things happened with utterly disorientating speed. Someone called 'Captain Karchenko!' in tones of shock and outrage. The gun left her face and spat a single shot that was agonizingly loud in the confines of the passage. Anna saw Mohammed Yamin spin away, tumbling back into the reactor-room corridor, clutching his shoulder. And a mighty voice, like the voice of God Himself boomed out in Richard's tones, 'Karchenko, we see you. You can't hide. Leave the woman alone or we'll hunt you down and give you to the Federal Prosecutor now!'

Karchenko snarled like a caged animal. Anna had simply never seen an expression like it on any face in her life. Frustrated, beaten for the moment, he pushed her away and she tumbled back into the lift car. As the doors hissed shut, she saw the chief of security turn away like a hunted beast and begin to run.

Richard stood in front of the CCTV display with his eyes narrow and the handset of the ship's address system shaking in his massive fist. He watched Karchenko, tracked by his own cameras, go fleeting from one screen to the next. 'Right,' he said to the security man standing rock-like at his side. 'You're temporarily in charge of security. Report to the Federal Prosecutor's MVD officers, and get that traitor now! Federal Prosecutor . . .' said Richard, turning.

'Yes,' said Yagula. 'I will take charge.' And off he went.

The chopper pilot stood, frowning, one calm point in the whirl of action on the bridge. 'Felix,' snapped Richard. 'I need you to get Anna up here and to check on Yamin. He's moving, trying to sit up. I want Anna here and I want Yamin in the dispensary. But first, we need to brief the pilot. Pilot. The weather is clearing fast. I want you to take Dr Ross and a team he will assemble down to the ice-barrier by Leningradskiy Bay. At full speed you should make it there and back before the weather closes in again. But only if you're quick. Will you confirm those orders, Mr Makorov?'

'Yes!' snapped Felix, and repeated the orders in Russian. The pilot saluted and turned on his heel. As he went out, followed by Felix, Anna pushed past them and tumbled on to the bridge, nearly falling in her eagerness. Felix caught her; steadied her. 'You all right?' he demanded.

'Yes, Mr Makarov,' she gasped, a small, round bruise already forming on her cheek from where Karchenko's pistol had been forced against her.

He nodded approvingly and let her go.

'Captain! You must see this,' she continued almost in the same breath, dismissing Felix and his approval without a second thought.

'What?' asked Richard. 'It had better be important, Anna, I have some delicate ship-handling to do here.'

'It's footnote one-five-seven,' she gasped, pulling the laptop out of Sholokhov's briefcase. 'Footnote one-five-seven among other things.' As she opened the computer's lid, the page Colin had been looking at came up on the screen. While she scrolled down, looking for the footnote, Richard began to sort through the mess of papers she had pulled out of the case along with his computer.

There were four bank books, two written in Russian. Richard thought he recognized the name St Petersburg. He rather thought he knew the bank name – it was one that Felix's companies used for direct payment of wages. He glanced idly at their balance. A couple of thousand roubles in each. But the other two were much more exotic. One came from the Rizal Commercial Banking Corporation, Manila, and the other was the United Timber Traders Bank, also of Manila. And these two accounts held American dollars. Tens of thousands of American dollars. And that brought a worried frown to his face. For he was all too well aware that the United Timber Traders Bank was an offshoot of Luzon Logging – under the direct, almost personal, control of Sittart.

His thoughts were disturbed by the sound of the chopper clattering away into the distance. He glanced across at the clear-view – and for once its name described what he could see. A clear view of calm weather. The sea ahead rolling emptily; the grey-green heave of Wrangel away to port. A cloud of gulls, wheeling across a blue sky. Somewhere in his mind, a countdown started. Sixty minutes and counting. 'What have you found?' he prompted Anna, gruffly, realizing suddenly that she was taking quite a time to find the footnote. 'Just a moment,' she said, her tone confused.

Amenably enough, he reached into the next bundle of paperwork and pulled out a photograph. Quite an old one to judge by the state of it. There were two men pictured in it, standing on a jetty with the forepeak of a freighter rearing behind them. Sholokhov stood, all aglow with youthful pride in captain's whites that looked brand new. Beside him stood what could only have been his chief engineer, in oily overalls, but with an engineering officer's cap at a jaunty angle and a jutting jaw extended by a full, square beard. It was just possible to read the name of the ship behind them. It was *Ocean's Bounty*. And, just as Richard knew where his fiercest and most dangerous competitor banked, so he knew the names of some of Luzon Logging's fleet of ships. And *Ocean's Bounty* was one of them.

'It's gone,' said Anna, her voice blank with astonishment.

'What has?' Richard glanced up from the photograph.

'The footnote. I didn't think that was possible!'

'It's not. Unless someone broke into the Internet site and changed it.'

'Not very likely, I'd have said . . .'

'Or unless someone's been tinkering with the computer itself. But anyway, what did footnote one-five-seven say that was so important?'

'As near as I can remember, it said something like, "Anoushka Molokov (aka Nana) married Gregor Potemkin, 26 April 2001. St Volodymyr's Cathedral, Kiev."'

'You're sure?' Richard was stunned by the neatness of the pattern. Almost the inevitability of it. 'Anoushka Molokov whose family all died because of Victor Vengerov at Chernobyl is actually Nana Potemkin? *Our* Nana Potemkin?'

Anna just nodded, her eyes huge.

Richard slammed the photograph he had been holding down on the table and turned, his mind racing. Turned, with the objective of grabbing the tannoy and telling Yagula he had better widen his search to include the computer expert as well. But then he froze as another apparently random piece of the puzzle fell into place in his mind. He picked up the picture and studied the smiling man with his jaunty cap standing beside Sholokhov on that long-ago Manila dockside.

It was Kulibin the engineer.

Worm

Richard was torn. Every shred of him demanded that he go below at once to lead the hunt for Karchenko, Potemkin and Kulibin. But he simply could not afford to be off the bridge. He had less than an hour to find a safe anchorage for *Zemlya*, with or without instruments. To get her in the lee of this island and out of the worst that the northerly hurricane could throw at them. On the other hand, it was impossible to calculate the damage that the three fugitives might do – might already have done – to the command that he had so reluctantly assumed.

But there was simply no one else aboard he could trust to man this bridge. Junior Lieutenant Kuznetsov was doing his best although the task was clearly far beyond him. The thought of leaving him here alone was chilling. Richard glanced down at his watch. Time to wake up Brodski, he decided. But he was not experienced enough either – and even the pair of them working together were hardly man enough. George Hebburn and Bill Beaumont could advise from the bridges of their respective tugs – and Captain Zak could put in his kopek's worth from *Ivan*, but even with their bridges and command systems all but turned into Siamese quads by the centralized computer system, it still needed someone here, in the central command position, who knew what they were doing, what they were likely to be facing, and what the odds were of pulling through.

So Richard had to content himself with jerking the ship's address system handset off its cradle once more. 'Federal Prosecutor,' he said briskly, his voice echoing through the ship and out across the Arctic Ocean, almost loud enough to echo from the slopes of Wrangel Island to the north. 'Will you please contact the captain on a secure line. And Mr Brodski, I want you on the bridge as soon as possible please. Mr Brodski, at the double.'

Richard's cell buzzed immediately after he hung up the handset. 'This line is as secure as possible,' growled Yagula. 'At least it is with my man guarding Spy Central in the Security Area. What do you want?'

'Bad news, I'm afraid. You will have to widen your searches to include Dr Potemkin and Engineer Kulibin. I should point out that the only area left aboard that I did not check myself was the turbine hall on the lowest deck of all.' He thought for a moment, his blood suddenly running cold as possible catastrophes reared in his imagination.

'Well?' prompted Yagula.

'I'd suggest you take some protective gear, dosimeters and maybe a couple of Geiger counters.'

'Of course. Especially as we'll be starting in the computer control room above the reactors if we're after Dr Potemkin.'

No sooner had Richard broken the connection with Yagula than his phone buzzed again. 'Yes?'

'It's Felix, Richard. I'm in the infirmary with Mohammed Yamin. He's shaken, but not too badly hurt. Bullet went through his shoulder muscles without hitting the bone. That's what the nurses say, anyway. Their speciality is radiation treatment, but their first aid is as good as yours. They've pumped him full of painkillers and he's settled down. Spaced out, actually, by the look of him. What do you want me to do next?'

It was a measure of how disorientated Felix was himself that he should ask Richard what to do. Richard had never heard his associate sound so indecisive. But he was the right man in the right place. And if what he said about the painkillers was correct, he might be in the best possible situation too. 'I want you to get as much information out of young Mohammed as you can,' said Richard. 'I want to know everything he knows about Indonesian Incorporated's involvement in this, from the nuts and bolts of computer equipment and Chinese anchor-chain to why so many of the people involved seem to have links with Luzon Logging, Professor Sittart and the rest.'

'Well,' huffed Felix. '*I* can tell you about most of that.'

'No, with all due respect, I don't think so,' said Richard. 'I think there's something going on here that's even more devious than you're aware of. But you're right. You do know a lot. Use what you know as bait to catch what he knows – then tell me at once if there's any important differences.' He began to speak more slowly as his mind changed up a gear. 'If Karchenko shot Yamin then that means Yamin isn't part of whatever Karchenko is part of. A possibility emphasized by the fact that Yamin seemed to be trying to stop Karchenko hurting Anna when the shot was fired. And that may well mean Yamin's just been put aboard as a distraction. A red herring. But even so, I'll bet he knows a good deal more than he realizes. A good deal more than we know, at the moment into the bargain.'

As soon as the preoccupied Richard broke the connection, Brodski came bustling in. He stopped and looked askance at Anna standing at the chart table, poring thoughtfully over the laptop. 'This isn't right,' she said to Richard, glancing over her shoulder.

But Brodski overrode her. 'What do you want done first, Captain? Kuznetsov and I should be able to get *Zemlya* to a nice safe spot for you. Will you want to anchor? Or will that restrict your freedom of movement too much?' He bounced across to Kuznetsov. 'Where are we, Kuznetsov? Have you learned how to use the GPS yet? What does the radar say about the coastline? What does the echo sounder say about depths beneath our keel? Thank God the weather has moderated. Swinging those reserve fuel barrels across to *Erebus* and *Terror* in the southerly storm was nothing short of a *ebanatyi pidaraz!*'

Richard was still preoccupied, even in the face of this overpowering ebullience. So when he turned back to Anna at last, his mind was too full to be sensitive to her worried frown. 'Any idea who went with Dr Ross in the chopper?' he asked.

'I know who the Federal Prosecutor ordered to go. I'd guess no one thought of refusing. So that would be Dr Ross and, to quote the Federal prosecutor, *all the ebanatyi journalists*. I think he hopes they'll go down in the ocean and drown.'

'Not with Dr Ross in charge they won't,' said Richard, half amused. Then her anxious expression registered. 'What's the matter?' he asked.

'There's something wrong with your laptop,' she replied. 'But it's nothing I've done.'

'Of course,' he smiled paternally. 'It's probably just a glitch. It'll sort itself out. Pop it back in my cabin. Take all this stuff back with you too.' He gestured at Sholokhov's paperwork. He saw the flash of nervousness and remembered Karchenko was still out there somewhere. Might still be hunting her. 'It's just a couple of steps across the corridor,' he said gently. 'I'll keep an eye on you. See you safely in. Then I want you to finish searching through Captain Sholokhov's kit for me. What you've found already is really important. There may be more still.'

After the cabin door closed behind Anna, Richard turned

and strode across towards the front of the bridge. 'Right, my trusty lieutenants,' he said briskly. 'Where are we and what's happening?'

'According to the GPS, we're here,' announced Kuznetsov excitedly. 'That's 70.80 north, minus 179.11 east. The radar confirms the lie of the land so to speak. We're just coming up on the first really promising bay.'

'The island is already causing the swell to moderate, even though it's still largely coming up from the south,' added Brodski. 'And, for the time being we have clear views and light airs. Looking eastwards dead ahead at least.'

'I wouldn't look behind us, however,' said Richard. 'That would put a bit of a damper on things.' In his head the countdown went below forty-five minutes. 'We'll head on east for the time being,' he decided. 'Maybe buy a few more minutes' grace before the monster catches up with us. Time to start considering where we want to drop anchor.'

Richard's next port of call was the communications centre where he stood in place of the Spetsnaz observer – who was now reassigned to tracking down his ex-commander and his confederates. The familiar faces of George Hebburn and Bill Beaumont lit up their respective screens, confirming Brodski and Kuznetsov's observations. But George, on the port side, was frowning. 'There's something . . .' he rumbled. 'Something just doesn't feel right, you know? But I just can't put my finger on it.'

'Never mind,' Richard answered bracingly. 'It'll come to you. In the meantime, we need to find a good sheltered spot. I'm keen to get at least one anchor down before the big wind hits us. Maybe one fore and one aft. You three tugs can rely on your hawsers, I think. But we've half an hour at the most.'

Richard was distracted once again even as he spoke, for on the other monitors, he could see the men under Yagula's command – and the command of his MVD majors – tracking from one screen to the next, in relentless pursuit of their prey. Prey who, disturbingly in Richard's mind, did not seem to feature at all on any of the other monitors. Where in hell's name could they have gone? he wondered. Where was there aboard that was not covered by those all-too intrusive CCTV security cameras?

But then the distraction became more immediate still. The

radio operator suddenly appeared. 'Dr Ross is reporting from Leningradskiy Bay, Captain. He says the ice-barrier is open. We should be able to get into the bay OK unless the barrier closes.'

'We'll have to sit out the hurricane at anchor where we are and hope for the best,' said Richard. 'Tell him he can go on to Mys Shmidta or come back here to Wrangel. The choice is his. Tell him we're at 70.80 north, minus 179.11 east. We'll run a little further north and east before we drop anchor, but not far.'

No sooner had the radio operator vanished than Marina Leonskaya arrived, dressed in her protective whites. And she didn't look happy. 'Can you tell me why all those bloody great Spetsnaz troops are tramping all over my reactor room?' she demanded. 'They have some blonde woman from the Hitler Youth in charge and no one will tell me anything! This is a fairly critical time you know. In all senses of the word! I realize I went a little overboard in emphasizing how safe the reactors are, but if the control programmes get mucked about with sufficiently, then they can still go critical. And I am talking *explosively* critical.'

'The patrol is looking for Nana Potemkin,' said Richard. 'Have you seen her?'

'No, now you mention it. Why would they be looking for Nana?'

Richard explained about footnote 157 and what it made him suspect. Marina gaped at him in simple wonder. 'It has to be someone else,' she said. 'It must be a mistake. God in Heaven . . .'

'You can go and check it all for yourself,' said Richard. 'Anna has my laptop in the captain's cabin. She'll show you.'

Marina stormed off, and Richard at last had the opportunity to stand by the helmsman and look out across the ocean dead ahead. The view was dominated by the green slopes of Wrangel Island close by on the port quarter rolling down past a lively surf-line awash with southerly swell to the wide view eastwards that seemed to stretch unbroken as far as the eye could see. To the Bering Strait. And, in his imagination at any rate, the promise of Alaska beyond. 'This is it,' he said decisively. 'Stop all and drop the starboard fore anchor.' *At least it'll wash the last of that poor bastard Vengerov clean away*, he thought grimly.

Richard lingered there for an instant, as his command slowed and the anchor went thundering down as he had ordered. He was simply enjoying the satisfying sense of the solid landmass rising like a good strong wall between himself and the distant Pole. He was just about to go back to the chart room to see if *Zemlya* had a decent chart of Wrangel that would allow him to assess the actual height of the protective wall he had chosen when he stopped, struck by something so glaringly obvious that he had come close to overlooking it.

In all the broad view of the ocean dead ahead, there was almost no sign at all of the tug *Ivan*. Just a hint of the communications system on her upper works, confusingly close beneath the forecastle. Her stern must be near as dammit hard up against the ice station's soaring cutwater. Richard paused, frowning, his mind a whirl of speculation. Captain Zak must have spent the last few hours as the southerly slowly moderated equally slowly shortening his tow rope. Richard did not count himself an expert in the art of towage, but he could see absolutely no reason why Zak would want to carry out such an eccentric manoeuvre.

He went back to the communications centre. The screen that communicated with Zak on the Ivan was blank. He hadn't really registered that before. 'George,' he called to Hebburn on *Terror*, 'have you been in contact with *Ivan* lately?'

'Nope.'

'Can you think of any reason why she should be wedged so tightly under my forecastle that I came damn close to dropping my anchor on to her poop?'

'Can't say's I do.'

'It's not some kind of advanced towing technique? Nothing like that?'

'Might be in Petersburg, but we'd never do aught so bloody silly on the Tyne.'

'It's not a towing technique,' chimed in Bill Beaumont. 'I mean, look at the physics. What sort of force is he going to exert wedged under your cutwater?'

'So just what in hell's name is he doing there?' asked Richard.

But before he could really turn his full attention to the unexpected conundrum, several more things conspired to

distract him yet again. The radio operator ran out on to the
bridge. 'Dr Ross says the Mil is coming back, but they can't
find us at the location you gave. They're searching along the
coast. And they want you to know that the hurricane front is
hard behind them. They say you have less than fifteen minutes
before the wind hits the west of the island.'

'Great . . .' Richard frowned. Another conundrum.

And Marina reappeared with an agonizingly anxious Anna
in tow. 'That laptop is totally fucked,' said the scientist
roundly. 'I mean it is what we Russians call *Polnyi pizdets*.
What the Americans call FUBAR! Fucked Up Beyond All
Recognition.'

'It wasn't me,' Anna repeated, hopelessly.

'Of course it wasn't!' snapped Marina. 'It's got a virus. A
worm. Something like that Stuxnet thing that hit the Iranian
facilities at Bushehr back in 2010.' Then she stopped. All
colour draining from her face as she realized the implication
of what she had just said. 'Oh shit,' she whispered. 'You
don't suppose . . .'

'What?' demanded Anna, pleased that suspicion seemed
to be moving away from her and keen to keep it moving that
way.

'The Stuxnet,' answered Marina. 'It was a worm designed
to hit computer-controlled power plants. Specifically *nuclear*
power plants . . .'

'What, you mean like fuck them up?' asked Anna. 'Close
them down?'

'No,' breathed Marina. 'To take them over, control them
from outside.' She looked at Richard wide-eyed, ashen-
faced. 'Could someone have taken over *Zemlya*'s computers
without us knowing?' she breathed. 'I mean, could
someone be overriding all our controls somehow even as
we speak?'

'How? How did the worm get into the system?' asked
Anna.

'As far as I know,' answered Richard, 'all it took was a
memory stick. The malware was on a memory stick and it
infected any machine the stick was plugged into. Then that
machine passed it on and so forth.'

'But who could do such a thing?' asked Anna, dazed.

'The three on my wanted list are Karchenko, Kulibin and

Potemkin,' grated Richard. 'If they got together, could they do that much damage?'

Marina nodded dumbly, apparently beyond speech now. And the radio operator burst on to the bridge for the third time. 'I've been speaking to the chopper,' he announced. 'They have us on their radar now and they think they'll make it just before the storm hits. But it'll be close, because they say we're not where we think we are. The coordinates we gave them are way off. They say that according to their instruments we're more than one hundred miles east of where we said. At the east of the island, almost in the Bering Strait.'

And Richard's eyes locked with Marina's. 'The GPS,' he said. 'It's controlled by the central computers. The same computers that control every system we have aboard. The same computers that control your reactors. Like Bushehr . . .'

When Richard assumed that the main power lines designed to connect the reactors and the turbines to the power grid were meant to run through the forepeak hawsehole currently occupied by the tow rope joining *Zemlya* and *Ivan*, he was wrong. The main power connection was designed to come through a lower opening that lay at the end of a walkway reaching from the very front of the massive turbine hall, through a sizeable portal on the ice-strengthened bows. Karchenko leaned forwards and unlatched the access hatchway at the heart of these big doors. It swung inwards. He pushed his head and shoulders out through, looking down a sharp-sided, sheer steel cliff to the after deck of the tug *Ivan*. It was a drop of maybe a dozen feet. But the men beside *Ivan*'s almost vertical tow rope were holding a ladder. '*Ivan*'s in place,' he grated. 'I'll go first.'

'Hurry up then,' prompted Nana. 'You know how dangerous it is down here.'

'In all sorts of ways,' snarled Kulibin behind her. 'The dosimeter on my shoulder is lit up such a bright red that it will make a perfect target for one of the trigger-happy security bastards you trained to kill on sight.'

His words were eerily prophetic, except that the crack shot which came from the distant end of the long, dark gallery to smash through Kulibin's chest and bury itself in Nana's forehead with sufficient force to blow her grey wig off, came

from the gun held by Colonel General Yagula, who was also
trained to kill on sight.

Karchenko gave a great bellow and threw himself backwards out through the hatch and, as it slammed shut above
and behind him, he scrambled wildly down the ladder on to
Ivan's deck, feeling the tug gather way as he landed.

Tempest

B y the time Yagula joined Richard on the bridge, *Ivan*
was out at the full length of her tow, far beyond all
hope of immediate access or retribution.

Marina had returned to the reactor room to check on
the disposition of the control computers. Anna was up on the
top deck awaiting the imminent arrival of the chopper, which
was due to arrive about now. Now or never, in fact; for if
the wind beat them to it then they were dead.

'I missed Karchenko,' grated the Federal Prosecutor, his
tone echoing the distant, tempestuous roaring, laden with
bitter regret. 'Got the other two. One shot. Heart and head.
Did you know the Potemkin woman wore a wig? She was
bald as an egg.'

'Result of radiation poisoning in her youth, I suppose. Hair
loss is a classic sign. She was probably riddled with cancer
too.'

'It's academic, now.' Satisfaction, almost pride, coloured
the bear-like growl.

'A blessed relief for her. And for the engineer, if I know
you,' said Richard. His narrow eyes were scrutinizing *Ivan*'s
bridge house as though for the first time. Cataloguing the
range of aerials and dishes he could see there.

'As Karchenko will find out when I get my hands on him,'
snarled Yagula.

'In the meantime we have a stand-off,' concluded Richard,
his voice rising to overcome a sudden blast of wind. 'With
a hurricane about to hit us.' The moment he spoke, the heavens

opened and *Ivan* became all but invisible behind a grey shroud of downpour and leaping spray. In a twinkling, the seascape went from softly dappled aquamarine to hard grey slate.

'What do you think the plan is?' asked Yagula, betraying a shadow of uncertainty for the first time in all their acquaintance.

'Send the reactors critical,' said Richard forthrightly. 'Override all the safety mechanisms – which are computer controlled in any case. Blow us up.'

He tersely explained his suspicions about the computer virus taking over the vessel's whole electronic command system.

'What's the point?' asked Yagula. 'Dr Leonskaya's convinced me that the reactors are so safe that even if they do go critical they'll only do a very limited amount of damage. Irradiate a couple of square kilometres tops.'

'Not if they're just the trigger,' said Richard. 'Not if the turbine hall is full of a much more dangerous substance – Uranium 235, say – that will get blown up into the atmosphere when the reactors go. Enough of it, for argument's sake to all but fill the turbine equipment – give or take enough to irradiate a couple of Vengerov brothers.'

'Even so,' said Yagula. 'What difference would that make? Out here? It's the middle of nowhere.'

'Here, at seventy one degrees north and minus one seven nine east – minus because we're just in the western hemisphere as near as I can judge – it will make very little difference, certainly in the short term.' He paused, as his mind shifted gear again. 'Except that it would put a radioactive wall across Russia's newly opened North East Passage and – at the very least – put a kink in their plans to move out into the Arctic Fields with BP. Which might look like a neat trick to our friends in the East. Especially as Gazprom froze them out of its new explorations in the Pechora Sea. And Sevmash has been pretty protective of its Kara Sea fields. But it's not supposed to happen here. It's supposed to happen at seventy one thirty one north, minus one five six sixty two east, well into the western hemisphere. And it's designed to happen when the hurricane clears and the standard prevailing westerly winds set in, blowing the radioactive plume east and south.'

'Why?' demanded Yagula. 'What's at seventy one north, one five six west?'

'Point Barrow in Alaska,' answered Richard. 'It's boxed in red ink on a piece of paper I found in Captain Sholokhov's quarters. I think the plan is to irradiate the North Slope oilfields which produce how many billions of barrels? Eight hundred thousand barrels a day? Two hundred and eighty-eight million a year. How many billions is that? Nearly three? Depends on how you calculate it I suppose. Still, with Texas running down and the Gulf of Mexico all but closed – California too – how hard will that hit?' Richard swung round and fixed Yagula with a stare as piercing as a blade of ice. 'And where are all the new fields opening up? Here in Siberia.'

'It's mad!' snarled Yagula. 'It would be Siberia that gets hit if any of this goes wrong! If *Zemlya* goes up during the hurricane instead of after it. If she goes up like you say and spreads radioactive uranium all over Leningradskiy and the huge new oilfields to the south, then who will benefit from that?'

It was Felix who answered. 'Indonesian Incorporated Oil will,' he said as he came in through the door on to the bridge, walking a little unsteadily as even the massive steadiness of *Zemlya* and her tethered tugs began to stir in the hurricane blast. 'They've apparently signed a huge deal with the Chinese to open up a massive new Indonesian field that makes even Exxon's Cepu field look modest. It's on the Andaman side, on that fault which runs down the eastern edge of the Bay of Bengal – which explains the importance of the new city of Hambantota in Sri Lanka. I'd guess that whether the North Slope or the Siberian fields are hit by this, Indonesian Incorporated will see a huge upsurge in demand.'

'Mohammed Yamin told you this?' demanded Yagula.

'Not in so many words. He told me about the city and the oilfield. He has no real idea they might be linked to any of this. He explained about the Chinese kit as well. What *Ivan* has aboard apparently is state of the art – a staging and control station. He has no idea what it's designed to do, but I'd guess it is designed to pass on and maybe amplify control signals via a satellite link.'

'Link is the right word,' said Richard thoughtfully. 'The

last link in the chain. Let's say *Ivan* is the link between Sittart and *Zemlya*'s computers. He put the worm in them – caused it to be put in; he won't have done it himself, though I know he was in St Petersburg. He controls them even from as far away as Manila via *Ivan*. Like the CIA pilots controlling drones in Afghanistan from their bases outside Washington. He has a dynamic situation he can stay on top of and make decisions about minute by minute. He's a control freak. He would like that. But how much information is he getting? How much control does he actually have? He has fooled the GPS systems in *Zemlya*, *Erebus* and *Terror* into putting us at the best possible place to attack Barrow after the hurricane. But not the GPS on the chopper because that's not controlled by the central computers. He can presumably make the reactors go critical at any time – though we'd have to check with Marina how precisely he would go about that. And logic dictates that he has access to all the information in the surveillance sections of the Security Suite. He might even be watching us and listening to us now.'

The Mil clattered urgently past the streaming clear-view, swinging in towards its landing area just above them. Its arrival emphasized how close the full force of the hurricane must be. Richard grabbed Felix by the arm and pulled him away into a secluded corner. 'The first thing we've got to do is get ready to cut *Ivan*'s tow line,' he said. 'I want you to take young Kuznetsov and see if he can work out how to undo all that good work on the foredeck. We'll have however long the hurricane lasts. Then we'll have to try and work out some way of overriding or shutting down the central computer. Push comes to shove, I guess we can simply shut off all the power. Mind you, if the oil we have aboard is as bad as Vengerov said it was on that recording, then the generators'll probably . . .'

Richard stopped mid sentence and strode across to where Brodski was standing by the helmsman. 'Helm, go below. We're at anchor, you can get some rest. Brodski, what oil did you swing across to the tugs while I was asleep?'

'We had spare barrels aboard in case any of the tugs needed refuelling. They all did, because we've come so far beyond our original planned journey.'

Richard was in motion once again, running back across

the bridge. 'Felix. Did Sittart or Indonesian Oil have anything to do with the spare bunkerage you had put aboard?'

'No. He had nothing to do with it. It was a job lot that we had to hand.'

Richard paused, his mind racing. He was so deep in thought that he hardly even registered the way the light suddenly vanished as though someone had switched off the sun. The first great gust of wind came roaring out of the north at sea level, booming across the peaks of Wrangel and exploding against the port side. But, blessedly, it brought with it neither big seas nor thick ice. Not yet at any rate. And not here in the lee of Wrangel Island.

But Richard stood, deep in thought, oblivious. Dare he risk contacting George Hebburn and Bill Beaumont? Or would every word he said to them be flashed via satellite to Sittart in Manila?

His mind was made up for him by Colin Ross who came on to the bridge then. 'Is your cell phone working?' he demanded, bellowing over the massive mayhem of the wind. 'I tried to call you direct from the ice-barrier but there was no signal, so I had to do it via the chopper's radio. Even the short-wave had trouble and that's a pretty powerful piece of kit. It's the interference from the storm.'

Richard pulled out his cell phone. Checked the screen. *No signal*, it said. He looked up, his expression clearing. The first great bolt of lightning smashed down on to a mountain top he could no longer see on the mercifully solid shore. Mercifully close at hand upwind. Of course there was no signal he thought. No signal between here and Leningradskiy. No signal between *Ivan* and Manila.

He turned away from his aggrieved friend and ran to the communications centre. *Ivan*'s screen was blessedly still blank. Unlike *Erebus'* and *Terror's*. 'George! Bill!' he called. Both men answered at once, though neither of them looked ready willing or able to indulge in lengthy conversation with the wild winds clawing at their suddenly puny vessels. 'That oil you took aboard during the southerly. What have you done with it?'

'Nothing, yet,' came the reply. Both captains estimated that they had enough bunkerage in hand for maybe twelve hours' sailing. But both planned to use the enforced idleness of the storm anchorage to top up with the extra that Brodski had swung aboard earlier.

'Don't,' ordered Richard roundly. 'What I want you to do is work out the quickest and most efficient way of closing down all power – without stopping your engines. Got that?'

Then Richard himself was off to find Marina. He found her in the little room outside the reactor room itself, climbing wearily out of her overalls. 'If we worked out how to shut down all the power aboard,' he asked, 'what would that do to your reactors? What would that do to the computers controlling them?'

'Nothing as far as I know. As I've already said, it would take a while to reboot them once they started up again, but that's all.' She straightened, the white lower section still covering her jeans.

'And the reactors? If we shut down the computers – shut down all the power aboard – what then?'

'As I told you and keep telling you, their default is the fail-safe mode. If everything shuts down, they go to sleep. Like Snow White and Sleeping Beauty.'

'OK,' said Richard. 'Get some warm clothes. And tell your people to wrap up warm as well. Then report back to the bridge. I'll have the next step under consideration then – even if I haven't worked out exactly what I want to do.'

He turned to leave her as she pulled up the top once more and started to shrug her arms into the white cotton sleeves.

'Brodski,' asked Richard a few moments later, bellowing over the incessant howling of the wind – which was trying its best to burst in through the clear-view – aided by sheets of rain and shrapnel-bursts of hail. 'How much do you know about the electrical systems aboard?'

'Well, as you can see from the monitoring systems on the bridge here, sir, the reactors power the main electrical systems aboard themselves. The main generator systems are immediately below the reactors, in the aft section of the turbine hall.'

'That would be the equivalent of one of my tankers or container ships powering the major systems from the main propulsion unit when she's under way,' nodded Richard. 'But there's always a back-up.'

'Just so, Captain. But there is a SOLAS requirement that

there should be at least one other generator aboard. That one
is oil-fired and it is located, as required by basic safety legis-
lation, well above the main deck. In fact it is in a smaller
generator room above the computers two decks above the
reactor room itself – at the rear of the bridge deck here.' His
gesture pointed vaguely back along the corridor to the solid
aft wall of the bridge house itself. A double wall, Richard
understood at once, with a generator room contained within
it. Accessible via the computer levels, through and above the
reactor room – for there were no doorways back there that
he had seen.

'And that's the one that powers the computers that start
up the reactors? As well as keeping the main heating, lighting
and ship-handling systems alive while the reactors are
asleep?'

Marina arrived most opportunely at that moment, reporting
back as ordered. Out of her whites at last. Though not yet,
he observed, wearing any cold-weather gear. Yet. 'Yes,' she
answered, fielding the question from Brodski as he began to
flounder at the outer edges of his knowledge. 'The oil-fired
generators have kept the power aboard running so far –
including the power to the reactor-control computers. The
moment the reactors came properly on line those generators
were designed to hand over to the much larger generators in
the turbine room. From there on in, the oil-fired generators
will only be needed in an emergency. In case the reactors
shut down for any reason.'

'But the reactors aren't on line yet. Or are they?' demanded
Richard.

'Yes they are!' she said, frowning. 'There was no reason
to hold things up just because of the storm.' Even as she said
the words a huge black wind tried to tear the superstructure
off. It seemed in the moment of her hesitation that every nut
and bolt above the waterline groaned with the almost unbear-
able strain of holding together. 'And anyway, Nana said . . .'
her voice trailed off into the cavernous silence between the
last blast and the next. The deck beneath them seemed to
swoop like a hawk after its prey. The swell was building,
thought Richard grimly, even this close to the lee of the land.

'Right,' snapped Richard. 'So we need to shut down the
big generators that keep the reactors running. Then we need

to shut down the smaller oil-fired generator back there at the aft of the bridge deck so that the whole system doesn't just start up again. Once the computers are down, there's no way anyone can control anything aboard.'

'Including us, Captain,' observed Brodski drily.

'But we don't need to,' answered Richard. 'We have tugs to do everything we need doing. As long as they can work independently of the computers.'

'And, if you are really thinking of cutting the tow line to *Ivan* at the same time as you switch off all the power aboard,' added Brodski, 'as long as you can work the ship without a guiding tug out there at her head. And, now I think of it, as long as you can get her through the Arctic Ocean and down to Leningradskiy Bay without the aid of communications, radar or GPS positioning.'

Richard's next port of call was the Mil's hangar. He took Anna with him, collecting her from his quarters en route. The short ride up in the lift seemed to take them to a new level of tempestuous violence. There was no doubt in Richard's mind as he reached the uppermost level that the whole of *Zemlya* was tossing with increasing force. He would have to get *Erebus* and *Terror* to ease off if this kept up, he thought, or their capstans would be torn out like *Ivan*'s had been when the cable broke so disastrously. And he would have to consider putting down at least one more anchor. But even having one down made a complicated situation more complex still. He would have to think that through a little further.

But then all deep thought stopped abruptly as the lift car stopped and gave a sudden lurch strong enough to throw Anna bodily into his arms. Her breasts were crushed against him. The fragrant cloud of her golden hair filled his face. Her hips and thighs ground briefly against his own as she tried to wriggle free. But his hands had found the slimness of her waist, the sudden, startling flare of her hips. They held her there, flattened against him as though they had a will of their own. And his arms were far too slow to let her go.

When she stepped back, there was a new look in her eyes. A look of almost naked speculation. The door hissed open and they stepped out into the chopper's hangar. As ever, the pilot was looking after his machine, with the engineers beside him.

Using Anna as interpreter, Richard checked their well-being, and the disposition of their machine. How well charged the batteries were. How full the fuel tank – and how recent and reliable the fuel supply. Then he asked the question that had brought him up here. What would they have to do to make best use of the chopper's on-board guidance system? Would the machine have to be flying? Out of the hangar? Powered up? Or simply switched on – as the readouts, dials and gauges on his own beloved Bentley Continental sprang to life long before he engaged the gears or began to roll her forward.

Captain Zak of the tug *Ivan* had chosen this spot himself, for he alone of the captains on and around the ice station had known where they really were. He knew the waters and had been in no doubt how bad the conditions might become. So he had positioned his vessel at the furthest possible extreme of her tow rope in a little area of relative calm where a headland hooked southwards, pushed out by the flank of a sheer cliff topped by a mountainous watershed ridge high enough to keep the worst of the wind away, as the headland kept the worst of the waves, and all of the ice off her, for the time being at least.

Nevertheless, the dazed, shocked and seasick Karchenko was beginning to regret the fact that he had ever come aboard. He stood at the captain's side, watching out through the whirling clear-view into the watery madness ahead. But *stood* was not the right word. He heaved. He rolled. He staggered and danced. He hung on for dear life and he prayed. After the steady solidity of the broad-beamed Ice Station *Zemlya*, the little tug seemed to be behaving with unimaginably wild abandon. She pitched – until the tow at her stern brought her up short, then she tossed, rearing back viciously like a bucking bronco. She rolled until the Spetsnaz captain was certain she was just about to be swamped. Not that that would make much difference, he thought. The sturdy little vessel seemed to be perpetually overwhelmed by rain and spray in any case. The hurricane howled through the aerials and dishes bolted, riveted and welded to her bridge house roof. All of them useless at the moment. Most of them seemingly destined to be torn off and whirled away like leaves in an autumn gale.

The tug's engineer stuck his head up into the bridge house.

'Bunkerage all made up, skipper,' he bellowed into a moment of cavernous silence. 'The tanks are as full as they will hold.' How can people work in this? Karchenko asked himself, simply awed.

'Good enough,' roared Zak in return. 'Go and get some rest. You'll have your work cut out when this lot moderates.' He turned to Karchenko. 'You too, Captain. You can have my bunk. You'll have your work cut out for you too when the storm calms down and communications open up again. Point Barrow is just less than twenty hours' hard sailing away. Twenty hours, then Chernobyl mark two. Armageddon on the North Slope. One way or another, tomorrow is going to be an extremely busy day.'

Ice

*I*van's engineer was by no means the only person busy during the hours that the hurricane winds tore down from the Pole and bellowed over Wrangel at more than a hundred and fifty miles an hour, generating over a hundred degrees of frost. Nor was Captain Zak the only commander who didn't see his bunk. And *Ivan* was not alone in pitching and tossing. Though *Zemlya*, with *Erebus* and *Terror* firmly lashed to her sides, could hardly have been said to roll, she developed a jarring see-saw motion as first her forecastle and then her poop went deeper and deeper under the heaving waters. As the hours passed and the wind chill factor continued to drop, so she became more and more laden with ice – so the swoops became more pronounced and the motion more extreme. She stayed relatively steady in the water, however, even at the peak of the storm, when the waves reached the highest they achieved in the little lee bay beneath the black, booming cliffs. Cliffs which seemed to shrug off a never-ending stream of freezing spume as though they were monstrous black shadows of the foaming, wild-headed rollers beating wildly at their feet.

At last, *Zemlya* became lively enough, and the hurricane became sufficiently fearsome, even downwind of the tall rock battlements, to start the ice station pulling her anchor, especially as the great slow wave of the storm surge pushed like a tsunami beneath her as it washed eastwards towards Alaska. A little sideways movement was acceptable, for it kept the vessels clear of that dangerous cascade of ice-chunks tumbling like a crystal avalanche into the bay at the cliffs' feet. But only so much drift could be allowed. Richard was forced to drop a second anchor. Then a third. And a fourth.

So that, as the storm at last began to ease, the gathering brightness found *Zemlya*, firmly anchored at each corner, sitting solidly in the lee of the still-streaming black cliffs, at the heart of the heaving bay, at the outer edge of yet another ice-barrier. To all intents and purposes almost another berg herself – ice-coated if steel-hearted. With both her generators still full on. For, no matter what the risk restoration of satellite access and ultimate loss of control of their computers might pose, Richard simply had to hang on to power long enough to get the great hooks back up if he was ever going to stand any chance of rescuing the ice station and her crew from their predicament.

By the time the weather began to moderate, he had a plan. It was detailed. Parts in it were assigned – rehearsed, even, where there had been the opportunity. Ready to go the instant he gave the word.

Richard was standing on *Zemlya*'s command bridge, towering at the point which would be occupied by the helmsman waiting in the canteen to be recalled the moment the screaming wind had dropped sufficiently – in octaves and decibels as well as strength. After his experience with the temperature in the hangar, he had changed into Felix's spare cold-weather gear, though there was little need for the fisherman's polo neck yet, and the thousand dollar parkas lay across the chart table – for the moment at least. He was alone, though he filled the bridge with the massiveness of his body, the strength of his will and the force of his personality.

Brodski was up in the generator room at the aft of this level of the bridge house, grim-faced with responsibility, leading a team who had to shut down the primary generators

– and be ready to start them up again at a moment's notice. Marina, pale with shock at the news of Nana's treachery and death, was in the secondary generator room below the reactors – and well back from the turbine hall with the second engineer from the chopper and the best of the late engineer Kulibin's people, waiting to do much the same – but in sequence with Brodski and one step behind. Ready to spring up into the reactor room – hence the larger team.

It had taken some time for Richard to trust her completely; but she had at last convinced him that what had seemed like an affair between herself and Karchenko had been cover for the Spetsnaz officer's actual liaison with her roommate, Nana. A liaison whose existence would have raised Richard's suspicions far earlier, had he known about it; had he not been led astray by her reaction to finding the Spetsnaz captain almost naked, waiting for Nana in the quarters they shared after the incident with Inspector Vengerov.

Young Kuznetsov was waiting in the shelter of the A Deck corridor with a small gang of seamen and an oxyacetylene rig, ready to brave the ice-rink that was the foredeck. Anna was up in the hanger with the chopper pilot, wearing every stitch of clothing she could beg, borrow or steal. The Security squad, under the command of the two MVD majors, was continuing to patrol, while the officers in question occupied the Security Room.

The chef and his men were ready to prepare endless supplies of hot food and drink. The chief steward and his rather more decorative boys and girls were ready to supply them to anyone anywhere aboard. At least the ranges and ovens in the galley were independent of the ship's heating systems as they used bottled gas. And to a certain extent they were independent of the lighting system too if the flames were turned up high enough. And if their fridges and freezers closed down when the electricity went off, the temperature in the vessel as a whole was likely to keep everything in them perfectly.

According to Bill Beaumont and George Hebburn, everyone aboard *Erebus* and *Terror* was in a parallel state of readiness. Colin, Felix and Yagula were in their various quarters, trying for some rest before the action started; like Karchenko aboard the distant *Ivan*, useless until the communication channels opened up again, and the action started once more. The only people Richard was not really sure about were the people in the medical facility and the journalists – because they were not part of his plans.

The instant Richard could hear himself think – a moment or two before he could see *Ivan* at the far end of her icicle-bearded tow, the plans went under way. He tapped the buttons of the cell phone he had placed on the console beneath the clear-view just above the helm itself. *No signal* said the phone's bright screen. Even so, Richard reached for the tannoy handset, feeling that there was precious little more time left. 'Helmsman report to the bridge,' he ordered. 'And Mr Kuznetsov, I want you up here too.' A frisson of expectation seemed to pass through the three close-linked vessels. 'Any moment now . . .' he said to himself. He tapped the cell phone again. *No signal* it said.

Kuznetsov arrived, all red cheeks and glinting glasses. 'Anchors up please, Second Lieutenant,' said Richard quietly. 'No particular order. All at once if you can. Easy to begin with in case the winches are frozen. Then as quick as you like.'

The eager young officer was still punching the orders into the bridge computer when the helmsman arrived. No sooner had he taken up position than Richard's cell phone started ringing. He looked down at the shrilling little instrument as though he had forgotten what it was for. Then, 'Here we go,' he said with the grim and gritty cheeriness of some ancient forbear leading his men over the top at the Somme. 'Incoming!'

He picked up the shrilling little machine. The signal had gone from *No signal* to a full five bars in an instant. And Robin's face filled the screen, called up from his incoming call memory. 'Sorry, love,' he said to himself, only pretending to talk to his importunate wife. 'No time to chat now.' And he cut her off.

'Wow!' breathed Kuznetsov. 'That was weird!'

'No,' explained Richard. 'When you marry you'll find that there are times . . .'

But the lieutenant was looking at him blankly. 'It's the computers,' he said. 'They just did . . . I don't know. They just did something *weird*. But the anchors are still coming up . . . I think . . .' And even as he spoke, the forecastle head tow began to tauten, spearing the heaving ocean with a couple of hundred harpoons of ice and George Hebburn suddenly bellowed, his voice echoing across the bridge from the communications centre, 'My engines are powering up!'

'Mine too,' bellowed Bill Beaumont. 'And all on their fucking own!'

Even with her anchors still part-way down, *Zemlya* shuddered into motion as she was tugged, relentlessly – apparently helplessly – out of her little haven and eastwards towards Point Barrow.

During the time it took for the four anchors to come fully out of the water, Richard had no choice but to let the computers run unchallenged. And it gave him just a little leisure to marvel at the manner in which the machines had been so totally overpowered. It was like something out of Richard Condon's thriller *The Manchurian Candidate*. Every system on board seemed to have been completely brain-washed. Reprogrammed from afar. It was simply wondrous. So much damage, done so swiftly – how long had his own computer vanished for when he first arrived aboard? Ten minutes? And the worm was in.

Oh Apple, thou art sick, he found himself thinking. *The invisible worm that flies in the night and the howling storm / Has found out thy bed of crimson joy. And his dark, secret love does thy life destroy.* And that's all it must have taken. A couple of infected memory sticks passing around like Typhoid Mary and the job was done. It was no wonder that all he could hear from *Erebus* and *Terror* were the fulminations of their captains, using language that even sailors rarely indulged in.

Then the alarms started sounding.

Marina had warned him of the sequence, so he was able to explain it to Yagula and Felix when they appeared on the bridge. 'That's the first alarm,' he said. 'It means that the computers are beginning to withdraw the control rods from the reactors. There are five levels. It's like terrorist threat levels. That first is the low warning, the green level.'

'Even so,' said Yagula, by no means pacified. 'How many more levels are there?'

'Four. Guarded, elevated, high, severe. Blue, yellow, orange and red.'

'And then?'

'There is nothing after red. There is no colour for melt-down. Black, maybe. Bible black – because you haven't got a prayer. And you're just about to see whether what they say about Heaven is true. Or of course Hell in your case, Federal Prosecutor.'

'Very funny,' snarled Yagula. 'Now, when do you propose doing something about it?'

'When the anchors are up and we have some freedom of movement. From what Dr Leonskaya has told me, we have the better part of thirty minutes before we get through blue to orange. The anchors will be up long before then.'

'And we will still have time to put things out of commission before we reach the red level, severe?' asked Felix.

'Yes. And in theory we can hold things at the top of the red level and still have the ability to recover when the computers come back under our control.'

It was only as he finished delivering himself of this little lecture that Richard realized Tom O'Neill, Joan and Mick were at the door.

'*In theory!*' spat Yagula, just as the camera light came on to him.

'It's nothing more dangerous than a test,' said Richard swiftly and a little more diplomatically than usual. 'We'll get things sorted long before we get to orange level. Remember, these aren't the old-fashioned RBMK reactors with flammable graphite control rods and enriched uranium fuel. As Dr Leonskaya explained . . .'

Colin shouldered his way on to the bridge then and Richard stopped talking to the truculent Russians – and Joan's world-wide audience. 'Colin,' he said with great relief. 'I'd like you to go with young Kuznetsov here, please. The foredeck is going to make the Petermann Ice Island look like Barbados. I really will need an ice master out there.'

'Anchors aweigh, Captain,' confirmed Kuznetsov then. 'All four are up.'

'Off you go, the pair of you,' said Richard. 'And wait for the word. Ladies and gentlemen, I would suggest you go down to the dining salon and get in some good hot food. Things are bound to get pretty chilly around here soon.'

But even as he spoke, the next alarm level chimed in as the status went from green to blue, from low danger to guarded as the computers continued to extract the reactors' control rods. 'Unless our carefully laid plans go wrong,' rumbled Yagula mutinously, under the sudden intensification of the sound. 'Then things will get very, very hot indeed.'

Once the bridge was clear, Richard crossed to the communications console. 'George? Bill?' he said. 'Go to it.' No sooner had he given the order – one which would hopefully mean nothing to anyone monitoring the communications – he crossed to the helm and picked up his cell phone. He dialled Brodski. 'Go to work.'

He dialled Marina. 'Go to work. We're coming up to yellow.' He broke the connection. Dialled Kuznestov. 'Go straight to work as soon as you join the team. And watch the ice.'

That last order was weirdly prophetic. Richard had meant the ice on the foredeck. But even as he said the words, *Zemlya* came out of the shadow of Wrangel entirely and into the full reach of the Arctic Ocean. Seemingly straight into the heart of an ice-field. White ice stretched from horizon to horizon as far as the eye could see; dazzling, seemingly solid, as though the great wind had blown the entire polar ice cap down into the Bering Strait. It was not a flat field. It was more like an infinitely huge quarry for blindingly white Carrara marble. It lay in a wild, heaving abandon, piled half on top of itself. Scattered through the floes there were the shattered remains of bergs – growlers, bergy bits and even a few small bergs. What was disturbing about the scene was that it all seemed to be sailing towards him. Had the wind been a brisk easterly, there might have been some explanation. But he was certain that the hurricane's tight little depression would be followed – as Sittart had calculated – by the prevailing westerlies. He was certain that there was a westerly wind pushing his command eastwards while something else, something strange, was pulling the ice westwards directly against the wind.

Richard paused, frowning. It was more than an optical illusion, he was sure – more than an impression arising from the gather in speed with which the little flotilla was beginning to bash into the outer edges of the dazzlingly dangerous scene. And, as his plans were beginning to run now, he reckoned he could risk continuing to be at the centre of things even if he wasn't on the bridge. Almost without further thought, he was on his way to the bridge lift, catching up

Felix's thousand dollar parka as he went. Five minutes later he was stepping out through the A Deck door and on to the weather deck in the wake of Kuznetsov, his oxyacetylene team and – most important of all – Colin the ice master.

In fact the foredeck was crowded. In spite of the fact that it was laden with a dangerously slick cowl of ice, deep enough and solid enough to coat the whole vessel in a couple of inches of clear crystal – like food preserved in aspic – it was the best vantage point for anyone eager to get the full effect of the ice field. Joan was there, with Mick and the sound-man Al, and Tom O'Neill was there too. Whether any of them really had a full appreciation of the deadly danger all around them, Richard had neither the leisure nor the inclination to find out. Instead, he tightened his harness and did his best to hurry forward along safety lines thickened with ice and hoar frost. As he moved forward, so he came further away from the wind-shadow of the bridge house and was able to confirm his suspicion. There was a westerly breeze gusting on the back of his hood. 'What's going on with this ice-field?' he asked Colin as soon as he was close enough to speak quietly. As quietly as possible, given the cacophony of the clashing ice ahead of them.

'What do you mean?' asked Colin, turning his face towards his friend and making Richard mentally curse himself for not thinking ahead. Colin was wearing dark glasses. Richard's tears were already beginning to freeze on his lashes.

'The breeze is blowing from the west. The ice is flowing from the east. It's moving exactly counter to the prevailing wind. Isn't that unusual?'

Colin reached into his parka pocket and handed Richard his spare Ray-Bans. 'Ice is moved as much by current as by wind,' he observed as Richard put the sunshades on. 'Current must be running counter to the wind. I guess those bergs and bergy bits are enough to have the whole of the ice-field in motion. Must be quite a current, though, now you mention it.'

Richard nodded once, decisively, lucky not to lose his glasses. 'Of course! The hurricane pushed a storm surge eastwards ahead of it as it came past. That's why the anchors dragged. Spring tide and storm surge; bloody great hill of water heading for Alaska. That will have left a hollow in the ocean behind it – and the current will probably flow back to even things out for a few more hours yet.' He opened his mouth to add more thoughts, but the distant alarm just audible from the bridge house suddenly went up an octave. 'That's the warning level up to elevated,' said Richard grimly. 'We're into the yellow zone. Halfway to heaven.' His phone started ringing. 'Time to go in,' he said. 'Tell Kuznetsov not to hang about; I want that cable cut. And for Christ's sake stand well clear when it goes!'

As he turned, he pulled the phone out of his pocket, vaguely aware of several more things going on around and behind him. Joan Rudd called Colin over to explain about the ice-field Mike was filming. Tom O'Neill went closer to Kuznetsov and the oxyacetylene team, attracted by the sudden violet flame of the torch exploding to life. Richard looked down. It was Marina. He was just about to answer when the little device stopped ringing. *Signal blocked* said the screen.

Automatically, Richard turned and looked across at *Ivan*'s array of electronic equipment. He hadn't counted on the ship carrying a jammer that specific. But even as he looked at the labouring tug's electronic array, he saw something more sinister still. There were two men up on the very top of the tug's bridge and they seemed to be carrying rifles. No sooner had the thought occurred than there was a puff of smoke. Tom O'Neill sagged sideways and the whip-crack of the shot rose briefly above the mad chorus of the grinding ice. 'DOWN!' he bellowed. Get . . .' But the second puff of smoke whipped away downwind. There was no sound of the shot this time – it was lost in the far louder explosion as the oxyacetylene rig exploded. Tom O'Neill's sagging body absorbed much of the blast – enough to save the lives of Kuznetsov and his team, all except the man holding the torch and his nearest mate. But the young officer was still blown back, his safety clip free of the ruined safety lines, to come sliding up the deck like a curling stone.

The explosion had a more terrible consequence still. It simply shattered the tow rope. Kuznetsov's bikini-bottom plate whipped up and back to land on the deck beside Richard with enough force to smash the ice. The crystal cowl covering the whole deck shattered into a spider's web of cracks. The section hit by the metal plate exploded upwards with enough power to cover him with shards like shrapnel. Mercifully, none of them sharp enough to cut or pierce. *Zemlya* reared back so powerfully that even Richard lost his footing as the shattered ice slid back towards the bridge house.

The other end of the guillotined tow rope whipped away to wrap itself in the electronic array that Richard had just been looking at. Appearing there so suddenly and absolutely that it took a stretch of memory to understand that it had not always been draped there, wrapped around the aerials and dishes like the tentacle of some monstrous polar squid. *Ivan* surged forward thrusting her ice-laden bow beneath the surface, like a submarine about to crash-dive.

As the noise of the explosion echoed away across the ocean, even the grinding of the restless, westward-flowing pack seemed to still for a moment. And there was silence. It took Richard an instant to realize. The reactor alarms had stopped sounding.

Go

The song *Go With The Flow* kept running through Richard's head as he stared past the helmsman's shoulder out of the clear-view at the eye-watering wilderness of ice ahead. It had been one of his son William's favourites when he was going through his rock and roll stage and the group Queens of the Stone Age had pride of place on his Spotify and iPod. The song was not only an unusual occupant of Richard's mind, which habitually leaned towards late German Romantic classical composers and the severely underrated ex-conductor of the Liverpool Philharmonic, Max Bruch. It was also, it seemed to him, wildly inappropriate, given the desperate situation *Zemlya* and all aboard her were in. Though it seemed that rock and roll by everyone from The Doors to Nirvana had accompanied various recent wars. And there was a war going on on the frozen foredeck. Albeit a small and extremely one-sided war.

Yagula and Felix had at last found something to occupy

themselves, though Richard wished it could have been something more positive. Having cleared away the mess left
after the explosion of the oxyacetylene canisters, they had
detailed Karchenko's ex-Spetsnaz security men to use every
weapon aboard to return fire on *Ivan*. And the security contingent was happy to oblige. Perhaps their loyalty had been
tested beyond breaking point, thought Richard cynically, by
the realization that Karchenko had planned for them all to
burn to radioactive cinders in a nuclear holocaust. The reaction seemed to him to be unnecessarily brutal, even in the
face of Tom O'Neill's death and those of two other crewmen
whose names he did not as yet know. And the scorching, if
not the outright slaughter, of young Second Lieutenant
Kuznetsov.

Had Richard really been moved to do so, of course, he
could have gone about stopping them, but he reckoned that,
at the least, the fusillade stood an outside chance of disabling
the hefty range of communications equipment surmounting
the tug's bridge and still controlling two of his own three
vessels. Though, given the fact that it appeared to be functioning in spite of the weight of ice moulded over it and the
length of heavy tow rope wrapped around it made him reckon
it must be pretty robust. On the other hand, it kept the people
he was least able to control fully if not gainfully occupied,
actually without putting too many more lives at risk as far
as he could see. Certainly, no one aboard *Ivan* had put their
head above the metaphorical parapet to return fire for a good
long time.

Ivan was sitting strangely, high at the stern, as though
weighted down by the massive accumulation of ice which
must be resting on her forecastle, just as there was on
Zemlya's. That was what Richard assumed, though it was
difficult to be certain. The Russian tug was precisely ahead
of them – in the same relative position as if the tow had been
still attached. He could see everything aft of her bridge,
therefore, but nothing forward of it, even with the binoculars
he was using every now and then to survey some detail of
the scene in front of him. She had been sitting like that ever
since the massive lurch of separation – which had thrown
Zemlya back and up while hurling *Ivan* far more fiercely
forward and down by the head. *Ivan* was sitting low in any

case, so her screws were still well under the surface and they continued to thrash wildly as she moved inexorably forward in spite of her strange disposition; while *Erebus* and *Terror*, still under the control of the viral computer programmes, pounded gamely after her, dragging the unwilling and stone dead *Zemlya* with them.

Stone dead and stone cold, thought Richard. More than that – ice cold. He had never, in fact, felt so cold in his life. Even though he was wearing every stitch of Felix's spare cold-weather outfit; even though he was clutching a huge mug of steaming coffee in his gloved and mittened hands, taking judicious sips as he stood in thought, every cell in his body seemed to be on the point of freezing solid. Even the coffee, so close to scalding on his lip, seemed to be little short of icy when it reached his stomach. And when he held the field glasses instead of the coffee mug, his fingers seemed to go numb in seconds.

But Richard's mind was occupied with far more important things than the cold, the firefight, the way their enemy vessel was sitting in the water at the edge of the ice field, the pounding of the twin tugs' engines or that distractingly persistent refrain pounding *Go With The Flow* in his head. He looked down past the gently steaming coffee mug to where his cell phone lay beside the binoculars on the ledge below the clear-view. The bright screen still read *Signal blocked*. He sighed and walked past the dead communication screens towards the port bridge wing, looking back at *Erebus*, frowning. Regretting the fact that he had lost the ability to communicate with Bill and George at the same moment as *Ivan* had lost the ability to control the computers above the reactor room. What was going on down there? he wondered. The tugs' problems just one step more complex than *Zemlya*'s – they had to cut off power to the computers while still being able to use their motors. Drifting powerless into an ice-field was what had destroyed their namesakes and Sir William Franklin more than a hundred and sixty years ago.

Unless they found some way of regaining control of their own power and destiny, and soon, they would follow *Ivan* deeper into the ice-field and likely as not get trapped there. Perhaps even nipped – crushed like a nut at Christmas between the jaws of the ice. It had been the fate of more Arctic exploration vessels than he cared to remember. Franklin's original *Erebus* and *Terror* amongst them. Everything turned, it seemed to Richard, on finding a way to pull *Zemlya*'s head round from the southeasterly course into the ice-field, towards Alaska – and towards the southwest, Leningradskiy Bay. If he could turn her head, through as little as ninety degrees, the fact that the twin tugs' engines seemed to be stuck on full-ahead would be an advantage rather than a danger. Give them a chance of outrunning the drifting ice-field instead of thrusting themselves ever deeper into it.

And that, it appeared to Richard, was a matter of increasing urgency, because, as they pushed slowly but surely out of the last of Wrangel Island's protection zone and into the deep water of the Bering Strait approaches, so the nature of the ice-field itself seemed to be changing, becoming more threatening – dangerous, in fact. He returned to the helmsman's shoulder, put down the cold coffee mug and picked up the binoculars again, pushed the dark glasses up his forehead, flinching at the dazzle, thrusting their freezing eyepieces beneath his frowning brows. There was something not quite right out there. Something amid the coruscating, the teardazzled and mist-shrouded distances that set the hairs on the back of his neck to prickling as though there were ghosts nearby.

As though summoned by Richard's superstitious thoughts, Colin Ross entered the bridge followed by Brodski, both wrapped up as though they were thinking of going for the Pole. 'The power is still down, Captain,' reported Brodski unnecessarily, reaching into his pocket for a pair of dark glasses as Colin did the same. 'Computers off line. Reactors safe. Dr Leonskaya is in the reactor room and she says things look OK there. Kuznetsov is still in the sickbay though he says he's well enough to report for duty now. Anna the air hostess has taken him under her wing, though, and she won't let him up. How's the battle on the ice going?'

'Still one-sided,' answered Richard. 'Pop back down to the sick bay would you? Tell the second lieutenant he can report to me here if he feels up to it. Grab something hot to eat or drink. You've done well, but we've still a way to go.'

'I don't like the look of that,' said Richard forthrightly to Colin as soon as Brodski had clattered away off the bridge.

He gestured forwards. There appeared to be a grey line stretching right across the ice-field dead ahead, north to south, horizon to horizon. It seemed to Richard that the ice beyond it was much more lively than the ice through which they were driving now, though much of the view beyond the grey line was shrouded in disorientating illusory billows of wind-driven mist and fog.

Colin grunted and took the binoculars Richard was offering as he spoke. He raised his Ray-Bans and took a look. He hissed – a sound that Richard had never heard him make before. 'What?' asked Richard at once.

The ice master slowly lowered the binoculars and the Ray-Bans slid down into place, making Colin's face inscrutable. 'Big ice,' he said. 'I expect if you were out there on the foredeck every now and then between the clouds of cordite you'd get a whiff of cucumbers.'

Richard knew about big ice, and the telltale smell of cucumbers it gave off. He had once towed an enormous iceberg from the North Atlantic to the west coast of Africa – one of the first to do so. 'There's a berg out there? A big one?' he demanded.

'Big enough,' said Colin. It's in that fogbank – it's why the fogbank is there, I'd say. And it's coming this way. That's what's causing the fracture in the ice field. You saw that?'

'The grey line? Yes. But it looks quite a way off still.'

'It's not. That's an optical illusion. It's close – and so is the berg as a matter of fact. Close and coming closer. And there's something else . . .'

'What?'

'The ice field is under enormous pressure. It's coming apart. Most of it looks to be one or two-year ice, maybe a couple of metres thick. Floating on the surface with a draft of maybe a metre and a half, raised in folds and ridges like the sails of sailing ships, mostly moving under the influence of the wind – or trying to. You noticed the other stuff, though. The growlers and the bergy bits.' Richard nodded in reply. 'Even a growler can have a good deal more draught,' continued Colin grimly. 'Bergy bits and small bergs can go down tens of metres. And a more substantial piece, like that one hiding in the fog-bank over there can go down even further. The rough guide is this: one measure up, five measures down. So if a berg is fifty meters high it may have a draft two hundred and fifty metres deep. And of course, the underwater section is far wider than the section above the surface, as the captain of *Titanic* found out the hard way. Something like that is really powerfully under the influence of the deep ocean currents.'

'I know,' said Richard. 'So it's pushing this lot southwest in spite of the fact that the wind's trying to push it eastwards.'

'More than that. The strain of the counteractive forces is a bit like a stone hitting a windshield. That grey area that looks like a line from here is actually an area of cracks – a spider's web of cracks. I think the whole of the ice-field is just about to shatter.'

'And that would mean? For *Zemlya*?'

'Unless you can turn her, she will push right into the ice-field when it breaks up. Be sucked in, effectively. Then she'll become trapped there when the whole lot settles again and freezes back into one great sheet. Unless she gets nipped and crushed by the ice. Unless she hits the berg that is coming towards us.'

'So the most likely scenario unless we get her head right round is that we sit in an ice-field freezing to death. Or we go down with the ship when she's crushed – we're certainly not equipped to survive on the ice itself. Or we put the power back on, the computers take over again and we all go up like Hiroshima.'

'That's about it,' agreed the ice master grimly.

Floe

Captain Zak had no ice master on the bridge of his tug *Ivan*, but he knew a little about the dynamics of ice-fields and icebergs. He had a much more limited view than Richard and was as yet unaware either of the grey line in the ice ahead or the approach of the fog-shrouded berg.

But he had a shrewd suspicion that all was not well – and was rapidly getting worse. He stood on one side of his helmsman, narrow-eyed, while Karchenko stood, sleepless and still stunned, on the other.

It took a lot to stun a seasoned Spetsnaz officer, but a lot had happened to Karchenko lately. He had seen his confederates – his lover – slaughtered by the Federal Prosecutor. He had almost killed himself tumbling down on to *Ivan*'s after deck. He had received short shrift from his secret employer communicating from faraway Manila; short shrift and no sympathy at all. He had tried to take out some of his rage and frustration by opening fire on the party on *Zemlya*'s foredeck. But even that had only led to greater disaster. For the explosion of the oxyacetylene canisters and the guillotining of the tow line had had a much more serious effect on the tug than on the vessel it was towing.

Ivan had been thrown forward and down. Her already ice-weighted forecastle had hurled deep beneath the surface of the sea ahead. Even in open water, this would have been a serious matter for a boat already rendered less than stable by the mass of ice in her upper works. The burden of ice now compounded by the added ponderousness of the tangled tow rope. But *Ivan* was not in open water. She had wedged her heavy forecastle beneath a sizeable ice-sheet; something larger, older and thicker than a mere floe. An ice sheet torn bodily by the hurricane off the southern edge of the permanent pack. Big enough, thick enough and heavy enough to hold her there, partly submerged and all but helpless. The propellers that Richard observed thrashing just beneath the surface were actually running in full reverse, the gauges on the command bridge reading well above the top of the green, as far into the red danger area as Zak dared go, burning up the tug's fuel at a dangerous rate. And all, it seemed, to no avail.

So much, thought Karchenko bitterly, for his boast to Richard Mariner that he would influence people. His unspoken plan then had been to influence the Americans by helping Satang Sittart irradiate their oil supply from behind the impunity of an apparently tragic accident. That had been a high point. He had harnessed Nana Potemkin's desire for revenge to his own ends. He ruled the doomed vessel with a deadly and faithful unit of men. He was the linchpin of Sittart's plan and he stood every chance of becoming even richer than Felix Makarov. But that was all gone now. The constant fusillade wasting itself on the ironwork behind the bridge house showed how few friends he had won. The only person not aboard *Ivan* – not physically at least – to whom he could turn was Sittart himself, whose distant hand still controlled the computers aboard the three vessels behind them via the ponderous but powerful communications equipment on the bridge house roof. Whose patience was, it seemed, at an end; whose support and sympathy were non-existent. Whose plan, as far as Karchenko could see, was still to cause a holocaust as soon as *Zemlya*'s reactors could be pushed past the critical limit. Whether or not *Ivan* was close enough to be caught up in it or not. And yet somehow it never occurred to him that he should try and get Zak to shut down the computers on the tug and shut off the signal boosters. Because they all knew that Sittart and his cohorts knew where they, and their families, lived.

'You do realize,' growled the ex-Spetsnaz captain, 'that if you don't get free of this pretty soon, then the best any of us can hope for during the rest of our lives is that we'll glow in the fucking dark.' He swung round, his eyes ablaze. 'I've seen what large doses of enriched uranium dust can do to people,' he snarled. 'And it isn't pretty!'

That was the straw. Captain Zak pushed the throttles up to their buffers. The motors screamed to the upper limit of their revs, the bridge monitor dials spinning resolutely to the top of the red. And just as the tug exerted the maximum pressure it could on the ice sheet holding it down, the effect of the invisible iceberg at last made itself felt. Like a bolt of black lightning, a crack appeared across the ice-sheet immediately ahead. The men on *Ivan*'s bridge stood frozen, half believing that their actions were responsible for this apparent earthquake. Another black-floored chasm appeared. Another. The whole great section disintegrated. *Ivan* bounded free. Reared up into the air, cascading water and chunks of ice as she did so. The screaming propellers bit back into the deep water as her stern settled. And the cheaply purchased, low quality water-contaminated fuel oil in the bunkerage that the unfortunate Lieutenant Vengerov had warned of in his interview the day before Karchenko crushed him with the anchor froze within the howling motors. The whole vessel went from bounding life to utter stasis in an instant. And even before the alarms could sound the engines' death-knell, the shock-wave of the ice-field's destruction hit her. And it was a real wave, a steep-sided wall of black water more than two metres high.

Had *Ivan* not been so ice-laden she would have ridden over it easily. Had she not had the extra weight of the tow rope tangled high above the substantial array of communications devices above her bridge. Had she been sitting deeper in the water she would have stood a chance. Had her motors still been thrusting her forward – or pulling her backward – with sufficient force to set up a gyroscopic effect like the motion of a motorcycle, then she would have lived. But as it was, the wave was enough to flip her over.

It was an instant thing. There was no warning, no rocking, no pitching. One moment her bridge was up in the air, the men within it staggering with the shock of sudden movement. The next it was under the water, and the weight of the ice was enough to hold her there as the buoyant air exploded out of her. Then the simple weight of her ice-strengthened bows and the massive communications array was enough to pull the tug towards the distant floor of the Arctic Ocean, everyone aboard her freezing to death so fast that they didn't even have time to drown.

The last thoughts to occupy Yuri Karchenko's mind were a vague surprise that he should be dying by cold and wet instead of nuclear fire. And that he wished Satang Sittart, who had got him into this, had been aboard with them in person instead of at the far end of some cell phone video link like a monster in a movie on satellite TV. That the whole sorry mess should have been tricked off by the one genuine accident – a road crash that killed a sad old man on his way to visit his wife's grave in Kuntsevo. Then his eardrums burst with the soaring water pressure, he gasped with agony and the shock of the Arctic Ocean entering his lungs stopped his heart mid-beat.

Richard's mind was also awash with indelible impressions, though, for once, Professor Sittart was not amongst them.

Even as he registered the fact that *Ivan* had simply vanished, turned turtle and gulped down in an instant, leaving nothing but a hill of foam half buried beneath a shell of ice, so the wave hit *Zemlya*. She heaved in a ladylike fashion, and swung round through perhaps five of the ninety degrees Richard had been praying for. The black comber swept past and broke against the lower slopes of the iceberg, defining, suddenly, both its presence and its proximity. As though summoned by the shattering of the ice-field, the west wind gusted more strongly and the veil of fog lifted for a moment, revealing a large berg that looked perhaps seventy metres high, seemingly a good half kilometre away. But the heaving seas betrayed the danger Colin had warned of, the subsurface section of the berg was reaching out towards them, as the undersea ledge had reached so fatally out towards *Titanic*.

Brodski, Kuznetsov and Anna erupted on to the bridge then. They had seen the loss of *Ivan* on their way up from the sickbay and were stunned by the suddenness and totality of the tug's destruction. 'Go down on to the foredeck, both of you,' Richard ordered his young officers. 'There may be survivors. Look out for them.' He glanced across at Colin's frowning profile. 'Normally I'd launch lifeboats but I want to know it's worth the risk, the time and the effort before I do so,' he explained. 'Especially as the davits will be frozen as solid as the foredeck. Anna, find the Mil's pilot. I want the chopper out and ready for lift-off as soon as possible. He might be more effective than a lifeboat anyway. In the meantime, I want his GPS.'

And as he said that, his cell phone started ringing. He caught it up, looking down into the screen, where Robin's smiling face looked back up at him. He blinked. 'That's it,' he said. 'The signal block has gone, Colin. We're back in control. *Brodski!*' he bellowed. 'Belay that last order. Don't go on to the foredeck, take your team back into the generator room. Start up the generators as soon as you can. Warn Dr Leonskaya on the way. She'll want to reverse the computer settings as the computers come back on line and quieten down the reactors. But I don't want them shut down altogether if we can help it. Then she'll need to start up the auxiliary generators too. Tell her I'll talk to her about running the reactors at the lowest effective setting later on and starting

to pump out some of that hot water she promised us as well
as generating extra power to warm us up post-haste. Mr
Kuznetsov. Down to the foredeck as quickly as you can! Take
the walkie-talkie and a cell phone. We have comms back as
well as computer control.'

As he spoke, Richard was tearing off his mittens and
gloves. Then he caught up his cell phone, refused Robin's
call – with the swiftest possible prayer that it wasn't about
anything too crucial – and dialled George Hebburn. 'George.
You should have control back. Reverse your engines. I want
to try and spin us round.'

No sooner had he broken contact than the phone was
ringing again. It was Brodski. 'We'll have the generator
running in fifteen minutes or so, Captain. Dr Leonskaya and
her team will take control of the reactors and put them in
safe running mode before she goes on down and fires up the
auxiliary generators. We'll be back on full power within a
couple of hours she says. Though she doesn't know when
she can guarantee the hot water.'

'Good enough,' snapped Richard. 'Go to work. First step
towards salvation almost complete,' he informed Colin.

He broke contact and walked back to the front of the
bridge, frowning again. He pulled up the dark glasses and
squinted. The water immediately in front of *Zemlya* had gone
from coal black to milky white. 'What's that?' he asked
Colin.

'That's a ledge from the iceberg,' said Colin. 'It's swinging
just under your bow by the look of things. You're bloody
lucky you're not sitting any deeper in the water or you'd
have found out what it's like to be in command of the *Titanic*.'

Richard stared at his friend for an instant, his face almost
blank as his mind raced into overdrive. And his subconscious
at last made full contact with his conscious. The Queens of
the Stone Age song pounded in his brain. He pushed the
phone to his lips again. 'Mr Kuznestov!' he ordered briskly.

'Yes, Captain?'

'Drop the forward anchors at once. Start with the starboard
hook. Do it by hand and take care. Override the winch
mechanism and stop as soon as the hook hits anything solid.
By the sound of things we'll have the power to pull it back
up again within an hour or so.'

'Anything solid, Captain? What is there? Other than the ocean floor?'

'There's the ice-ledge,' answered Richard. 'The ledge sticking out of the side of the berg. It's just below out fore-castle and its heading south-west with the current. If we can get our anchors on to that ledge in time, then the berg will pull us round.'

He glanced across at Colin, suddenly hilarious with hope. 'Saved by Queens Of The Stone Age, near as dammit!' he said. 'Who'd have believed it?'

'What?' asked Colin, who had no teenage children and whose personal taste in music ran to bagpipes, big bands and the Rat Pack.

'*Go With The Flow!*' explained Richard. 'We're going to *go with the floe . . .*'

AFTERMATH

Hot

Robin Mariner was hot. London was sweltering under a late summer heatwave and Heritage Mariner was keeping its carbon footprint small by keeping the air conditioning on low power. It was her decision – so she was as always leading from the front. Her office was the hottest in the building. She had shed her tailored jacket some time ago and was wondering whether her silk blouse might be darkening with perspiration. Without thinking, she undid another button and fanned her cleavage distractedly. Had she crossed to her window high in Heritage House she could have looked down on a vision of Leadenhall made vague and sinister – almost fogbound by the warmth. The fearsome heat-haze covered the distant ground like one of the pea-soupers familiar to Dickens and Conan Doyle. The spectral figures thronging the pavements could have been Fagin's boys out picking pockets, or Professor Moriarty's minions hunting Sherlock Holmes.

But Robin was too busy looking at the screen of her laptop

to be bothered with such fanciful nonsense. The Skype alert lit up on the toolbar asking her to accept or refuse the contact. She refused and continued reading. Her screen was filled with the front page of today's *Times Online*. 'ICE STATION *ZEMLYA* FINALLY REACHES SAFETY' said the headline. The sub-head immediately below it read: 'Journalist Dies Aboard.' She focused on the story, her forehead folding into the faintest of frowns.

'The Russian floating nuclear facility which has become known to the world as Ice Station *Zemlya* anchored in Leningradskiy Bay in the early hours of the morning BST. Russian sources have informed this reporter that the vessel has reached safe haven after a series of unfortunate accidents and incidents. These have included the tragic death of Newscorp reporter Tom O'Neill . . .'

Robin clicked on a link beside the story and the screen filled with a live broadcast. A disturbingly familiar face stared out at her. Her frown deepened. She shivered, but the sudden chill was nothing physical. Federal Prosecutor Lavrenty Yagula was speaking rapidly in Russian. The instantaneous translation ran along the bottom of the screen: 'I went on board *Zemlya* to investigate an alleged case of international financial malfeasance which may have included the late Captain Sholokhov and some companies in China and Indonesia. Fortunately, I was able to remain aboard throughout the final sections of the voyage. I am therefore able to assure you that nothing untoward or even sinister occurred. There were deaths, yes. The tug *Ivan* was lost with all hands. Tragic. The ship's doctor, Mussorgsky, was found at the bottom of a . . . ah . . . of a companionway with his neck sadly broken. Another tug *Ilya* was damaged, members of her crew killed too, but she made it to safety in the end. But you must understand that this was the first voyage of a highly experimental vessel, and it sailed through several severe storms and a full-blown hurricane. It very nearly became wedged in an ice field and was only saved by an outstanding feat of seamanship. Men were lost overboard, certainly. The captain and some officers were killed when a tow line snapped. Others, including the journalist Mr Tom O'Neill, were killed and injured in the explosion of oxyacetylene equipment. These are the kinds of accidents that can happen in any industrial situation. But rumours of crewmen dying through radioactive contamination are utterly unfounded. However, in the spirit of openness and cooperation, we will be sending a team from the Nuclear Safety Inspectorate aboard during the next few days. There will be no criminal prosecutions because there were no crimes committed to my sure and certain knowledge. Now, I would like to hand over to the vessel's owner, Mr Felix Makarov . . .'

Felix's face filled Robin's laptop screen. The Russian dialogue and the English subtitles continued with hardly a pause. 'Thank you, Prosecutor General. The point I would like to make most forcefully is the fact that Ice Station *Zemlya* has proved what a solid and dependable vessel she is. As Dr Leonskaya will explain at greater length and more technical detail in a moment, the reactors are the safest ever designed. We never had a moment of concern about them. The ice station itself has withstood extremes of weather and environment far beyond anything we could have dreamed of, let alone planned for – and she has survived. Not merely survived, but survived triumphantly. She is, I can assure you, the first of a new generation of such vessels which, as representatives of the pinnacle of Russian design and technology, will soon be bringing power and progress to any part of the world which has access by water. And at an absolutely unbeatable price.'

There was a discrete tap at Robin's door. 'Come!' she called. The door swung wide and Robin's hot new PA stepped into the room. She glanced up and closed the laptop. His simple size and presence always made an impact. Half the secretaries in the building were propositioning him; most of them single girls – but by no means all. He had the shoulders and hips of a rowing blue, though he had been a fly-half of awesome speed on the rugby pitch as well, by all accounts. He still played for Wasps. Or was it Saracens? That explained why his nose was broken ever so slightly out of line. And the scar of a stud-mark on his cheekbone. 'What is it, Alex?' she asked.

Alex glanced down at the bundle of papers clutched to the breast of a navy-blue blazer that had been perfectly crafted by Gieves and Hawkes. As had the grey flannel slacks. His father was a retired Commodore. His hair fell forward across his forehead, so black that it seemed to catch a hint of blue. He took another step forward, and the faintest fragrance of Roger and Gallet aftershave filled the torrid air, though, as it was mid-afternoon, his square jaw was beginning to darken with a hint of blue-black shadow. He was wearing a finely striped shirt in Cambridge blue with Oxford weave and his Trinity college tie. When he looked up again, his ice blue gaze seemed to pierce her in a way that no other gaze had ever done. Except Richard's.

'They've moved the meeting forward,' he said, his voice a gravelly growl that raised goosebumps all along her thighs. 'Are you ready?'

Robin's Blackberry started to ring. Like the Skype, it would be Richard. She refused the call and eased herself sensuously to her feet. 'Ready when you are,' she purred.